THE SECOND MARRIAGE

REBECCA DE WINTER

Storm
PUBLISHING

This is a work of fiction. Names, characters, business, events and incidents are the products of the author's imagination. Any resemblance to actual persons, living or dead, or actual events is purely coincidental.

Copyright © Rebecca Williams, 2024

The moral right of the author has been asserted.

All rights reserved. No part of this book may be reproduced or used in any manner without the prior written permission of the copyright owner.

To request permissions, contact the publisher at rights@stormpublishing.co

Ebook ISBN: 978-1-80508-330-6
Paperback ISBN: 978-1-80508-332-0

Cover design: Henry Steadman
Cover images: Getty Images, Shutterstock

Published by Storm Publishing.
For further information, visit:
www.stormpublishing.co

ALSO BY REBECCA DE WINTER

Best Friends

As ever, this book is dedicated to my dragons, the big one and our babies.
Diolch cariads, caru ti x

PROLOGUE

January 2023
Naomi

It wasn't like I didn't know who Emily Brigham was.

Her trial had taken up the whole summer after I graduated, My mother and I watched the news together every evening, catching up on the latest sordid details when my little sisters were in bed.

Throughout the trial, I pressed my mother for her thoughts – after all, they'd known each other for years. What was she like? But Mum refused to talk about her, I guess she felt bad about the way things had worked out.

It wasn't until I was floundering around, desperate for women to interview for my PhD thesis, a year or so later, that I thought of her, and read the court files. Listened to the audio of that call to the hotel concierge.

She's perfect, I told my supervisor, imagining how I would describe her, remembering that iconic picture of her being led out of the hotel in handcuffs, still in her wedding dress.

But I wanted to know the woman behind it all, the one who

twisted and wrung her hands when she spoke. And surely if I did, others would too.

Because who was she – a Mata Hari, a seductive, dangerous, sociopath – or someone else entirely?

As much as I always believed a victim, that didn't mean they were perfect, and it was the lowest form of sexism to paint a woman as feeble.

A quote though, in part of her testimony, nagged at me as I waited for my first visit.

'Don't you know, a wolf on a leash is still a wolf?'

And each time I read it, I'd second guess myself – and her – all over again.

The first time I meet Brigham she tells me I'm asking the wrong questions.

It throws me off balance, even as I know to be careful around her.

Max wasn't happy from the start, typical man, I just took it as him being a protective boyfriend. He believed everything they said about her. *I'm only looking out for you, you're too nice, please try to remember she was found guilty.*

I said that she was a victim too. That, despite the verdict, she had her husband's confession on tape. Everything that man did to her – and to the others.

It's not that I haven't had difficult subjects before. Or been in difficult situations. Especially writing this thesis. I've deliberately picked controversial subjects. I'm planning to write a book. I know what sells.

She'd refused every interview request during her trial, and after. So, whilst part of me wants to know why now, and why me, a larger part knows that's a risky road to go down. My supervisor wasn't enthusiastic about her inclusion in my thesis, but agreed on the proviso that I also spoke to the victim's family, to avoid painting Brigham as some sort of martyr.

When I arrive at the prison, the sky and the brickwork blend together in a mass of icy grey. Sleet pelts down on me, biting my face and the slivers of skin between my coat and my mittens. It's an imposing building, lurking behind rows of houses and a big park. Even in the height of summer, I can't imagine any light penetrating the gloom.

Right away, I know she's not like the other women I've spoken to. Well, aside from being incarcerated. I interviewed them in their own homes, mostly; they were jittery, tearful, angry, scared even. It's understandable, after what they'd been through. I told them it's not trauma porn; I'm not making entertainment out of their stories. Even so, many asked to be anonymous. Brigham doesn't have that option.

The room is bare, but well lit, despite the dreary day outside. When Brigham enters, she's not alone. Her escort remains present the entire time we talk. But she seems unbothered, her self-possession impressive. She takes a seat across from me, in a chair bolted to the ground, just like mine, whilst her guard remains standing.

She's a beautiful woman, still – or, as Max would add, *for her age*.

She's in her early forties, petite, groomed. I wonder how she does it, stuck in here. I don't want to think about the favours she gives, what she trades, to access beauty products.

Still that incredible bone structure – she's a model prisoner I'm told, in all senses of the phrase. The papers struggled with her looks; how could someone who looked like she did, do what they said? But as the case dragged on, the tide turned against her – she was too beautiful, full of herself, icy.

Swamped in her grey sweatshirt and jogging bottoms, she's child-like, doll sized. Rumour has it she manages twenty thousand steps a day, pacing her cell, and it's true that she emanates a certain wiry energy. I can see how charismatic she must have been, at work, as a consultant; when I initially saw her, she demanded my attention without even saying a single word.

When I get home, I'm going to be straight on the phone to Mum, asking her if Brigham had always been like this, dominant, irresistible. It makes Mum's decisions back then even more inexplicable – wasn't she afraid of the consequences? – but she told me that no one had any idea what Brigham was capable of.

Rain patters on the windowpanes as Brigham starts to speak, drips crawling down the shadowy reflection on the wall behind her.

'Everyone wants to know why,' Brigham tells me, 'but no one ever wants to know how. They think they know how. But they don't, not really. And they don't understand that you don't need to be behind a locked door, to have limitations on how you live your life.'

She talks like this a lot, in riddles and ambiguity. But what I need for my thesis is the truth and I tell her so. That I'm not here to play games, only to understand what happened.

'Darling, there's more than one version of the truth. Surely you know that by now?'

Brigham can be quite maternal at times, and it shocks me when she calls me darling. Then I'm told she calls everyone darling. That her nickname in prison is darling. When I ask her why, she laughs.

'Mrs Brigham, you said that no one wants to know how. So... tell me how.'

'That's easy, I mean Harley Quinn said it best: "I've got daddy issues".'

The prison guard, allegedly not listening, rolls their eyes.

It would be easy to react, to give her what I can see she

wants. But I simply smile and bide my time, knowing she'll fill the silence with words.

'I jest, I jest. I have mommy issues too.'

But I meet her eyes, the smile on her lips hasn't reached them, and there is a hardness there.

'You know, sometimes I think they didn't believe I could be a victim. As if men can't help themselves, so I should have accepted it all.'

And she smiled a wide beautiful smile, all shiny white teeth and full lips. I thought then of the Wolf from *Little Red Riding Hood*: *All the better to eat you with.*

I met with the prison warden first, and she told me that Brigham is popular with inmates and guards alike. That she runs creative writing classes, holds impromptu yoga sessions, that she is a trusted confidante of even the most dangerous prisoners.

This spooked Max, but I was resolute, unafraid. What harm could she do to me, behind bars; all I needed was her story. Even as I reassured him, Max had asked me, *but what will it cost you?*

'I get frustrated when people focus on my husband,' Brigham says, 'Always centring the man in my story. Always putting him first.'

'Is that not because, in this case, he's the victim?'

'Can't you be both victim and perpetrator? What's that stat about abusers? That they themselves are quite often abused first?'

'Were you abused? Is that what you're saying?'

When my subject's story is as complex as I suspect Brigham's is, I let them go down the rabbit holes. It takes skill though, to listen to what's left unsaid, because the narrative comes in the telling, not the plot.

'The world is so insistent on pathologising women. Telling us we're hysterical and crazy, we're too much and not enough.

Sit down and be quiet but don't be a little mouse, but don't be bossy, don't take up too much space, ask nicely, all the sugar and spice. It's like they want to medicate us for the disease of being women in a man's world. It's no wonder I stopped taking the medication.'

'Were you on medication?'

Brigham has been heavily pathologised in the media, all the armchair experts diagnosing her with everything from autism to schizophrenia to psychopathy.

When I read the court mandated reports from the psychiatrist who reviewed her, there were no surprises, but they were equally careful not to label – or libel her, as she claims. She has traits of antisocial personality disorder, but not enough to merit treatment or a full diagnosis, and besides, she loves her daughter, she'll tell anyone who cares to know.

'It's so easy to call someone sociopathic, psychotic, sadistic,' she continues, warming to her theme. 'We accuse anyone who has a different version of the truth of being a gaslighter. But nothing happens in a vacuum.'

Brigham has always maintained her innocence to the media, despite her guilty plea for manslaughter. She says this is what her defence team advised her to do. But it was all really an accident.

'Are you saying you felt alone?'

'I'm saying nothing is straightforward. The hand that holds the knife isn't always the hand of a killer.'

I just stare at her.

'Don't you have a list of questions for me?'

'Mrs Brigham—'

'Call me Emily.' She smiles at me as she speaks, her mouth closed, saturnine.

'Emily, then. What would you like to talk about today? I'm happy to hear whatever you feel is relevant to your story.'

'My story.' She sniffs. 'What kind of bullshit is that? It's not a story, it's the truth.'

She pauses and looks to the side. In another situation she'd take a drag of a cigarette, breathe smoke from her nostrils.

'But to answer your question, I'll start where any good story starts. At the beginning.'

There's a silence in the room as she takes a sip of water, and it makes me think about how most stories are made up.

Before she starts though she surprises me. 'You look like her, you know.'

'Who?'

'Your mother. Did you think I didn't know who you were?'

She smiles again, that Cheshire cat grin, and then she begins to speak, unspooling away the time until we are back where someone like Brigham is made – her teenage years.

Recording #1 – January 2023

The first time a man beeped his horn at me – I was maybe fourteen. I was walking to the library, on a Saturday morning, down past a road of expensive houses.

I wasn't one of those fourteen-year-olds who looked sixteen who looked eighteen. I looked like the child I was, breast buds nestled in the soft cotton cups of my trainer bra, gangly and awkward on legs that had sprouted from nowhere. But that of course, was the attraction.

It didn't stop, after the man in the car. That was only the beginning.

The times that boys at school felt it was fine to snap my bra, brush past me, that bit too close. The dread of walking past a building site, a white van, a group of drunk men, a pub. The comments, the leers, the whistles. The way I learned that beauty was the price I paid to exist in a world built for men.

And eventually I took that cost and I made it my weapon.

Oh, I know what the papers say, that I hate men. But it's not true. Because I've loved them too. I love the way I feel with a man who wants me, who desires me, who would crawl across coals for the dark heat inside of me.

But I can't even begin to list every time, since then, that I've been written off or underestimated. And the trouble is, it's not only me – every woman has these stories.

But, here is mine.

PART 1

BEFORE

ONE

Spring 2015
Emily

I hate checking the pockets of clothes, it's like a really bad prize draw. At best I find desiccated tissues, at worst... well, at worst I find a torn condom packet in my husband, Pete's jeans pocket.

The main problem being, we don't use condoms; we haven't for years. And just to hammer the point home, the expiry date is February 2021, so I know it's new.

I'm in front of the washing machine, so I put the wrapper in my pocket to throw away when next I walk back through the kitchen, and continue loading the machine. On autopilot, I add the washing liquid and set the cycle. My mind doesn't dwell on my find too much, veering away every time I am tempted to think about it, what it might mean. It's time for the school run anyway and as much as I hate small talk at the school gates, I'm grateful for the distraction, especially when Anouk comes running out to show me her wonkily written love letter to 'Mumy' and a necklace made from uncooked pasta shapes.

In the end, I forget about the condom wrapper until I'm

changing for bed. I'm too caught up in after-school dramas in ballet class – the woman who runs it is a total dictator about the correct way to put Anouk's hair in a bun, despite my protests that my little girl has a bob and it's not easy!

I then provide the wrong sort of pizza for dinner – apparently Anouk now won't eat any toppings except plain cheese – and it takes forever to shepherd my mini-dictator in pink through her bath and bedtime routine. And that's before Pete even deigns to walk through the door, discarding his jacket on the floor, his shoes outside the cupboard, chucking loose coins and whatever from his pockets on the delicate grey-painted wood of our vintage sideboard.

I still don't ask Pete about the wrapper though. I don't know why. Something makes me hold fire. I'm sure it'll be to do with the boys' weekend he came home from on Sunday night, the reason I've had to navigate round his half-unpacked weekend bag all week.

But on Thursday, when I meet Sarah for our weekly coffee, I don't know what comes over me – I mention it to her.

'So, do you think he cheated on you?'

Straight in for the kill, she fixes me in her laser-like gaze.

'Well, I'd like to think he wouldn't...'

'But the evidence suggests otherwise?'

'I was hoping you'd tell me I was imagining it.'

'You could be. He did go away after all, maybe they did some sort of competition to see who could fit a condom over their head or something. Why don't you ask him about it?'

'Mmmmm. Something keeps stopping me. That whole "don't ask questions you don't want the answer to".'

I'm scared, is the truth. I've had a thing about being cheated on since I was young; once someone breaks your trust, that's it.

'You could be massively overthinking it all. Is there anything on his Instagram?'

'I doubt it. I mean, they went to Amsterdam, I'm pretty sure nothing they did is safe for Instagram.'

'It's worth a look though, isn't it? Put your mind at rest. And then you don't have to talk to him about it.'

'I don't want to make a big deal about it if it's nothing to worry about.'

One of the first things Pete told me he loved about me was my independence, and it wasn't accidental that he loved that about me; after all, my mother had lectured me practically from birth on how to keep a man.

You need a little mystery, darling, a little distance. Keeps him wondering.

I excel at being the cool girlfriend, the cool wife, always have done. And I'm pretty sure the cool wife does not go through her husband's pockets. The cool wife does not question her husband as to what she finds in his pockets. The cool wife does not overthink and overanalyse. The cool wife is not paranoid, or sitting in coffee shops with her friends, discussing her husband's activities on a boys' weekend. The cool wife has better things to do.

The clink of Sarah's latte cup on its saucer brings me back to earth.

'I guess you need to decide how much it's going to eat away at you, not knowing.'

'What would you do, in my place?'

I don't know why I'm asking, I know the answer.

'Greg doesn't go on boys' weekends, so I wouldn't know.'

She doesn't let Greg go on boys' weekends, is what she means. Also, Greg doesn't have any friends outside of us – at least, not ones that don't live on the internet – and it's clear he worships the ground Sarah walks on.

'But you trust Pete, right?'

'Yeah, completely.'

. . .

When Pete gets home that evening, I watch him like a hawk. How he is with Anouk, how often he looks at his phone, how he speaks to me, what he says about his day – what he doesn't say.

'What?'

'Nothing.'

'You've been weird all evening, Em. Have I done something?'

'I don't know... have you?'

'What?'

'Is there something you're not telling me?'

Pete's never been a good liar. He couldn't fake the confused expression that crosses his face, the way his brow crinkles.

'I'm not with you here.'

'Are you sure?'

'Yeeeeessss?'

I can't take this. Even if he has done something, it's clearly not significant enough for him to worry about. Although I also know how easy lying can be for some.

'Ignore me, I'm being ridiculous. Sarah made some crack about Amsterdam and boys' weekends today, you must think I'm crazy.'

This is not cool wife behaviour, I need to get a hold of myself.

He catches my eye in the mirror as I turn to unzip my dress, it slithers to the ground into a silky pool. I step out of it and face him.

'Em, if you're crazy, you're my crazy. Why would I want anyone else when I have you?'

'Aren't you bored of me?'

'Never.' He walks across the room, kisses me, cups my face in his hands, and then moves his hands down my body, bringing me in close against him.

He kisses my neck, my collarbone, my belly – and lower,

falling to his knees in front of me, but my brain worries away, because words are easy... and so are men.

Sarah and Beckie are over for a play date as it's another teacher training day and school is closed. I planned to take Anouk out for the day, but I'm too tired. I lay awake last night, worrying about Pete and the what-ifs, despite our antics in bed.

Sarah and I have quite an unusual friendship. After all, how many women are besties with their husband's childhood sweetheart? But when we moved out here to Ranthmere, she was straight round with wine and a casserole, and we've been super close ever since.

Much like us, our daughters are besties also, despite their differences. Anouk loves her primary coloured Mini Rodini tops and dresses. I buy her limited-edition Converse and Vans. Her wardrobe is almost as expensive as mine. Sarah teases me about it, how they'll only end up torn and filthy, like Beckie's.

Beckie loves those synthetic Disney princess fancy dresses and pastel and white Adidas. She's adorable, with blond hair to her waist, but Sarah despairs of all the plastic pink femininity, and also because of the sea of pink and lilac glittery plastic that dominates her sitting room.

Today the two of them are screaming joyfully in our garden, I beckon Anouk over.

'Darling, children should be seen and not heard!'

I'm half serious, my curtain-twitching neighbours love making pointed comments about how they had lovely peaceful afternoons before we moved in.

'Oh, Mummy,' Anouk giggles, her hands over her mouth, 'you're so funny,' and her gap-toothed smile peeps out from behind her chipped pink glitter manicure.

I want to frown but hear my mother's voice say, *careful darling, wrinkles.*

'I wasn't joking!' I call after her as she tears off into the garden, covering her limited-edition Nikes in mud and compost and god knows what.

The gardener is here too, though he's not doing a very good job, too busy making TikToks of his muscles as he mows the lawn; it's not for our benefit though – next door's daughter is home from university, she's lying on their balcony in a tiny bikini top and cut-offs.

Sarah clocks him, and then her, and raises an eyebrow.

'I bet you used to eat boys like that for breakfast, Ems.'

I only laugh, as she continues, gesturing at the neighbour's balcony. 'Remember when we looked like that?'

For a moment, I think of how when she looked like that, she was with Pete. Even so, I smile at her and gesture at the girls.

'I don't know where Anouk gets her attitude from.'

'Hmmm, yes I wonder.' Sarah snorts into her coffee and I stifle a yawn.

Sarah and Beckie have been here for over an hour now and, as much as I enjoy Sarah's company, I'm struggling with small talk. Today it's more like tiny talk, miniscule even.

Sarah is droning on about her new air-fryer, how it's revolutionised meal planning, what she makes for dinner. I really should listen, but I let Sarah's words wash over me, as my mind wanders to the last time someone cheated on me. The way I felt in that hotel room after, the humiliation, everything I did to forget him...

Eventually Sarah notices I'm not listening, so I change the subject to the new teachers the girls have this term – both men, unbelievably. Male teachers are like hen's teeth in any primary school.

Sarah talks about them in a breathy voice, *they're so good with the kids*. I roll my eyes and wonder how much credit they get for doing the work that we take for granted from the female teachers; even so, they could both put me in detention any day.

I only realise I've said this out loud by the expression on Sarah's face.

'Oh, don't look like that. Pete is constantly going on about the year-five teacher, can't we look too?'

I often wonder what it's like to be someone like Sarah, her life mapped out in school terms and holidays to Spain, weekly takeaways and *Love Island, Strictly Come Dancing, Bake Off*. I love her dearly, but she's always so predictable, so good.

She's trying to persuade me to come on a mums' night out with the rest of the year group, I'm not enthusiastic, but I bite my tongue and murmur in a noncommittal way.

'And maybe a curry? Or will they want to go for drinks instead? There's that new bar – you know, where that vape shop was...'

I tune out again, looking at the garden. Wonder if Pete will notice that the £500 a month we're paying the gardener doesn't appear to be making any difference, apart from brightening up the landscape even if it's not for my benefit.

Although sometimes I feel like I could be having affairs with half the neighbourhood and Pete wouldn't notice. He's been more distant recently. He used to message me every day on the train home, funny memes and videos, but when I check my phone, I realise he's not sent me anything silly for ages.

This is why I'm scared of becoming complacent like Sarah. Assuming he'll love me no matter what and not putting in the hard work, the maintenance and grooming. Although it feels a bit like painting the Firth of Forth bridge – as soon as I finish, I have to start all over again.

I'm scared that one day all my worst fears will come true and Pete will get bored of me, and then where will I be – and more importantly, Anouk? I've worked so hard to give her the security I never had. If we split up, where would we live? How would I manage? I've been out of the workforce for years. My thoughts start to spiral again, but then I'm distracted by Sarah clearing away the mugs.

'Oh, don't worry about that, I'll do it later.'

I bellow in an unladylike fashion for Beckie and Anouk to come in from the garden.

When they appear, Sarah and I laugh. Their hair is loose from whatever plait or pigtail it had been forced into, socks falling down, muddy scuffed knees, faces pink with excitement and exercise.

Anouk likes to remind me that Beckie is excellent at football and cricket and ask why can't she do those instead of ballet and gymnastics? I make Anouk practise her box splits in front of the TV, watch her pick the sequins off her leotard, probably hand glued on by girls her age in a sweatshop in China.

Pete tells me to let her be, that girls can do anything boys can do now, but I remain unconvinced. When you grow up like I do, you want your children to have everything you didn't. You don't want them to have to do the things you do to get by.

When Sarah and Beckie finally leave – not without protracted goodbyes – I leave Anouk to her own devices, quite literally, and make myself a cup of tea, even though the Sauvignon in the fridge looks tempting.

I consider what to make for dinner; it's annoying that my brain, which was once used to plan multi-million-dollar marketing campaigns, is now used to plan three, delicious nutritious meals a day for someone whose idea of *haute cuisine* comes in a box with a free plastic toy. And that's just Pete.

It's so relentless, and that's without the shopping and the prep and the cleaning up. I wonder what the teenage me would say if she saw me now; I thought I could change the world, but now I'm just a suburban housewife.

Pete knows I'm restless, he's said maybe it's my hormones. I had to bite my tongue from telling him where he could stick that suggestion. Moving out of the city has been great, it really is – I don't regret it at all, I know it was the right thing to do, especially for Anouk.

But I do miss my old life. I can't explain why. It's like I've lost a part of myself moving here – the fun part that went to festivals and exhibitions and house parties and travelled to other countries on a whim.

Oh, I know I'm being silly. Now, whenever I'm in London, I'm overwhelmed by the noise and the people; I wouldn't like the commute, as Pete tells me all the time.

I keep meaning to get involved with the PTA and the Women's Institute and all the other activities that are part of small-town life. There must be things going on somewhere – what was *Midsomer Murders* based on after all.

It's only... I've always had a low tolerance for tedium and the school WhatsApps are full of competitive mothering – about phonic groups and bake offs and activities to do on inset days.

I know teenage girls are like a grenade with its pin pulled, but sometimes I can't wait until Anouk is responsible for all elements of her friendships and I don't have to constantly talk to women I have nothing in common with.

When we first moved here, it was different. I had high hopes. Maybe it was the way Pete presented it all to me, on holiday – with a glossy brochure for the house and some subtle mentions about local shops and good schools.

We were in a five-star resort on some Greek island, I forget which. Anouk was a toddler and obsessed with the kids' club, so was quite happy to be dispatched there most days, which meant I had time to myself, time to think.

I knew we should have booked that place with the swim-up bar, Pete grumbled at me. I rolled my eyes behind my sunnies and sat up on my sun lounger. I flicked through the thick pages of the sales brochure Pete had given me, like a caveman throwing the carcass of a deer at my feet.

It's detached, acres of land, seventeenth century, all modernised though. There's planning permission for a pool. Think about it, babe.

We had enough money for a deposit on a house further into Southwest London, but the repayments were pretty hefty. Despite his '*detail is for the little people*' attitude, Pete did get antsy about how he had the entire weight of the mortgage on his shoulders, all the pressure.

Moving was a constant source of tension, even though Pete himself had said that he wasn't prepared to raise a child in a house where we could hear our next-door neighbours' every bowel movement. It seemed this new house he'd found was the solution to all our woes – a move to a small town, like so many before us.

On the holiday loungers, Pete patted my thigh even as he watched a woman in a white string bikini apply sun oil to her legs.

'See, I do listen, babe, I know it's been hard for you, with Anouk. But this place, yeah, look at the garden. I can have a ride-on mower!' He made a *vroom vroom* noise and ran his fingers up my arm. Despite myself, I laughed.

I paged through the brochure again.

'Okay, I'll go and see it with you.'

'Excellent! You'll love it, I promise, it's exactly what we need.'

In the end, the holiday was a success. Pete bought me a little white bikini just like Miss Sun Oil and persuaded me to wear it, telling me I was more beautiful than her, even Anouk liked it – *Mama pwetty!*

We moved house six months later, but that was five years ago now.

. . .

The other day Pete asked me if I'd thought about going back to work.

'Why?'

'Thought you might want to, now that Anouk's older?'

We'd delayed my return to work because of the move and the work on the house, and the cost of childcare.

'What about baby number two?'

'I thought you didn't want another? And you don't seem yourself. You haven't for a while.'

I twist my body round to face him and stop loading the dishwasher. He's standing at the kitchen island, scarfing down peanuts and a beer.

'But, Pete, I was a consultant. What would I consult on now – the benefits of baby-led weaning versus purees? I'm so out of the loop...'

'You could have some chats though? You were great and there's loads of return-to-work programmes now. I'm always being asked to attend events to help recruit them.'

'Maybe... but let's not rush into anything. And if we do try for another, then there's not much point in me going back if I'm only going to have to go off again pretty quickly.'

He chews his lip.

'Okay but... but it might take a while for you to get pregnant?'

'It didn't with Anouk.'

'I know but you're a bit older now and...'

I glare at him, I'm not that old.

'What's with me suddenly needing to go back to work anyway, everything okay?'

'No – no, all good, all fine.'

Something crosses his face though and even though I know we're not going to go bankrupt – it's not like when I was little – old habits die hard. I make a mental note to check the bank statements.

'And if I didn't go back to consulting, what would I do? I'm not exactly employable. What should I put on my CV?'

'Expert in kids' fashion, drinking Prosecco and spending all my money?' Pete quips.

And before I can say anything else, he takes the nuts and beer and disappears into the family room, calling for Anouk as he goes.

It's a few days later that I spot an email notification on his phone, about risk of redundancy and consultation periods, and then the penny drops.

I really, really don't want to go back to work. I *can't* go back, even to a different company, because of how it all ended.

It's a few weeks later when I get a message on Instagram when I'm posting a picture of my wine glass, that I find a solution.

It's the account I used to document our move and subsequent house renovation. I've got a decent following and I get the odd freebie and sponsorship deal. And I do the odd 'outfit of the day' post and 'get ready with me' video, usually skincare stuff about anti-ageing. Sometimes I post a workout – though I'm careful with that because ninety per cent of the comments I get are from strange men, telling me I'm gorgeous. This message is different though, it's from a man asking for a photo of my legs – and, more importantly, offering to pay a lot of money for it.

I let it sit for a few days... I mean, how awful would it really be? Because... well, who would know? It's just my legs. My real name isn't on my account, and no one knows on here who I am in real life.

Curious, I google at-home glamour shoots and photography tips, it doesn't look too difficult. I read articles about women making thousands of pounds each month and their photos are incredible – but then I think I'd have to be insane to do anything like that. Insane and stupid.

It's not like we need the money per se, but I also really, really don't want to go back to work.

Would taking the odd photo be that bad?

So, one day, after I drop Anouk at school, I lie to Sarah and tell her I can't make our weekly coffee. I go home, set up my ring light and apply make-up to my legs. I have a gin and tonic at ten in the morning and before I let myself think about it too much, I take a photo – a few photos – of my legs. And then, knocking back another drink, dizzy with alcohol, I send them in a private message, along with my bank details.

Within seconds, my phone chimes, it's a notification from my bank.

It's the easiest money I have ever made in my life.

TWO

Between Anouk, my new Instagram activities, and general life admin, I forget all about that condom wrapper in Pete's pocket. But then it all comes rushing back, one weekend. I've been away for a spa weekend with Billie and Sarah. It's very convenient that my closest friends are married to Pete's closest friends. Although, seeing as they've all known each other since school, I'm still counted as the newcomer – even once being referred to as Yoko to Pete's John! How nice...

The spa trip is some sort of nominal thank you from the husbands for all our hard work as mums and wives. Billie and Sarah love it, thinking that the boys are doing us a huge favour. But as much as I love a bit of luxury and a deep tissue massage – even if it's from a hairy Scandinavian called Bjorn – I feel like we're missing a trick here. Don't get me wrong, Pete tries hard, he does – even though he calls his time with Anouk 'daddy daycare', a phrase that makes my teeth itch. I mean, at least I don't work – not like Billie – but I also can't help thinking that if the guys helped out a little more, we wouldn't need a break in the first place.

Sometimes I wonder if Pete likes it better this way though.

Work is tiring but it gives him a ready-made excuse not to help out more – working late or extra projects on the weekends. Though every time I stick my head round the study door he's gaming – on a break, apparently.

I also feel a bit guilty about the cost of the getaway. I can't really blame peer pressure, but I might have gone a bit overboard in the spa. Billie and Sarah went all in, full-body massage, facials, mani/pedi; I did get a wax too, it's not like there's nothing in it for him. I probably shouldn't have had the champagne afternoon tea though…

The boys have been at our house all day – even though Sarah lives close by, Billie and Dan are still in London. Pete sold it to them as a trip to the country, and of course our heated pool is a big win. They're staying overnight, obviously, so I'm expecting a party atmosphere when we get home and I'm not disappointed.

Billie is driving, so I tell her to park up in front of the garage on our drive. Even as the electric gates at the front of our house open, giving access onto our drive, and we park up, we can hear the music and squeals from the kids. I don't bother going in the front door, the gate to the path running down the side of the house is open and we shimmy down it like ninjas.

We've all had at least one glass of champagne – even Billie – and Sarah and I are definitely a little worse for wear. As we go past the recycling, we notice the empties stacking up here too.

Sarah smiles at me. 'The boys have been on it…' There's something in her tone implying this could only be a good thing. I'm less sure. I know all the clearing up will fall to me and sometimes I'm just not in the mood for Pete trying to relive his younger days until 3am or whatever. It's not that I don't like a party, but it seems it's harder for me to forget my responsibilities than the others. It's also me who will have to get up with Anouk if she wakes in the night.

Sarah and Billie push past me and run into the garden, Pete

spots them both and Sarah flings her arms around him whooping before the kids and her own husband comes running up.

'Mummy!' Anouk, slippery as an eel in her bathing suit, goggles on her head, grabs my hand, pulling me over to everyone.

There is a lot of kissing and hugging and shrieking – from the adults too, not just the kids. The pool is full of every inflatable we own, and then some. The sprinkler is going at one end of the garden and there are discarded toys, towels and shoes everywhere.

Billie reads my mind. 'You're freaking out, aren't you?'

'Mmmm, little bit.'

'Don't waste your energy.' She passes me a glass of Pimm's. 'If you can't beat them, join them.'

'Where did you get that drink? We've been back less than two minutes.'

She taps the side of her nose. 'I have my ways.'

We sip our drinks and watch the unfolding chaos. Sarah is still clinging onto Pete's arm now. Next to me, Billie watches them too, and then turns to me, frowning at my expression.

'Does it bother you when she's like that? It shouldn't. She doesn't mean anything by it...'

'I know, I know. I'm being silly.'

'It's all in the past now. You're his wife, not her. He chose you, she's like a sister to him.'

'Seems like whenever she has a few drinks she wants to remind me that he was hers, first.'

Sarah isn't unattractive. In fact, we look quite similar in some respects – dark hair, pale skin, petite. But I have curves, where she is still sylph-like, and I have green eyes, not blue.

'Sometimes I think I should drape myself all over Greg, see how she likes it.'

'She'd know you were doing it to trick her though, bless Greg.'

Bless Greg indeed. Time has not been kind to him, balding, paunchy, years of rugby – and drinking – have not left him looking like Pete does. It's a shame though, because Greg is kind, behind all the buffoonery and banter. I watch him not only with his own children, but also Anouk and Billie's little boys, Isaac and Kaiden. The way he takes time to make sure they each get a turn playing, the way he crouches down on their level, smiling, making sure no one is hurt, no one is left out.

I know he does more than Pete also. He works from home two days a week and Sarah told me he splits the school run with her. He does the cooking and laundry. It's not a military operation for her to have a night away.

Finally, Pete disentangles himself from Sarah and comes over.

'Did you have a nice time?' He gives me a peck on the lips, but I kiss him back, more passionately than he was expecting. He smells of Acqua di Parma and sweat.

He pulls away from me to the sound of Billie clearing her throat.

'Nice to see you too, Pete. Shall I give you two some space?' She's laughing though and he leans over to hug her.

'Sorry, B, wasn't expecting my wife to be quite so excited to see me!'

I spot Sarah watching us and I smile and wave at her. She stays where she is, her expression unreadable, but after a second she waves back at me.

Billie heads off to greet her boys and Dan, her husband.

I don't like Dan one bit and I cannot understand what Billie – who is beautiful, intelligent and funny – sees in him. He's a sales director for some software company, but you'd think he was Elon Musk the way he tells it. He seems to spend any time not at work – and I use the term work loosely – at the gym and given any opportunity will bore the face off you talking about protein shakes and ratios. There's nothing wrong with looking after yourself, but with Dan, it's his entire personality. I can't spend more than about five minutes with him before wanting to punch him in the face and I have no idea why Pete is still friends with him.

I tell Pete I'm heading upstairs to change into my bikini and does anything need sorting in the kitchen?

'It's all good, you don't need to worry about a thing. But I'm available for bikini tying support.' He raises his eyebrows at me, smirking. I swat at him and smile.

'Down, boy!'

He feigns a pout, but heads for Anouk and the kids. As I get indoors I hear him throwing them all in the pool as they scream with delight.

Inside, my normally immaculate kitchen is a war zone, the floor is gritty underfoot, there are used plates and glasses and empty packets all over our black granite worktops.

There's a crunching behind me and I turn to find Dan has followed me in.

'Hey, Ems... have fun at the spa, being oiled up and rubbed down?' He smirks at me.

'Lovely, thank you.'

'I bet it was.'

I treat Dan like a toddler when he gets like this – ignore the bad behaviour and praise the good.

'Can I get you something?'

'Depends if you've got what I need?'

'Well, if you can find it, help yourself,' I say mildly and head upstairs.

He follows me though, telling me he's getting something from their room.

All the way down the corridor, to my room – in the opposite direction of his, the skin on the back of my neck prickles. I don't turn around though, I don't want to give him the satisfaction.

Closing my bedroom door – I debate locking it even – I strip off my Boden sundress and espadrilles, and chuck on a cheapo bathing suit, deciding against a bikini. What with the kids and Dan on the prowl, there's too great a chance it'll 'accidentally' come untied.

I find my denim cut-offs and a racer-back vest and slide my feet into Havaianas. When I go back downstairs, Dan is out in the garden, but as soon as he spots me, he comes over.

Greg, Pete, the kids and Sarah are in the pool playing some sort of bastardised game of water polo with a beach ball, and Billie is nowhere to be seen. I can only assume she's getting changed, I hope she hurries up so I'm not stuck with Dan for too long.

'And now it's beach Barbie, I assume?' Dan offers me another glass of Pimm's and looks at me smugly.

'Pardon?'

'Your outfit? You've got something for every occasion – like Barbie.'

He slurps a bottle of IPA, how very East London of him.

'You know, I always tell Pete how lucky he is to have you.'

'You do?'

'Yeah! You're well out of his league, we all know that.'

'I like to think I'm more than just an attractive accessory.'

'Of course you are!' He winks.

He's definitely drunk. Sober Dan likes to think he's a feminist. He talks about body positivity and role models and being an ally with a meaningful look on his face, as if to say, look at me, I'm hot *and* a good guy. But when he's on the booze, the real Dan creeps out.

'Well, thank you, I think.'

He leans in close to me now, I can see the open pores on his nose, the spikes of his stubble, the white crust beginning to form in the corners of his mouth. I want to run away but I'm trapped against the fence, and the drinks table in front of me.

Where are Billie and Sarah – or Pete even – when I need them?

'I said to him, *mate, you don't know how good you've got it, don't risk it*. But he ignored me.'

His words make a churning feeling start up in my stomach.

'He's so fucking lucky you didn't chuck him out when he told you. I mean, Billie, she'd have had my balls as earrings.'

'Told me what?'

A strange expression crosses his face as I speak. It's almost like he wants to smile, but it's quickly replaced by alarm as he realises he's put his foot in it.

'Told you about what happened in Krakow?'

Between the drama of me dropping my glass and it shattering everywhere, the clear up and trying to keep the kids away, realising it's starting to get chilly and people are tired and need food – mostly the kids – I don't even get to speak to Pete, or Dan, to find out what the hell is going on.

Instead, I wipe and sweep and wash and clear for what seems like aeons until finally, the pool is clear of toys, the cover back on, the tables are empty outside and the kids are inside in fleecy onesies watching a movie with pizza and popcorn. They're all in sleeping bags for a sleepover which I didn't have the energy to veto and I was tired of being the party pooper anyway.

In a way the distraction helps me, buys me time. Again, part of me wonders if I'm jumping to conclusions, that Dan didn't mean what he said, that I've misunderstood.

I'm standing outside, watching the stars appear in the sky, one by one as if someone has pressed a switch, when Billie comes over to me. She's changed into a maxi dress and her braids are up in a headscarf. I feel pretty scummy next to her, still in my pool 'fit.

She looks at me.

'Dan told you, didn't he?'

'I... well, I don't know what he told me. But it didn't sound good... I'm so confused now.'

'Shit.' She claps a hand to her forehead. 'I told him not to say anything.'

'I still don't know what Pete's done, but if you two know, then Sarah and Greg do too. So that doesn't feel great.'

I haven't had a cigarette since university, but God I want one now.

'Okay, look, I don't know exactly what happened. You need to speak to Pete, but for what it's worth, I'm on your side, not Sarah's. I blame her, not Pete... well, not as much.'

A chill runs down my spine. I wasn't imagining things.

'Wait... what has Sarah got to do with all this? I don't understand?'

'Shit, I'd sell a child for a cigarette right now.' Billie sits down on one of the wicker chairs on the patio, leans on her elbows, and the slumps low in her seat.

'And anyway, I thought they went to Amsterdam, not Krakow?'

'What? Oh, Dan's just getting confused, they did go to Amsterdam, not Krakow. Pete's not lying about that at least.'

'Right, well forgive me if I'm not seeing the silver lining.'

'No, of course. Look, she wasn't supposed to be there. I heard something about a city break with a friend and late cancellations and whatever, they bumped into each other on the Eurostar.'

'So they thought they'd party in Amsterdam?'

I don't even know what to do with myself right now. I want to get in the car and drive away, but I've drunk too much. And the kids are here.

'Billie, I found a condom wrapper a few weeks ago and I wondered if he'd slept with someone else – a stranger on his weekend away. A terrible mistake, but a one off. But Sarah? He slept with Sarah?' The betrayal feels like someone's poured petrol through my veins and set it alight.

I don't know what expression is on my face right now, but Billie sits back, away from me. If I'm scaring Billie then I really must look how I feel.

'I don't want to ask, but I feel I have to... where did you find the condom wrapper?'

'In his jeans pocket. We don't use them. I ultimately decided it was some boys' weekend nonsense.'

'Okay. Shit. Look, let's not jump to conclusions yet. And can I get you something? Anything? A glass of wine – in fact, a bottle? All the wine?'

You can bring me my husband's balls on a plate, is what I want to say. And Sarah's... I don't even know where to start with unpicking this.

'Just... give me a minute, yeah? By myself?'

'Sure, hon. Of course.' Billie chews the inside of her cheek and looks at me intently as she gets up. 'I wish there was something I could do.'

'I know. But you can't. No one can.'

I sit out there, staring at the sky until it darkens from royal blue to violet, to inky navy, and the moon hangs like a fishhook in the sky.

No one disturbs me. I'm guessing Pete's gone to bed without me as I see lights wink on and off upstairs and in the kitchen, until the only glow comes from the candles lit in the sitting room. When a fox skulks through the shrubbery and heads for the bins, I decide it's probably time to go inside.

Annoyingly I have to sleep in my bed, as Sarah and Greg –

staying over because of the kids and the booze – and Billie and Dan are in the spare rooms.

When I get upstairs, Pete is already snoring away, but thankfully not doing his usual trick of starfishing across the bed. I creep in and curl up under the blankets, clinging to the edge of the bed. I don't want a single part of my body to touch Pete's.

And, despite everything, the exhaustion hits me like a wave and I pass out straight away.

THREE

When I wake up, the bed is empty and cold beside me, but the shower is running in the en suite. From the sunshine filtering through the blinds, I'm guessing it's about eight-ish and my phone confirms the fact. I'm surprised I haven't been woken earlier, but I guess Anouk had a late one. I should go and sort her out, check she's got her overnight oats with berries that I make her.

I don't want to see Pete, but he emerges in a cloud of steam from the bathroom as I'm pulling on my robe, a sheepish expression on his face.

'Babe...'

I put a hand up as if to physically stop the words exiting his mouth.

'Not now.'

'It's not what you think.'

I look at him, raise an eyebrow. 'So, they're lying?'

'All I'm saying is you don't know the whole story. People make mistakes.'

'So, you did do something? A mistake is... I don't know, putting a pink shirt in with the whites or making tea not coffee.

Whatever this is, it's a little bit bigger!'

He steps back at my tone.

'All I'm saying is that we need to talk. You're never around anymore.'

'Excuse me?'

'Come on, you've got to accept things have been different recently.'

'If I've been a bit distracted, can you blame me? You're the one coming home telling me I desperately need to get a job when you know I want another baby. I'm so sorry if I've not been around to pander to your every whim!' My voice cracks as I shout at him. I can't stand for him to see me cry, so I take a deep breath and go downstairs.

There are voices coming from the kitchen but when I walk in they stop, creating an awkward silence, before everyone starts talking at once. Dan asks me how I slept. Anouk is clamouring for pancakes and Billie's boys are screeching and dancing around next to her. Of Sarah and Greg, there is no sign. *Shit, Greg.* Last night I was too caught up in my own dramas to even think about him. And to be honest, until I know exactly what happened I can't think about him.

Billie passes me a coffee.

'Thanks.'

I take a big gulp, letting it burn my mouth, as Billie looks at me, her face close to mine. 'You okay?'

I can only shrug. I really need everyone to leave, but can't say that. Though surely it's obvious?

'Greg and Sarah have gone already.'

'They forgot they had some family thing on at lunch.'

'Right.'

'I hope they get stuck behind a tractor,' I say.

'Ouch.' Dan laughs, his teeth white and shiny. How is he looking so together this morning? If there was any justice in the world he'd be vomiting in the toilet, especially after what he's done to my marriage.

Anouk continues nagging for pancakes, but I can't face any cooking.

'Go and ask Daddy if he wants to go to the farm shop for breakfast.'

As she bolts upstairs, I explain to Billie that they do epic buttermilk pancakes and my favourite, eggs royale.

'Sounds perfect. We'll probably head home from there – Dan, can you get the rest of the stuff?'

As he also disappears out of the room, I laugh to myself. 'Subtle, Billie.'

'How else am I supposed to get you alone?'

'Look, I'm okay, really.'

She looks at me, as if to say *yeah, right*, but doesn't call me out, just pulls me in for a hug.

'Are you sure you don't want us to go now? Give you both some space?'

Suddenly, I want her to stay more than anything. 'Nah, I could do with the time to calm down. If I get too emotional, we won't get anywhere and somehow I'll end up being the bad guy.'

'Ah yes, the typical defence of any guilty man, blame the woman.'

It hurts when she says the word 'guilty'. That there's no room for doubt in her mind. A part of me was still hoping maybe it wasn't true, that perhaps Dan had misunderstood. I take another deep breath.

'The farm has a massive play area, so I figured we could send the kids off there with Dan and Pete, and you and me can drink coffee in the sunshine.'

'Sounds good. If you're sure. Though I'm not sure I'll be any good at talking you down.'

Billie likes to think she's a fiery one, and don't get me wrong, she's bad-ass when she needs to be, but she's actually the calmest person I know.

She'll be objective and help me work through my feelings, to think about how to deal with Pete. It's always good to have a friend who is a lawyer, if anyone knows how to create a complex and unbreakable argument, it's them.

Time at the farm kills an extra couple of hours and I manage to avoid speaking to Pete beyond asking him to take Anouk to the toilet and barking my coffee order at him. He skulks around me, all hangdog, a pleading look on his face. Billie, true to her word, counsels me to ask him to be honest, to give me the facts if he values his marriage at all. To tell him that I'm not jumping to conclusions and it's worse if he lies more. She also tells me that if I need an alibi, she'll give me one. She thinks she's joking, but the way I feel right now, I wouldn't rule anything out.

Several cups of strong coffee and a plate of eggs helps me gird my loins or whatever the expression is, and as we wave Billie and Dan off in their Porsche Cayenne, I take the car keys off Pete.

'I'll drive us back.'

'Are you sure?'

'Yep.'

I call for Anouk, who is mucking about in the gravel path, watching the dust trail left by her friends. She climbs into her car seat and, sensing a potential opportunity to have the upper hand, given how quiet and tired we are, commences a very convincing argument to be allowed a *Frozen* movie marathon when we return home. I don't even bother negotiating for a tidy room or some homework and relent immediately.

'...and Domino's for tea?'

I've taught Anouk that if you don't ask, you don't get, and she's making the most of it.

When I acquiesce to even this demand, knowing how much I hate Domino's, I swear Pete's face goes pale. If Domino's is allowed, anything is possible.

The journey home is quick and quiet, Anouk gazing out of the window in satisfaction, Pete fiddling with his phone.

I wait until Anouk is ensconced in our room on our super king size bed with the remote and the promise to notify her *immediately* when it is time for Domino's later. As it's only just after lunch, she'll be waiting awhile, but that's good, it gives me time.

When I go back downstairs, Pete is in the kitchen looking as if he's never been in our house before. He's opening and closing cupboards, faffing around with our selection of herbal teas and the kettle.

'I didn't know what to do, Em. Do you want tea – or a glass of wine?'

'I don't know, what pairs best with an unfaithful husband?'

'Are you going to let me explain myself, or are you just going to believe hearsay?'

'Is it hearsay, though?'

I press my lips together to stop them trembling. I wish I could rewind, go back to before Dan said anything. Ignorance is bliss. My mind is starting to spiral about the realities I might have to face now. I love Pete, I do. And I thought he loved me too.

My phone vibrates and an Instagram message comes through. For a moment, I wonder how Pete would feel, if he knew about the photo – well, photos. I've sent a couple more. It's such easy money. But it's not the same, it really isn't.

'Look, Em, I hold my hands up. Like I said, made a mistake, and you've got to know, I've regretted it ever since.'

'A pretty big mistake it seems.'

'You don't even know what happened.'

'So, tell me.' He won't meet my eyes; my whole body aches

with tension and nerves. There's no going back from whatever he says now.

'First of all, you need to know it wasn't planned, okay? I didn't know Sarah was going to be there. She was on a girls' weekend.'

'Right.'

But she knew he'd be there.

Pete rubs a hand across his jaw and braces himself against the kitchen counter. He looks everywhere, except at me.

'Look, maybe someone mentioned I would be there to her, okay. But I swear, I had no idea.'

'So what, you went for some drinks and then fell over and landed with your dick in her?'

'Emily!'

'I'm sorry, please continue.' I'm not sorry though. Why does he get to have this nice and easy, when he's the one in the wrong?

'We'd been drinking all day and I didn't feel great and neither did Luke, so we decided to sneak off and head back to the hotel to grab some food, try and sober up a bit. Remember this was Friday and we weren't coming home until Sunday. I can't hack it like I used to.'

I don't remember him being able to hack it all that well back then either.

'When we walked into the hotel lobby, Sarah was the first person I saw.'

I can imagine the squealy hugs, the way drunk people are effusive with affection, their bodies remembering how well they fit together. It's all hurting so much, I need him to rip the plaster off.

'And then what happened?'

He looks down at the floor. Does that mean lying or remembering? Or is that looking up to the left?

'She invited me to grab some food with her and her mates –

Luke came too, I wasn't on my own. Honestly it was all innocent—'

'Pete...' I blink and tears start to run down my face. 'Just tell me what happened.'

He looks at me and bites his lip and tries to hug me, but I bat him away.

'I'm so sorry, Ems, really I am. You've got to believe me... God, this is so hard... okay, so we went to a bar, but I was still really tired so said I wanted to call it a night... and she offered to walk back with me.'

'I bet she fucking did.' I'm crying properly now, despite myself.

'Please, Ems, you're making this so hard... I can't...'

'Are you kidding me? I didn't sleep with someone else! You're in no position to tell me that.'

'Shhh, keep your voice down!'

From upstairs, Anouk's reedy little voice calls down to us. 'Mummy, why are you shouting?'

'I saw a spider, that's all,' I call back.

'Can I see it?'

I grab the kitchen roll and dab at my face, take a gulp of water.

Her little feet come clomping down the stairs. She's changed into her furry white unicorn onesie and something in my heart squeezes at the sight of her, her little black bob all rumpled at the back from where she's been snuggled in our bed. Pete might be a dickhead, but God we created a beautiful child. Sometimes I want to eat her. I pull her little body close to mine, press her perfectly smooth cheek against my lips and kiss her.

'Is it time for Domino's?' She wriggles out of my arms and looks up at us both.

'Baby, it's only just gone lunchtime. How can you possibly be hungry again? Domino's is for dinner. Have some fruit.'

She rolls her eyes at the concept of fruit as an acceptable snack. So much sass, I have no idea where she gets it from.

'Sweetie, here you go.' Pete passes her a sharing bag of Doritos and tells her to go back up to our room.

'Great, crumbs all over our bed.'

'I'll clear it up later.'

The dulcet tones of Elsa singing about letting it go soon reach us and I gesture to Pete to continue.

'She walked you back to the hotel and then what happened?'

'I didn't sleep with her. I need you to know that.'

'But clearly something did happen...'

I know all too well how many other options there are, aside from sex, when you're alone in a hotel room. That's all a long time ago now though, before Pete. In any case, his attempt at reassurance isn't working.

'We went back to her room for a nightcap. Honestly it was purely platonic at that point. She's a good mate, I've known her for a long time.'

'And therein lies the problem... she thinks she can pick up where you left off as kids.'

'I didn't mean for it to happen, but one thing lead to another and—'

'Who made the first move?'

'I can't remember okay. I'm sorry.'

'You expect me to believe it was some sort of cosmic coming together of hearts and minds? Who kissed who?'

'Please don't make me do this.'

'Pete!'

'Fine. She kissed me.'

He's lying. I know my husband.

'And then what.'

He squirms and shifts on his feet now, turning to the sink and rinsing out his coffee cup.

'Babe...'

'Oh, I'm sorry, is this embarrassing you? Maybe you should have thought of that in the first place?' My sadness is replaced by a tidal wave of anger.

I don't actually want to know the details, I don't need to know the sordid account of who put what where. But I'm desperate for him to feel as bad as I feel.

'I regret every minute of it, I do.'

'Did she blow you? Did you eat her out? Did you fuck her, Pete? Did she come?!'

His face flushes red and his fists clench.

'Fine.' He spits the words out at me. 'We kissed, I went down on her, she blew me for a bit, then we were going to fuck but I stopped at the last minute. Because I knew it was wrong! Happy now?'

'What do you want? A medal? Should I congratulate you on only putting your penis in one of Sarah's holes?'

'Emily! There's no need to be so crude.'

'Isn't there?'

'Look, we stopped, I told her I was sorry. She cried. We agreed it was a terrible mistake and I went back to my room. I know I should have told you, but I thought you were better off not knowing. It was a one-off, I swear.' He's petulant though, in his apology, I feel like I've forced it out of him. *Is he really sorry?*

'How can I believe you?'

Billie had asked me what I was going to do once I'd spoken to Pete. *You need to think about what you want to do.* Is this worth ending my marriage over?

'I'll do anything, I promise. I love you. I love Anouk. I love this.' He gestures to the house, our home. 'I love our life together.'

He's calm again now. I want to forgive him, I think... But how can I? Doesn't this go against everything we're supposed to stand for?

'Why risk it then?'

Perhaps he didn't think it was such a big risk. Am I such a pushover? But then again... Aren't I taking risks also, with those photos? And doesn't he deserve a second chance, after all these years. I wasn't so perfect, when we met. I've made mistakes before. Some he knows about.

'I don't know, Emily!'

'It's that you chose her, of all people, to cheat on me with. You must realise how much that hurts.'

Because it does. As much as I love her as a friend, the knowledge of their history always needled me. How could one man love two so very different women?

'I do, I do. God, I'm so so so sorry.'

This time when he reaches out to hold me, I let him. I rest my head on his shoulder, curl into his arms, his familiar smell. I don't know how we're here. How can the only person I want to comfort me, also be the person who hurts me the most?

'Tell me what to do, how to make it up to you please.'

He's expecting me to know how to make it right.

'I don't know. I really don't.' I shake my head and extricate myself from his arms, bite my lip and try to stop the tears from coming again. 'I wasn't prepared for any of this.' I feel unmoored, lost.

Outside, the sky is clouding over and it reminds me that I need to bring the laundry in. That life needs to carry on, despite everything.

He puts his arms around me again and we stand there for a few moments, until images of him and Sarah fill my head, and then I have to push him away.

'I can't tell you what to do here, Pete. You did this to us, not me.'

He cries then, like I haven't seen him do since Anouk was born.

I know he's sorry, I do. Or at least, I believe he's sorry for hurting me. I'm less sure that he regrets it. Anything seems possible now.

'I just need some space.'

And then, although it kills me to do it, I walk away from him and head upstairs to Anouk.

For the rest of the day and evening, Pete does what I ask and leaves me alone. He gets the laundry in without being asked and then clears and wipes down the kitchen. He also strips and remakes the beds in both spare rooms and orders Domino's for Anouk.

When it arrives, we all sit around the kitchen table. She eyes both of us, head swivelling like she's watching a tennis match.

'Why are you being weird, Daddy?'

'What? I'm not being weird.'

'You are. And you too, Mummy.' She narrows her eyes at me, as if trying to laser open my skull.

'Everything is fine, sweetheart, eat up.' I load another disgustingly oily slice onto her plate.

'Are you getting divorced?'

'What? No! Where did you hear that?'

'I heard Auntie Billie say it to Uncle Dan.'

Good to know our friends are gossiping about us in front of their kids. Dan must be loving it. I can only imagine Pete confessing, shamed-faced to him, on the flight back, Dan clapping him on the back and congratulating him – *what happens on boys' trips, stays on boys' trips, hey!*

'Auntie Billie doesn't know what she's talking about. Now, how about we do home pedicures after your bath?'

Her little mouth twists, she knows I'm trying to distract her, but her own self-interest wins out and she immediately starts asking if she can use my Rouge Noir nail polish.

After Anouk is in bed, Pete and I watch some nonsense on Netflix in silence, a million miles between us on the sofa. But both of us are on our phones the whole time. I'm messaging Billie to update her. As for Pete, well... I can only hope he's not messaging Sarah.

Eventually I go up before Pete and move my stuff into the spare room, closing the door behind me.

FOUR

Autumn 2015

It's been three months since the spa weekend. I'm still struggling with it all, to be honest. But because of Anouk and Beckie's friendship, I'm trying to be civil. As Pete reminded me, he didn't actually sleep with Sarah, they stopped before then.

And things with Pete have eased up a little; we've found a way through all this, somehow. After all, if our marriage had been good, surely Pete wouldn't have strayed in the first place...?

So, although I don't think things will ever go back to the way they were, and even though I'm still not really at the having-coffee-after-the-school-run stage, I'm meeting her this morning after the school run. Billie is staying with her for the weekend, but has come down early today so we can get some child-free time. Dan, amazingly enough, is bringing Billie's boys down this evening after school..

Billie's been WhatsApping me, telling me Sarah has hot gossip. Billie loves all our mall town non-dramas, finds them hilarious – all the fighting over who has the best roses or makes the best Victoria sponge. She's convinced that secretly it's all code for wife-swapping and cocaine. Sarah and I wound her up for ages about the real meaning of the pampas grass in front of the vicarage.

Before everything that happened, I loved my coffees with Sarah. Despite her mild-mannered persona, Sarah has a nose for gossip like I've never known. In another life she'd be a tabloid journalist – or perhaps a spy.

Meeting them both for coffee also allows me to escape the house, where Pete has taken to working from home, three days a week, in a bid to show his commitment to our marriage. I do appreciate it, but sometimes his presence is stifling and him being around isn't actually solving anything. I almost feel like his jailer, which I don't want to be. I want to be able to trust him when temptation is in his path, not keep him locked away.

Also, when I'm doing my shoots for Instagram, he gets in the way. I did stop for a little while, right after everything. But Pete's worries about redundancy weren't going anywhere, having a few hundred quid extra every month to cover coffees and shopping and various activities for Anouk was pretty handy. Pete himself was impressed – still thinking it came from photos of lamps or nicely arranged plates of food – and told me to carry on. Each time I take a photo of myself – my legs, my breasts – separate myself into pieces, I have a sick feeling in my stomach, and tell myself it would be the last time. But then another request will come in, and Anouk comes home asking for a new pair of trainers like Beckie, and I didn't have the heart to say no.

In the end I decided to just do a whole batch of photos during a weekend when Pete was taking Anouk camping. And then that would be it, no more. I'd be done with the whole thing.

On the evening they were due to return, I had dinner ready on the patio: grilled chicken, salad, home-made potato wedges, a Shirley Temple for Anouk, a jug of Pimm's for us, and Eton mess for dessert. I put on a dress I knew Pete loved, did my hair and make-up.

'Wow!' Pete came in, dumped the bags on the floor, and gave me a kiss.

'Mummy! You look so pretty!'

The house glowed with light at this time of year, early evening. I knew where to stand to benefit, turning my dress semi-sheer. I spotted the moment Pete clocked it too.

'Why don't you guys go shower and then we can have dinner outside – and maybe a movie?'

'Yay!' Anouk squealed as Pete picked her up rugby ball style and carried her upstairs.

We ate dinner and watched the movie and when Anouk, as predicted, fell asleep on the sofa, Pete again carried her upstairs.

When he came back down, I was in the hallway.

'I missed you.'

'I missed you, too.'

I let him press me up against the wall and kiss me.

'I love you so much.'

I don't reply, but pull him close again, his mouth cool and minty from brushing his teeth with Anouk. I can't say the words back to him, but I want to.

We hadn't slept together since that weekend, though I moved back into our room after a few days. But I'd not been able to let him near me, not properly. Something about the little break though, distance, has helped.

We make our way from the hall to the sitting room. He kisses my neck, and I pull his T-shirt off, his skin hot against my hands, fiery with desire. He tangles his hands in my hair, runs them down my back, around my waist, cups my breasts and he keeps kissing me, frantic with need.

We have the kind of sex I remember from when we were first together, fast and urgent, the need to be as close as possible.

Somehow we work our way to the sofa and as I fall backwards on it he kisses his way down my body, removing unnecessary items of clothing in his way. As he pushes himself into me and moves over me, he looks at me, tells me he loves me, that I'm incredible. He works his fingers between us, against me, telling me he wants to make me come. But when I do, before him, even as I say his name, I think about that nameless, faceless man, looking at my photos. As he drives into me harder and faster, pulling me tight against him, I realise that maybe, despite tonight, we're not as easily fixed as I thought.

The café is busy when I get there, but Sarah, who drove, has secured us a decent table at the back, away from the buggies and breastfeeding women. I never breastfed Anouk. Sometimes I wonder if I should have tried harder, but my milk didn't seem to come in and she had tongue tie. I remember crying in our bed, delirious with sleep deprivation, burping Anouk, watching her spit up milk, tinged red from my bleeding nipples. She wouldn't stop crying. When Pete suggested formula and then fed it to her, I cried as had a shower and made a sandwich and but then fell asleep – and slept for four hours solid. Despite the angst and guilt, it was worth it. I got a little of myself back when I let go of trying.

Pete loved giving Anouk a bottle anyway, cracking jokes and enjoying the adoring looks of the mothers at the baby groups.

Sarah and Billie are at the table with lattes and cake, but they've ordered my usual – an americano.

'I don't know how you can drink that. It's like rocket fuel.'

I'm not sure I'm ready quite yet to joke and laugh with Sarah, even if it's Billie making the remarks. This whole set up seems artificial. I can't just forget that Pete and Sarah almost slept together, but I can at least pretend to, for Billie's sake.

'Calories, babe – a latte is like a whole meal in itself.'

'There is more to life than calories counting, Emily. Can't you ever just enjoy yourself?'

I know they're right. But I've always been careful around food. And right now, I don't want to give Pete any reason for straying again. After all, I'm reminded of it almost daily when I see Sarah in the playground. But I want to make things better between us all, try to move on.

'So, what's this gossip you promised? It'd better be good, I've got a busy day.'

'A busy day – you? What does that involve, hot yoga "and" a massage?' Billie quips.

'That's rich coming from you.' But I smile at Billie, so she knows I'm only joking.

'Anyway, yeah, Sarah, spit it out! Has someone been sabotaging the world's largest marrow or overwatering their roses?' Billie is already giggling, but Sarah shakes her head.

'Nothing to do with gardening this time. Well not really.' Sarah takes a sip of her latte, 'So apparently there's a school mum with a dodgy Instagram account.'

Coffee spurts out of my nose as I cough and choke.

'Ems? You okay?' Billie and Sarah pat me on the back like they're winding a baby.

'Yes, sorry, went down the wrong way – but so what, I'm not with you. What's wrong with that?'

'Emily, you naive little bunny, it's not pictures of their lunch or their latest camping trip, they're nude pictures or whatever.'

Billie is gleeful at my perceived lack of knowledge here. To be fair, it *is* pretty good gossip compared to the usual storm-in-a-tea-cup incidents. Even so I can barely breathe – surely no one knows about my photos? There's hundreds of parents at the school, it's just a coincidence, a wardrobe malfunction or something.

'I don't get it...' I fish for information, this is the most Sarah and I have spoken in weeks.

'There's a mum at the school that is taking racy pictures of herself and posting them online. Can you even believe it? Why would you do that?'

I haven't posted them online, I sent them in a private message, but they're making it sound like they're on a billboard in Piccadilly Circus.

'Haven't you ever made a home movie?' I ask, trying to distract them.

'No!'

'Bet Greg would love it.' Billie is laughing at us.

'Greg might love it, but there is no way on God's earth I'm doing it.'

'Why not?' I ask.

'Have you done it?'

'What do you think?'

'You have!'

'It can't just be me, surely.'

'No, you're not alone, I have too,' says Billie.

Of course she has, although I expect Dan probably wants to look at himself when he watches it back, not her.

Sarah stares at us both in surprise.

'That's not my point here – why *don't* you do it?' I ask. I know it's a weird thing to press her on, and I can see Billie is thinking that too, from the expression on her face. But I want to steer the conversation away from guessing who it is in those pictures.

'Because I don't want to. It's not because I don't like sex or I don't like my body, it just doesn't appeal. Plus, somehow I know it would get leaked and then I'd be the one all over the school WhatsApps.'

'You can delete them after.'

'It's so risky though, whoever you send them to can share them however they like. ANYWAY! Everyone is talking about who the mum could be.'

Shit.

'Don't they know from the pictures?'

'No, no one knows... or if they do, they're not saying. I mean, I'm not really surprised because that would mean implicating their own husbands. I wouldn't be shouting about Greg perusing porn.'

'How do they know it's a dad who found it?'

Billie nods along as I grill Sarah. I've given up trying to be subtle. I'm hoping my intense interest is being taken for vicarious pleasure in someone else's misfortune.

'Good point. There is that lesbian couple in year four,' Sarah concedes.

'Hmm, so what else do we know? I wonder if we can help you work out who it is?'

I love Billie, but right now I could murder her. I drink my americano but the squirming in my stomach makes me want to spit it right back out again.

'Well, we know that she's got dark hair, she's petite and has small boobs.' Sarah checks her phone. 'Here – have a look yourself.'

She holds out her phone, but I don't take it.

'What are you waiting for, Ems?'

Billie reaches out and grabs it, holding the screen so we can both see the tiny screenshot.

It is me.

Thankfully it's a blurry picture of me from the side, my hair covering my face. I could be any dark-haired woman. And then I notice something. *Shit*. My mouth goes dry and my Fitbit beeps to tell me my heart rate is climbing. *No kidding!*

'How funny, she's got a bracelet just like mine, look.'

I hold up my wrist. I figure it's best to hide in plain sight, call out anything that could identify me. I haven't done any more shoots since the summer, and I've sent nearly all the pictures I took. I'm going to have to go back through them all again, thoroughly, to check for anything that might identify me. How could I be so stupid? I want to be sick.

'So she does. Haha! It's not you, is it?'

I force out a laugh, trying to sound jolly, and take some deep breaths, bring my breathing under control.

'I'd hardly be sitting here telling you about the bracelet if it was!'

'Good point. Still, it's an unusual bracelet that – where did you get it again? Maybe we can use that to work out who she is?'

'Alright Inspector Morse, it was a present from Pete. So... I've no idea. For all I know he got it off Facebook marketplace.'

It's platinum and diamonds. It's from De Beers, and it isn't from Pete. It was a gift, from a very long time ago, from someone I don't speak to anymore.

'Well anyway, that doesn't help us work it out.' Sarah sighs.

'Plus, she might be wearing a wig. It could be anyone. How do they even know it's a mum from school?'

Thank God for Billie, asking the question that hadn't even crossed my mind. I'm really no good at all this sneaking around, not anymore.

'The other photos, apparently. Even though they don't show her face, there's a St Mark's jacket in the background of one.'

This is news to me. That was very remiss of me if so. I'm going to have to see if I can get that photo back, send the recipient a replacement. Although I have no idea how to explain why. Also, how the hell did it get onto the parents' WhatsApp groups? Who would even share the photos? My insides churn, I don't want to talk about this anymore.

I rest my elbows on the table. 'Why does it even matter anyway, who cares?'

'Are you seriously telling me this is not top gossip? In our school, the biggest beef is over parking or whose child got to play Mary in the school nativity. This is proper suburban, wife-swapping goodness.'

I've never seen Billie so excited, and it makes me smile despite myself.

'Go on, guess who it is, let's have some fun,' Billie continues.

'Bills, you don't even know the people here, why do you care?' I'm surprised at Sarah, but she smiles at me. It's nice to have someone on my side, even if it's her and she doesn't realise.

'Spoilsports.' Billie pouts at us and drains her latte.

'S'pose we'd better be going then – come on, Sarah, you promised me a trip to that shoe store all those celebs go to.'

'Okay, okay.' Sarah pushes her chair back and stands up. 'But, Ems, I didn't even get to tell you about the new single dad at school.'

'Tell me, tell me!' Billie is beside herself again. God knows what she tells all her trendy friends in Herne Hill about us. They must have a right laugh.

As we make our way out, there's a man with his back to us, placing an order. He's standing with his head tilted to one side. Something about the way he holds himself, even in jeans and a shirt, the sleeves rolled up to mid-forearm, causes me to feel like I've taken a bend too fast in the car.

It can't be him. Surely.

'Ems? Are you okay? You've gone all white.'

Sarah goes to take my arm, but I bat her away.

'I'm fine, don't be silly. I just remembered something – somewhere I need to be.'

But as we reach the door I hear his voice, that deep, throaty voice, the slight rasp that had me on my knees.

And when I turn around for one last look, he's looking right back at me.

Shit.
It is him.

FIVE

February 2023
Naomi

It rains the next time I see Brigham, the grey arch of the prison gates looming over me. She makes a joke about Manderley, and dreaming about going back there, except she's always here. I don't laugh, but she smiles her saturnine smile anyway.

It's been a tough week, Max and I fought about silly things – the washing up, the laundry. He forgot to take the bins out, I forgot to pay a bill. It's like we're constantly rubbing each other up the wrong way. It's a shock though, after a few months of newly living together bliss. Mum would tell me it's normal. I don't call her though, moaning about Max to her feels somehow disloyal. He's not done anything wrong, and neither have I. And I don't want her to love him any less.

Max grumbled this morning when my alarm woke him also. Days he doesn't go into the office he likes to sleep until nine, but it's an early start for me, catching the train down to London. He tried to coax me back under the warm blankets, curving his arm around me, spooning around me, kissing my neck. It was tempting – his clever mouth, his clever fingers. I didn't give in though, gave him promises for this evening, told him I wouldn't be late. He frowned and burrowed back under the duvet, asleep again before I even got in the shower.

I have two coffees on my way to the prison, endeavouring to jolt myself awake, preparing for Brigham's complex call and response way of answering my questions.

As it turns out, she doesn't want to talk about the case today, no digging into what led her to do what she allegedly did or didn't do. Instead, she wants to talk about him, about Liam.

It's odd, talking about someone I almost met, and that Mum knew; she even went to the wedding.

Brigham tells me that it wasn't love at first sight.

'You need to know that. Or lust even. Although there was plenty of that later on.'

'Did you think he was a predator, then?'

'Of course not! What kind of stupid question is that.'

'Well, you strike me as far too intelligent to fall for some sleazy older man.'

'This is the problem with the reporting of the case. With everything!' She throws her hands up in the air and then clasps them in her lap, fixing me with that steely gaze.

'You're all so narrow-minded, so binary about relationships. God, it must be so boring to be ordinary.'

Brigham talks a lot about being ordinary and how she despises it. She says ordinary people were just jealous. It's hard to reconcile the assertive, aggressive woman in front of me with the fragile victim her defence painted her to be. The victim of a manipulative predator, controlling her every move, what she wore, what she ate, what she drank, when she went to the toilet, who she slept with.

'I'm confused, that's all.'

'Oh, darling, so am I sometimes. But don't you know better

than to believe everything you read? Don't you want to know what really happened?'

I get my phone out, place it on the table, press record.

'Yes please.'

And she starts.

Recording #2 – 16th March 2023

I met him at work. It's a predictable story in some ways. He was my boss. It's not what you're thinking. It wasn't lust at first sight, bending me backwards over his desk, long lunches, and quickies in the stationery cupboard.

I don't know what I expected when I left university. Perhaps that everyone in my new job would be on my side. Not that everyone would like me – far from it – but the way that school engenders a kind of pastoral bubble around everyone and everything. Competition is limited and defined. If people sink, there are, to lesser or greater degrees, support networks – even if they're only a bunch of teenagers, able to call the police or break down a door to catch someone mid-overdose. Sit with them whilst they have their stomach pumped. That's not to say it's not possible to disappear at university, it's more that you still have the expectation that someone, somewhere, is looking out for you.

But in the real world, it is entirely possible to become invisible.

One of the first things he said to me – well, to the cohort of grads that had joined his team – was that no one gave a shit about who you were there, where you'd studied, your grades, who you'd shagged. Your colleagues weren't your mummy or your daddy. There was no safety net. This was real life, wake up and smell the coffee. The grad next to me whispered to a friend, 'What else – life's a bitch and then you die?' and they sniggered quietly.

At the time I thought it was more likely that *he* was having a midlife crisis, that he wasn't having enough sex – are any of us? – and that he couldn't relate to his kids. I wasn't surprised to find out later he had a motorbike. Not that it got a lot of use, being ridden from his house in Surrey to the station and back every day. And is it even a midlife crisis if you're only in your late thirties?

It started small – almost nothing really. No playing footsie, no meaningful looks. I mean, that's not to say he didn't check me out, because he definitely did. And I heard him when he came back from a meeting once, talking about a pregnant woman's breasts as if they were shrink-wrapped and on display in Sainsbury's, ready for him to consume. He liked looking at women, he never hid that. But he somehow got away with it when another man – less handsome, less able to make you feel like the centre of the universe – wouldn't.

He had opinions, all the time, on everything about us. The length of my skirt, the colour of someone's socks, the angle of the coffee cups stacked in the reception area. He was a typical consultant, excellent at borrowing your watch and then selling it back to you. He was a total asshole, and he was the most charming, charismatic man I'd ever met.

Obviously I know now how he did it. I went through the same sales training, after all. The mirroring of body language, the attention to detail. Love bombing, I think they call it. He knew how to win you over – how to find anyone's Achilles' heel and use it against them.

Also, you have to remember I was used to scruffy art-student boys, with baggy jeans and band T-shirts, still skateboarding to lectures. Not that I dated much… in fact, you could blame university for why things turned out the way they did.

I was in my second year at Oxford when a visiting professor came to give a guest lecture one night. I'd been asked by a course tutor to escort him across campus and ensure he had everything he needed – by which they meant, skivvy for him. He was tall, middle-aged, American, divorced, no doubt he'd left a trail of tearful under-grads in his expensively cologned wake everywhere he went.

Like Liam, he was clever, taking a more passive approach I'd not seen before. Making sure I was thanked, included, taken out for dinner after. And somehow he finagled it that I was sat next to him, and he asked me about my studies – History of Art – and my life, boring as it was, growing up in a suburban, single-parent family. He asked me about my hopes and dreams and he acted like I was the visiting professor, the sun around which the room and its associated hangers-on revolved.

He told me how promising I was, that he had heard excellent things about my essays, my insight, and wit. He kept his eyes on my face, never once dipping below my neck. He remained within his own personal space, there were no accidental leg bumps, no brushing of arms – it was a masterclass in seduction.

When the dinner began to end, it was me who suggested continuing the conversation over a nightcap, and where better than his suite? And, of course, it was natural for him to say that he would go up first, to give him a minute to clear up when in fact, I now know he was simply avoiding anyone seeing us go up in the lift together.

It was me who made the first move, me that couldn't take the tension, pressed my lips against his. And he was the one who asked me if I was sure, if I consented, if I wanted it. And I did – yes, I said. Every time, to everything he did to me.

It only took that one time, but once I had a taste for older men, I was addicted. I couldn't explain it. There were rumours later of course – why I was always asked to help with departmental guests, the abundant references I received for extra courses over the holidays, the excellent grades I maintained, seemingly effortlessly. But I never confirmed or denied anything, I never spoke of it at all. Still, none of those men prepared me for Liam.

Although maybe 'prepare' is the wrong word, because in some ways I absolutely was prepared for him – low expectations, little interest in younger men. Liam always swore that he noticed me straight away and liked that I was different. I know better now, but back then I liked that someone with experience, power, intellect, had singled me out.

The age gap wasn't insurmountable – although someone in their late thirties seemed remote to most graduates, I was used to it. Where we were playing at grown-ups – pushing around budget figures, putting things on expenses, packing our schedules with meetings – he really was one. And I knew why I was of interest to him, or at least I thought I did. I thought I came as part of his midlife crisis set, something to tick off along with his motorbike and new gym membership.

I could have been any attractive, standoffish young woman. He didn't have a reputation back then, not for seducing grads anyway. Not like 'the Octopus' – a nickname for a senior director, who had a hands-on approach to learning and development. Or the low-level rumours about the sales director sleeping with the publicity assistant and the boys-only client trips and evenings out – destination unspecified – but resulting in late appearances in the office, accompanied by monstrous hangovers and bacon rolls.

Liam also – and it is with some sense of irony that I say this – was not like the others.

He was openly a complete shit to work with. Low tolerance and high standards. If you made a spelling error, mismatched a colour on a deck, didn't check print margins on a P+L sheet, then he'd ball you out. And this was from the start.

There was no grace period, no time to ramp up. As he said himself, it wasn't so much a steep learning curve as a vertical trajectory upwards.

I overheard some other analysts on a project with him, muttering over frantically gasped cigarettes, that if you hadn't cried in your first week with him, you were most likely a psychopath.

It wasn't until we'd been seeing each other for some time, when he told me that for most people, their bark was much worse than their bite, but not him. He was proud of how self-aware he was. His other favourite saying was to believe people the first time when they showed you who they were.

The night he told me that, he also told me his wife didn't understand him. That she hadn't for a long time. That he'd never felt this way before. That he knew he was a cliché.

It's the folly of youth to believe that no one could ever come before you. That you are the freshly minted zeitgeist, cracking the mould and being the change you wanted to see. After all, how often are we told when we graduate that the world is our oyster. When I look back at the pictures, that nacre still gleams across my collarbones, freshly hatched, ready for anything it seemed.

How little I knew.

SIX

Autumn 2015

'Emily?'

That voice, that reduced me to tears or drove me wild with a single word. Sarah and Billie's faces are a picture – heads swivelling between us as if they're watching a tennis match on centre court at Wimbledon.

'Is it really you?'

He strides towards me and closes the gap between us in seconds.

The coffee shop has fallen silent. Honestly, social media has nothing on the speed of local mums with juicy dirt.

I take one step backwards as he comes in close and kisses my cheek. Still, that expensive scent he wears, and behind it his own smell, dark, musky. It catches me unawares.

'Liam! How lovely to see you.'

I try to regain control of my wildly galloping heartbeat, my body remembering, even as I try to forget. I kiss him back, prickles of stubble he never had before under my lips, acting as if I only saw him yesterday.

'How long has it been? Five years? Longer?'

'Something like that.' I smile back at him.

'You're looking well.'

He is, too. The whole silver fox thing is working for him. He's still big, still tall. Still making me breathless.

I try to think of Pete, the way he felt the other night, but it doesn't help. So I distract us both, point at the barista over his shoulder, who is holding out a to-go cup with his name scrawled across it in big letters.

'Still a scalding hot americano?'

'Some things never change.'

And again he meets my gaze with his and the world around me falls away. Distantly I'm aware of Sarah calling me.

'Ems!' And then she's right next to me. 'We need to make a move!' Her eyebrows are semaphoring questions at me and Billie is half out the door, but I know I will be grilled by them in the car. I need to get a grip.

'Oh God, yes. Sorry, Sarah. Liam, it was lovely to see you... lovely, but random...'

'Same here. I... do you come here often?'

Even Sarah laughs at this.

He grins. 'God, what a cliché. I mean, only... I've just moved to the area. Finally dragged my arse out of London – so maybe I'll see you again soon? Can I get your number?'

Sarah is fidgeting next to me, looking at her Fitbit and tapping her phone. 'Em, we really need to go now. Remember you wanted to go shoe shopping?' She's lying, we don't have plans, but I sense she's trying to bail me out of this – which seems oddly loyal after what she did with Pete, but then she does have ground to make up here.

'You're busy, I'm sorry. I'll let you go. But let's catch up soon.' And then he takes his coffee and brushes past us on his way out of the door.

It's as if a button is pressed and the coffee shop comes back to life again, the clinking of cups and saucers, children crying, mothers nagging. The baristas yelling orders to each other across the whirr and grind of the coffee machines.

Sarah only looks at me, wide-eyed, before grabbing my arm and dragging me outside to her car where Billie is waiting also.

It takes a while to extract myself from them both after. Sarah gives me a lift home and all the way I can tell she and Billie are itching to ask me questions, but I manage to hold them at bay with a comment about how we'd worked together, a long time ago.

'I meant to tell you that there was a new dad at school. And that he's a right silver fox. Maddy was telling me all about him at pick up!'

I want to ask Sarah if she's going to sleep with him also, but I know I'm better than that. It's tempting though.

'Well, now you can tell her you've met him.'

And the rest, I think. I know our coffee shop reunion will be all over the playground by the time I collect Anouk. And if I try to stop it, I'll only get Sarah more intrigued.

'He's single as well.'

That's news to me though, that he's single. He was definitely *not* single when we were together. I wonder what finally made his wife divorce him. He was always discreet, but I now know I wasn't the first and I highly doubt I was the last.

'Well, good for him. I'm sure someone will snap him up.'

Sarah looks at me.

'Not me, obviously.'

Sarah blushes as I say this. The subtext being that *I'm* not the one who sleeps with the dad from school.

'Obviously,' she mumbles and focuses on navigating across a roundabout behind a cyclist.

Never have I been so grateful for Sarah's tendency to see the speed limit as a sort of suggested guidance rather than a legal requirement. I'm home within ten minutes and I leap out of the car with a quick shout that I'll see her – and Billie, who's staying at hers – at pick up.

Now I'm sitting at my kitchen table with another black coffee trying to ignore every memory that is trying to rush through my mind. How is he here, now, after all this time? This is the last thing I need – that my marriage needs.

The last time Liam and I saw each other was eight years ago, in a grubby hotel room in Swindon. A Travelodge or a Premier Inn, I can't remember now. How the mighty fall. We weren't even together then. It was months after we'd ended – and I was with someone else. And yet, somehow, I'd ended up on a project he was leading. And all it took was one glass of wine and for him to look at me a certain way. I'm not proud of myself.

It wasn't even nice that last time. It hurt. I was dry and yet I still let him, did what I was told. Up against a badly painted and plastered wall. My back bled afterwards. I remember him asking me if I needed a hand, but I could tell from the speedy noise of his zip as he redressed that he didn't want to be there anymore. He'd got what he came for.

I still feel bad about what I did next.

What are you doing here?

The look of surprise on Pete's face when I buzzed his flat at midnight, after I told him I'd be away overnight. We'd been together a few months by then, not exactly super serious, but it had potential. We'd never said we were exclusive, but I knew I was walking a fine line.

Conference finished early, babe. Aren't you going to let me in?

The way he held the door open for me, the pleasure in his expression when he realised what I wanted. The way he felt like home right then, how Liam didn't.

Despite that night, it only took another couple of months

before Pete asked me to move in, and here we are, eight years later. Happy... or at least, attempting to be.

For the rest of the day, I am ambushed by flashbacks of my life before Pete. A life that no one has any idea about – at least no one I am friends with now.

I hear snippets of music that aren't there, the ozone smell of the ocean accosts me as I walk upstairs, the whisper of a man's voice in my ear low and demanding. Telling me I'm a good girl, to *be* a good girl.

And also, though I try to stop myself, behind it all are memories of Anna.

We don't see Billie and Dan over the weekend, it's still too weird for me and Pete to be hanging out with them and Greg and Sarah like nothing's happened. Billie texts me, promises we'll catch up soon, but I can't help feeling a little left out. Watching their Instagram stories of fun dinners and taking the kids to a National Trust place, it occurs to me that Pete's mistake has cost us more than he thought. Monday comes round soon enough though and then rest of the week passes in a blur of school runs, ferrying Anouk to her various activities, and the usual house and life admin. But when I get a moment, I remember what Sarah said in the coffee shop, about the rumours of the school mum. I decide not to send any more pictures for a while.

I knew there was a risk I would be found out, but I never thought it would actually happen. And, of course, what were the chances that the man messaging me would be someone local?

I feel so stupid. It seemed like such a simple fix to our financial problems. I know better than anyone though – there's no such thing as a free lunch.

Part of me is angry too. How unfair it seems. Really, what's wrong with it, when you come down to it? I'm not showing anything they wouldn't see if I swam at the local pool. Why can't I monetise all the pervy looks at my page? I know though that Pete wouldn't see it like that. That it's not that simple.

I'm on edge at every school run now too, in case I bump into Liam. I'm avoiding Sarah again too. I don't want to see her because she'll talk to me about him and then I'll be tempted to talk about him. And I know once I start, I won't be able to stop. The Pandora's box in my head is already cracking open. I've kept it shut for so long, for good reason. There are things in there that could do real damage, and not just to me.

Billie offered me a free trial at the swanky gym in the local country manor house spa – it's part of a boutique chain that she's a member of – so one day I take myself off there, as a distraction, book in a session with a personal trainer, Alex.

I was expecting a woman, but when I arrive, I see why the receptionist winked at me and told me to have a good time. Alex is ripped and charming, very attentive, but it only makes my skin crawl. He's all fake tan and macros and bleached teeth. Asking me if I've considered collagen supplements.

When he's leaning over me, because apparently I need to stretch out my groin, I catch him watching us in the mirror. After our session, I can't get away fast enough, but Alex is persistent. He's a tennis coach too, he tells me, as he queues behind me at the café to get his daily superfood smoothie – custom blended for him of course.

When I sit down with my post-workout latte, he joins me without asking, and points out all the calories I'm drinking right now, but that he can message me some good links for meal replacement shakes.

'Not that you need to lose weight. You look fantastic...'

I wait for him to say what usually follows, *for your age*, but he doesn't.

'Thank you.' I wonder how much longer he's going to sit

here; my coffee is hotter than hell, so I can't even down it and be free.

'I wish all my clients were like you. Diligent, understanding the importance of looking after yourself. The whole holistic approach. And you know...' He nods discreetly at a table next to us, full of women around my age but several dress sizes bigger, they're laughing and toasting to something.

'Your husband is a lucky man.'

'I don't know what to say.'

'Well, if you're looking for a regular trainer, hit me up!'

It's giving me eye strain trying not to roll my eyes.

And then another voice snaps me out of my boredom.

'Emily, we really must stop meeting like this.'

It's Liam, fresh in tennis whites, a little sweaty and flushed. Why is he here, why must we keep bumping into each other? *Dammit.*

'It's a small town,' I remind him, and my overactive imagination. It's not like we're in the movie *Serendipity* – I don't want him thinking there's some greater force at play here. I can't even take the bins out without seeing people I know.

Even so, I stand up, kiss him hello.

When I first met Liam he smoked. He used to complain about the smoking bans in bars –- and I'd lecture him about how bad it was for him, snatching cigarettes out of his hand when we were outside; but not before taking a drag myself, watching him watch me as I put it to my lips and inhaled.

'Hi, I'm Alex.'

Liam looks from me to him.

'I'm Emma's personal trainer.' And he flashes his pearly whites, crossing his arms, his shirt pulling across his biceps.

'Her name is Emily,' Liam corrects him. 'Nice to meet you.' Liam hides a smile as he turns back to me. 'The Emily I knew didn't even go to the gym. Said she was above such a banal, vain activity.'

I can feel Alex bristle. I guarantee he has no idea what banal means, but he'll know that someone has insulted him.

'Well, Liam, people can – and do – change.'

'So they can.'

'How do you two know each other?'

Alex is shorter than Liam. Not by much, an inch or two – although to men, we know that's everything – but he's doing his best to crowbar his way into whatever it is that's happening here.

'That's a good question. How do we know each other, Ems?'

And Liam smiles that crooked smile at me. A million images tumble through my mind, times he smiled that same smile, but for very different reasons.

I remind myself a crooked little smile is nothing. *I am better than this*. I take a deep breath.

'We worked together a very long time ago.'

Liam puts a hand to his heart, a hand that no longer bears a wedding ring, Sarah's intel was correct.

'Was it really that long ago? Seems like yesterday to me.'

Despite myself, I can't take my eyes off him, that same magnetic pull that drew me to him all those years ago. I know I need to escape, but somehow I'm powerless, a pinned and chloroformed butterfly under his gaze.

I'm not the only one transfixed; Alex looks like he's about ready to lamp Liam. He's underestimating him though. Despite the accent and the fancy education, there's an edge to Liam, a wildness. And I know what he's really capable of. I have the scars to prove it.

'Ems, we are long overdue a catch up.'

It's interesting to me how Liam isn't playing it cool, not like he used to. I can't even start to think about how else he might have changed though.

'A lot's happened.'

'I can tell.' His eyes flick to *my* left hand.

Out of the corner of my eye I notice Alex getting up and slinging his kit over his shoulder.

'I'm going to leave you guys to your reunion. Emily, see you next week... maybe?'

'Sure!'

As he walks off, Liam tells me he hopes there isn't a snowball's chance in hell that I'll be booking another session with Alex.

'Definitely not!' And I can't help but laugh.

'Shall we sit down?'

Liam pulls out my chair for me. He always did have beautiful manners. It was part of his allure.

He sits in Alex's seat, and I duly sit in mine.

I flash back to that final hotel meeting. His last words to me. How much they hurt, remember how long it took me to get over him.

'Do you want another? I can put it on my account.'

He beckons over a waiter, orders a macchiato and then waves in my direction – 'and whatever she's having.'

'Nothing for me thanks.'

Liam frowns at me. I need to make my excuses and leave.

Because I need to forget the taste of the hollows beneath his hip bones. The timbre of his voice when it is low and quiet, muttering in my ear, for no one else but me. The look on his face when he sees me across a room full of hundreds of people.

I think of Pete instead, his easy humour, his bouncy energy. The way people are drawn to his extraversion, the way everyone always wants to be his friend. Despite everything, right now with Liam, Pete is my anchor, my safety net. Or, at least, I need to believe that...

When the waiter bustles off, there is silence and Liam only looks at me. I chew the inside of my cheek.

'So...'

'Alone at last,' he says.

I shake my head. 'Liam... what are you doing here? What are we doing here?'

'It's like your mate Alex said – we're old friends, catching up.'

'We were never friends, Liam. You know that.'

He tips his head to the side and smiles.

'If you say so.'

The anger comes over me so suddenly the room is almost tinted red.

'What are you playing at? Don't pretend like it's a friendly reunion for us.'

He leans back in his chair, legs out, crossed at the ankle. Relaxed.

'I never meant to hurt you. I never wanted it to end the way it did.'

'It's all just words, Liam. What do you want from me? I've not got time for your games. In fact, I should be going...'

The muscle in his jaw twitches.

'I'm not playing games. I saw you and I genuinely thought it would be nice to catch up. It wasn't all bad, back then, was it?'

That's the problem though. It wasn't bad at all, far from it. That's why I shouldn't be here. I look at my phone. I need to get out of here, put the laundry on before I pick up Anouk.

'I just don't know what we've got to say to each other.'

I'm kidding myself though, there's a big part of me that wants to throw myself into his arms, tell him all about Pete cheating. About how this perfect life is nothing like I imagined. Have him whisper to me in the darkness like he used to.

'I'm glad you're happy now, Ems – honestly. I didn't mean to upset you or cause any drama. I guess... I don't know, I saw you and I... well, I missed you. I still miss you. I miss us. What we had. But it looks like everything is going great for you.'

'It *is* going great. I am really happy. I've moved on. It's all in the past. There's no point looking back.'

'Isn't there? Don't you ever think about us?'

Sometimes, more than I should, I want to say. But I really don't need to know that he thinks about us.

'Not really.'

'So, you do.'

How has he got that out of my answer? I forgot that his trick is to wear you down drip by drip, the way water wears away stone, until nothing is left.

'No. I mean, you've crossed my mind but only when stuff pops up on LinkedIn or whatever.'

'Right.'

But he smiles wolfishly and folds his arms across his chest. A memory flashes back to me, him with that same expression and pose. Lying on the floor beneath him, a locked door between me and freedom.

'Look, you're right. It wasn't all bad. But lots of it wasn't good. You were my boss!' I hiss at him across the table.

'So what? We weren't the first, and we definitely weren't the last. When did you get so law-abiding? Don't tell me you've gone all trad-wife like the rest of them out here. I thought you were better than that.'

Here is the man I knew, acting like he's something special.

'Fuck off, Liam.'

He laughs, he knows I'm rattled. It kills me to admit it, but Liam always saw straight to the heart of me.

You like it, don't you, here in the dark, with me? We're night people. We're not like others. Don't you know? We're better than them. I see you, Emily. No one else does. But I do.

His voice is a memory. But he's here all the same.

More than ever, I want to go home and tidy the house and pick up Anouk and pretend none of this ever happened.

'I know she's still there, the Emily I knew. People don't change that much. Does your husband know what you're really like?'

And he smiles at me again. Every time I meet his gaze it burns, I'm staring at the sun in an eclipse.

'It's none of your business who I am and what my husband does and doesn't know. You could have had me, but you made it quite clear you didn't want me. Or only on your terms. Don't come here now, with your puppy-dog eyes, telling me you miss me and you think of me.'

I stand up and grab my bag, walk out. I know the other tables and the staff are staring. I'm sure someone here will know someone at school, the jungle drums will be beating even before I get to my car, but I don't care.

I almost make it, I almost escape. Freedom is so close.

But as I get to the door, a hand grabs my arm and pulls me out into the corridor, pressing me against the wall. The door slams behind us, there's no one around. I'm shaking with adrenaline. Isn't it strange how fear and excitement can feel the same?

'Ems. Please. I'm sorry.'

And I really, really want to believe him. But what's the point? We can't ever be just friends, and besides I've got enough friends. Rage sears through me all over again.

'Stay away from me, Liam.'

But even as I say the words, my heart is pounding and I'm breathing like I've finished a workout.

'Let go of me.'

'I've made that mistake before. I'm not doing it again.'

'It's not your choice.'

'Please. Give me another chance? Just one more?'

'No. Take your hands off me, there's nothing to give a chance to. We're done, over, finished, eight years ago.'

He lets go of me. But then runs one hand down the side of my face, murmurs to me.

'I know I fucked up, so badly. I've regretted it every day since.'

'So why now then, Liam. Did you cry every night for

months after we ended? Did it hurt to breathe, to exist? Did you forget who you were? Because I don't think you did. You carried on, like nothing happened, just like you always do.'

I pull his hand away from my face. Before I can stop him, he twines his fingers in mine, pulls me close against him.

'I thought of you – think of you – every single day. I wanted you every day... I still do. I wasn't ready then. But I am now.'

I remember the addictive delight of raw chemistry, how irresistible it is when you find someone just like you. It takes every ounce of willpower and self-control to remove my hand from Liam's. My wedding ring winks in the lights.

Then I whisper in his ear. Tell him what I wish I'd been brave enough to say all those years ago.

And then I walk away. I don't look back.

It's not until I get home that I find the fresh bruises he left me with.

SEVEN

Pete's been working on a big project launch for several weeks now. We're like ships in the night. I'm comforted by the fact that I know – well, I hope – he's not seeing Sarah. But also, it seems like the effort he went to a few months ago, to reassure me he was sorry, is ebbing away. And right now, I need him more than ever.

I'm being good, I am. I've stopped the photos completely now. Even though the demand is still there. And I've managed to avoid Liam as much as possible, apart from the odd wave across the playground. Instead, I dig out my wedding album, rewatch the video we had made. Let Anouk try on my wedding dress. We looked so happy back then. Where is that Pete now, because I need him back. The one who wiped away my tears when we had our first scans, who fed me ice chips in labour, who helped me prep for client presentations, who brought me flowers every week.

And all the time I try to stay away from the shoebox at the back of my wardrobe that has a handful of mementoes from Liam; a couple of Polaroids, gift receipts from La Perla, a diamond pendant and matching bracelet, and an old phone. I wonder what Liam kept, if anything, aside from secrets.

I know Pete doesn't mean to make me feel this lonely. I know he loves me. I know he'd be here if he could. And I know better than anyone that the grass isn't greener. But I'd give anything for Liam not to be here, where I live, reminding me of a past that is best left exactly there.

It's a surprise then, when Anouk and I get in from school on a Thursday afternoon, to find the front door unlocked and music coming from upstairs. There's an epic bouquet on the kitchen table – all glossy leaves, showy peonies, in wild dark green foliage and puffs of babies' breath.

'Mummy. What's Daddy done now?'

I only laugh and shake my head.

For an eight-year-old she's very perceptive. Beauty and brains, my girl has it all. Woe betide the man – or woman – who messes with her in future.

'Maybe he wanted to do something nice for Mummy?'

Pete walks into the room behind me. 'You're home!'

He pulls me to him and kisses me. He's sweaty and in his running kit – I can only assume he's been on the treadmill upstairs.

'Why did you buy Mummy flowers?'

There's my little barrister.

'Can't I do something nice for her?'

Anouk only looks at me and then stalks out of the room. The shoe cupboard swings open and her classic black converse thud inside.

'Moody, isn't she? I thought we had a few years until the girly hormones set in.'

'Pete.' I roll my eyes at him.

Pete holds his hands up, defending himself. 'Hey I'm sorry, I was only joking.'

'Well, it's not funny, hey. Not everything about women is to do with our menstrual cycles.'

I push past him, pick up the flowers and take them over to the sink, start stripping them of their paper and ribbons, hunt for the scissors to trim the stems.

'Thank you though, for these, they're beautiful.'

'I know you hate flowers normally – I know they're a faff – but I wanted to treat you.'

He's right – even though I never complained when he bought me them – I'm terrible with flower arranging. Plus it annoys me that they're such a short-hand for an apology for bad behaviour – that us little women can be placated with something pretty. I know Pete doesn't mean it like that though. And I'm happy he's making an effort.

Liam never, not once, bought me flowers, but I do still have some of the presents he gave me, hidden in plain sight, on my bookshelves, on my playlists, on my walls. They used to fade into the background, but now, with the flowers, it occurs to me that I should probably get rid of them all. *Should* being the key word here. Whether I do is another matter entirely.

'I know I've not been around much and you've done so much for me and Anouk. I wanted you to know it hasn't gone unnoticed.' His expression is both hopeful and wary. Like a puppy that's pissed on the kitchen floor but knows it's still cute.

'It's okay. I know work is full on. We miss you though. Would be nice if you could work from home more again.' And I reach up and kiss him again. 'Urgh, you're all sweaty!'

He puts his arm around me. 'You love it really.' His smile is so warm, so kind, I don't even know why Liam is taking up space in my head at all. What am I thinking?

The doorbell goes.

'Who's that? Are you expecting anyone?'

'Maybe.' He winks at me. 'I'll get it.'

He heads off to answer the door, and I sort the flowers, smiling to myself.

As I rinse down the sink and put the wrapping in the bin, my mother's voice carries down the corridor to me.

'Darling!' Mum bustles towards me, weighed down with expensive cardboard shopping bags, hair freshly blow dried into a blond helmet, nails and lips a perfect shade of neutral pink. 'I'm here now, off you go!' She ushers me away from my own sink, still talking at me: 'Scoot, scoot. The taxi will be here soon.'

Pete comes back into the kitchen, holding a clean shirt and jeans. They look like he's ironed them.

'Is someone going to tell me what's going on?'

I stand there, hands dripping water on the floor, leaves clinging to my fingers.

Mum doesn't come over all that often. It's a bit of a journey from her bungalow in Southampton, and usually there's a reason – a birthday or anniversary – when she does show up. I know I should visit her more – as Pete reminds me, she's getting on a bit. It's tricky though, conversations with her can be like navigating a minefield. I never know what will detonate a bomb for either of us.

I know it was difficult for her, when I was young – raising me by herself, working three jobs, cleaning the houses of my school friends. But sometimes, I don't think the lessons she taught me are all that relevant anymore. Sometimes I think they've made my life harder. Nevertheless, she adores Pete and of course, Anouk, and spoils her rotten. So I tell myself I can I put up with the odd dig about my parenting or my style and remind myself that Anouk is the most important person here – and she loves her Baba equally.

She bustles around the kitchen, settling herself by the breakfast nook, telling Pete that *a tea would be lovely, darling.*

'Your mum knew how tough things had been recently and offered to babysit, so I can take you out for dinner.'

'Isn't he a lovely man!' Mum gazes at Pete as if he holds the key to all of life's mysteries, when most of the time he can't even find his own keys. I know she wishes she'd found a Pete for herself – she's told me often enough.

She tried hard though, after Dad left us. But no one really stuck, despite the effort she put in. All she ever wanted in life was a rich husband to adore her. Now I have one – well, maybe not rich, maybe not adoring all the time – and she is so proud. It would break her heart to know how things feel like they're starting to get off track between us.

'Wait... I don't have anything to wear and I'm not ready.' I gesture to myself – unwashed hair, chipped manicure, sweaty from ferrying Anouk around this afternoon.

The doorbell rings again, confusing me further.

'Don't worry about any of that. I've sorted it for you.' As Pete disappears to open the front door, Mum looks secretive and excited, a gleam in her eye as she leans towards me.

'He's booked you a hairdresser and a home beauty session – make-up, nails, the works! Isn't he lovely? Oh – and he's bought you an outfit.'

Ah, has he now? *Yikes*, I think. Pete might be good at dressing himself, but when it comes to women, his tastes are very mainstream – anything tight, low cut, short, lacy. It might be okay for the bedroom, but I hope he remembers I'm in my late thirties, not a twenty-something party girl anymore.

Mum must read the look on my face though and rushes to reassure me. 'It's lovely, darling, don't worry. He didn't choose it alone. He had a look at your wish list and browsing history.'

I have to hold on to the table so I don't fall over. My browsing history has some not-so-subtle Google searches for Liam. *Note to self, delete browsing history. Another note to self, this doesn't feel right, keeping secrets.*

Pete comes back holding what looks like a folding table, followed by a woman with a pink bob, and a man with an expensive looking tan.

They both smile vacantly at me. I get the impression behind their blinding white veneers, I am the zillionth pampered housewife they've seen today, and it's only a little nip of something in a hip flask that's keeping them in high spirits.

They both bound over and hug me as if we're long-lost friends, start to play with my hair and examine my nails and face, commenting on how good my skin is, what colours will suit me, how gorgeous I am. Mum looks on, beaming with delight.

Two hours later I am coiffured and dressed. Heels, dress, jewellery, the works. Even Pete looks surprised when I walk downstairs to meet them.

'Darling! You look wonderful! And you get it all from me – haha!' I ignore Mum though, focus on Pete's reaction. The dress he's bought me isn't something I would have chosen, but I can't fault his taste. It's a silk wrap dress that clings in all the right places with a pencil style skirt and a deep V-neck, in a forest green with a delicate floral pattern. He's in slim fit charcoal jeans, and a duck-egg blue sweater that makes his eyes glow. We make a good pair; I'll give us that.

'Hey.'

'Hey yourself.'

I feel a pull towards him, his eyes unreadable, his smile unmistakeable. I think he does still want me, despite it all. He wouldn't have gone to all this trouble otherwise.

But then for a moment, I imagine it's Liam waiting for me, at the bottom of the stairs, with that unfathomable stare, and a chill runs down my back. Pete has always been uncomplicated in comparison.

When Pete and I first met at work, I was in a bad place. I wasn't looking for anyone. But Pete was kind. And that was a rare commodity in my life, where at work everyone jostled constantly to be at the top. I didn't like it, but, like the rest, I wanted to be the best.

And the few friendships I had were with girls who I knew, despite how much time we spent partying together, wouldn't hesitate to climb over me in their studded Louboutins to get what they wanted.

Pete was different. Everyone at work loved Pete. He was funny, he took the piss out of himself, he'd save a seat for you in the pub, he'd make sure you knew where the meeting was. He had your back.

At first I wasn't sure, when he asked me for drinks one evening.

'I eat boys like you for breakfast,' I told him. Shameless, confident, putting up walls that most men couldn't break down.

Without missing a beat, he replied with 'Some of us want to be eaten'. And then I was curious. I let him take my hand, pull me over to an empty table in that crowded bar, ply me with food and drink – and despite myself, I unbent a little. You see, he didn't talk about himself. Not like the other men I met. And he didn't seem absorbed in me, the way Liam had been, as if I were a precious specimen, to be collected.

Instead, we just chatted – about books, films, TV, music, bands. We liked all the same things, and had all the same cultural references. I relaxed as I sat there. For once not just someone's ornament, but interesting and funny in my own right. Not someone to push to the limits, but enough as I was. It wasn't until a couple of weeks later that I discovered that Pete was also very good at doing other things with his mouth. And then it was too late.

He describes our beginnings differently. That I was like a feral cat he had to coax to come to him. That I didn't always laugh at his jokes. That I put him on edge. That he was scared when he first met me, didn't think he stood a chance. The Pete I know now is very different though. Age, wealth, seniority at work does that to a man. Back then, the power lay with me. Now, I'm not so sure. And I've changed too – mellowed, happy to be more in his shadow, the supporting actor, moving everything around behind the scenes.

When I'm ready to leave, we're picked up in a shiny Uber and are shortly dispatched to a nearby manor house that houses a Michelin starred restaurant. Pete has wanted to come here for ages. I'm less keen because these types of hotels remind me of the kind of places I went with Liam – and his friends. For 'parties'. I don't want to think about those now. Especially the last party I went to. Again, Anna's memory flickers in my mind's eye. I shut it down, interlink Pete's fingers with mine and smile up at him as we walk into the building.

The restaurant is moderately busy when we arrive. We're seated by a maître d', with a fake French accent that is so bad, I have to muffle my giggles when Pete raises his eyebrows at me.

We order champagne and oysters to start, Pete has steak for his main, obviously. I dither between ravioli and seafood risotto, but finally land on the swordfish.

'Very good, madam,' says our mock French friend, with a deep bow as he gathers our leather-bound menus.

Pete and I are nestled together in a deep sided booth. We had a glass of champagne in the car, but despite this, the buzz of chemistry that we had at home starts to crackle and dissipate. I order a martini, Pete a whisky sour, to try to regain lost ground. It doesn't work.

He puts his arm around me, but it feels weird, like a stranger's. I don't understand what's wrong. He waffles on about work, how the redundancy risk is lifting.

'They've made some cuts. I'm pretty sure I'm safe now. But thank God for your extra income. You've done really well with that twittergram influencing stuff.'

Pete dabbles in social media, to try to maintain some sense of being *down with the kids in the office*, but he doesn't really understand it, which has worked in my favour with everything I did – and shouldn't have done – online. But his comment grates on me – maintaining a high following online isn't easy and takes time and effort, but he's using the same tone of voice he uses when Anouk brings home a piece of artwork.

'My little heroine,' he adds, 'keeping herself in cappuccinos and expensive make-up.'

He can't see me as I roll my eyes. Why does he have to be like this? He was the one wanting me to go back to work.

'You can probably stop doing it all soon though.'

Even though I already have, it feels weird to have him make the decision for me.

'What if I don't want to?' The words come out of my mouth before I realise I've said them.

'Well... I didn't think you wanted to work.'

'But I'm enjoying it, I'm good at something beyond doing the laundry and cooking your dinner. Plus, think of all those freebies!'

I didn't realise how little I wanted to give it up until now. Even though I feel guilty, and I know it's wrong, it's something that's all mine – Emily the person, not Emily the wife, Emily the mother. I've not been that person in so long, I'm not even sure who she is anymore, but it would be nice to be allowed to find out.

'But we can buy those things. You don't need them.'

'You were right though, Anouk won't be little for much longer. I need something else to do. I can't be a housewife forever.'

'I thought you wanted me to look after you? I like looking after you.'

I look directly at him when he says this. He has the grace to blush as he thinks about what he's said.

'But, Pete, be real for a moment, it makes no sense now, for me to be completely reliant on you. It's not the 1950s anymore.

Everything that's happened–' He winces as I say this –'made me think about our situation – what if something happened to you? What if you actually lost your job?'

Although I hadn't planned to say this, it's how I feel. I'm scared. I don't want to end up like my mum.

'I know, I get it, I do. But then don't you want a job that's a little more... stable?'

The waiter brings over our mains before I can respond, offering different condiments and sauces. Pete chats away with him, grateful for the interruption.

Pete's got a point. This isn't the most secure of careers. I definitely need to work on my – our – financial security. Mum believed the best way for a woman to be financially secure was to have a wealthy husband. We lived through the flaw in her plans, and yet here I am, still dependent on a man. Am I making all the same mistakes?

I watch other couples at the other tables as we eat. It's not super busy and mostly it seems to be groups of four – parents with adult children, out for dinner. There's one other couple on a date though.

'Look at those two over there. Remember when we were like that?'

Pete smiles as I point out the couple, feeding each other morsels of bread and holding out glasses of cocktails to sip. They're sitting so close they're almost in each other's laps.

'Was it that long ago?'

He runs his hand across my thighs and winks at me, much more interested in this than talking about me going back to work, but my head's still a beat or two behind, after everything.

'Feels like it.'

'Maybe we should give them a run for their money.'

His hand inches up my thigh, under my skirt, his eyes boring into mine. And I remember being in other restaurants like this, doing the same thing. Burning up with desire, at the mercy of someone else. But that wasn't Pete.

'How are your mains?'

The officious waiter is back. Pete withdraws his hand from my lap.

'Lovely, thank you!'

'Can I top you up here?' The bottle of champagne is whisked to my side and gold bubbles fizz and crest as it's poured out.

As he walks away, Pete laughs.

'We were so busted there.'

'You think?'

My cheeks flush. It's a fine line I'm walking, trying to figure out what I want and how to negotiate for it. We continue to eat our mains, commenting on the loved-up couple – who departed giggling and hand in hand, barely sparing time between kisses to make their way from the table to the lifts.

'Dirty weekend?'

'Probably. Remember when we did those?'

We had a few of them – it's pretty standard fare for dating before getting married. *Can you survive food poisoning in a hotel room with paper for bathroom doors, getting lost in a souk in Marrakech, getting on the wrong train in Lisbon? If so, then you should mate for life.*

I'm struggling though. Every time Pete touches me, smiles at me, part of me recoils. I drink more champagne, hoping it'll work its magic, make me chatty and flirtatious, but all I feel is light-headed and a distant sense of unease.

It doesn't help that Pete keeps checking his phone, tapping away. Apparently there's some work issues, something in America, time difference, et cetera, et cetera.

The waiter comes over again when it's time to order dessert. Pete flicks his eyes to his phone before gesturing for me to go first.

'Limoncello sorbet please – and a fresh mint tea.'

'I'll take a chocolate pudding and an espresso martini.'

Men never worry about calories, do they?

'Very good, sir, madam, those will be right with you.'

As soon as he's gone, gathering the menus with him, Pete disappears to the toilet. But leaves his phone behind.

Within two seconds it's flashing with a notification. Even on the other side of the table I can read the name of the sender.

It's Sarah. I don't need to read the words to know what it says.

We travel home in silence, I bite my lip to muffle my sobs. Pete tried to apologise in the restaurant, but I can't do it. Not again. I shrink into my seat and face the window, away from him. All those broken promises, all those meaningless words. The house is dark when we get in, Mum is already in the spare room, tucked up for the night. Not a peep from Anouk.

I head straight for the freezer and excavate the ancient bottle of Grey Goose from the ice, pour myself a healthy measure before Pete even has his shoes off. It's not like me, but right now, I don't know who I even am. I think I'm allowed to be unpredictable. Pete walks into the kitchen, opens his mouth to speak but I shake my head, somehow holding tears at bay with the burn of the alcohol in me.

'Don't. I don't want to hear it. You're not sorry. You're just sorry you got caught.' I turn away from him, pour myself another measure. It sears through me, all the way down inside.

Pete protests, tells me it's not what it looks like, that Sarah is having a tough time, and needs a friend. It's all lies though, all meaningless words. We sleep in our bed together, but the space between us could be miles. The next day, I move Pete's stuff into the spare room.

EIGHT

Winter 2015

Somehow I make it through the next few days, the next week, without saying anything to anyone. Or speaking to Pete. We communicate in terse WhatsApp and voice notes. Requests to pick up milk or bread, navigating Anouk's social schedule. Plans for the weekend we've already committed to. But I know we're going to have to have it out at some point. I just can't face it.

Thankfully, Pete has to go to a conference in Birmingham, so I take advantage of his absence – and the weather, to do a photoshoot for my private fans. After everything that's happened, I don't waste time feeling guilty – and besides, I might need the money soon. Whenever I think about that though – separation, divorce – my whole body hurts and I can't breathe. How do you even unpick a life together? The cycle of anger and sadness has me trapped like a hamster on a wheel.

I've got more fans now, I get messages and requests everyday. Which I know means my reach is spreading. And with it, the risk that I get found out is increasing. I know I need to find a better way to make money. But in fairness, it works with the school hours. It's easy. I'm my own boss. And also, it's addictive. It reminds me of a person I used to be. Someone who sought validation, satisfaction – power. It's like, with every pose, every picture, every message, every ping as money lands in my PayPal, I'm showing Pete what he's missing.

It all makes up for the fact that Pete – and Sarah – have shattered my life, not only my marriage. I used to see Sarah on the school run every day, her daughter Beckie is Anouk's best friend. We went for coffee and lunches every week, we had a mums' night out every month.

I've left the WhatsApp group we had with Billie, who messages me every day, desperate to know what's happening. Sarah, I assume, has filled her in. I can't talk to anyone though, all my friends here are Sarah's too. And I'm no longer in touch with any friends I had before we moved. And I've not seen Liam in a while. Not since I bumped into him at the gym. And even so, I wouldn't talk to him. All I have is my Instagram and Anouk.

A few days later, I'm on the school run, head down, hood up, hurrying home before the forecasted snow hits us, when I get a message from a new follower.

> Still beautiful. You haven't changed a bit.

I don't normally reply to messages, unless they're specific requests. It's a business transaction, not a relationship. Besides, a lot of the messages are the same, telling me I'm hot, what they'd like to do to me, pictures of their anatomy. It's pretty gross, but a necessary evil. This message though, implying they know me, intrigues me. I can't take the risk of being found out.

> Who is this?

Guess.

> No thank you.

Go on. Aren't you curious?

> No.

So why reply?

> Because you're invading my private space and I have a right to defend myself

Okay, okay *Hands up emoji* You don't need to worry though. Your secret's safe with me.

And then he stops messaging me. At least, I assume it's a he.

I've been so careful since the incident with the school WhatsApp. I decide that it must be a troll, he's probably messaging loads of women, trying to spook them. Probably going to ask me for full nudes or he'll tell everyone who I am.

I can't see much from his profile, he's got no photo, just the name N33son3110. Something niggles in my brain, but whatever it is won't stick.

I decide not to worry about it unless he messages again, it's not like I don't have enough to deal with. Unfortunately, he does – my phone pings with a notification from him, late on Friday night.

I'm in the sitting room, watching *Tell Me Lies* on Hulu, the college partying scenes reminding me of that one semester I had abroad. Those days feel so far away, when I was so carefree, so happy. So beautiful too, so young. Even though I thought I was fat, constantly on a diet, Anna was telling me to stop obsessing about it, that I didn't need to worry.

Everyone is out – Anouk is at a sleepover and Pete's gone over to Dan's for a drink. I'm drinking too. I probably shouldn't.

All my restraint has gone out of the window in the past few weeks, since everything. Nothing seems to fill the void inside me though, no matter how much wine I drink or pizza I eat. The only thing that helps is my photos – and, weirdly, going running. Which I've taken to doing after I drop off Anouk, more to avoid talking to anyone than for fitness reasons.

I'm nestled on our grey velveteen modular sofa, legs up on the chaise, covered in a fur throw, the remote and my wine on one side, my phone on the other. I'm a little drunk, I'm not going to lie.

> Miss me?

And then, another message.

> Worked out who I am yet?

> Yeah

I reply, even though I haven't.

> Clever girl.

> You're a troll

> You're sending these messages to anyone to get what you want. I'm not stupid.

Grey dots move on my screen and I take a gulp of wine as his reply pings back to me.

> I never said you were stupid. But you're wrong.

> That's what they all say

I don't even know why I'm bothering, trolls live for this. He doesn't know who I am. But then he sends another message.

> Why are you messaging me then? Bored in that big house of yours?

The hair prickles on the back of my neck, I'm suddenly aware that I've not drawn the curtain and, with the lights on in here, anyone could see in from the street. The door to the hallway is dark and shadowy, when I blink it seems like something moves, even though I know it's my wine-fuelled imagination. I shake my head at how ridiculous I'm being.

I reply, telling him to do one. That I'm not interested in his nonsense.

> Your husband doesn't know what he's missing… besides, I thought you liked playing games.

I drink more wine before replying, telling him I don't play games with strange perverts and then get up to refill my glass. I'm bored, drunk, and messaging a random man who is probably touching himself as we chat. I should feel shame, but I don't feel anything.

The grey dots ripple again, and then his message comes through.

> The Emily I knew was pretty perverted herself. Haven't you remembered anything I taught you?

My heart flutters inside me, I don't use my full name on this account. How does he know who I am?

My mind jumps ahead, skittering around memories of his hands, his lips, his tongue. It can't be him. I shouldn't be thinking this.

> I'm not Emily.

> No?

> No.

> Who are you then?

My response is a test, to pull my demons out into the light, in all ways. And I know I shouldn't be doing this. If it is him. But then I remember Pete is out tonight – with Dan, he says, but he could be with her, he could be with anyone. So, I can too.

> My name is Anna.

> I know it's you Ems.

> What's wrong with the name Anna? Don't you like it?

> I like it just fine. But you're not Anna. So stop pretending.

I'm not even remotely watching TV anymore. I'm gripping my phone so tightly it hurts, my breathing coming fast now as I type my response:

> You used to like me to pretend.

> So, you know who I am then?

I can picture the satisfaction on his face, as he knows he has me. I've seen that expression many times. I never thought I'd see it again. I shouldn't *want* to see it again. Why am I doing this? Anna would tell me not to. But I am.

I ask him how he found me, how he knew it was me.

> That would be telling.

Later, much later, he tells me he'd know my body anywhere, he'd recognise it blindfolded, purely by touch. Every mole, the texture of my skin, the smell of me. The way I respond under his hands, so well trained, so Pavlovian. I hate myself for wanting this so much.

I ask him how he knows I'm not catfishing him. What if I'm some bored middle-aged stranger? Sitting on her sofa in her pyjamas, drinking cheap wine.

> How do you know I'm not catfishing •you•?

Is all he comes back with.

> I don't

I reply, but I know he's not though. I know him. And this has his fingerprints all over it.

> I can prove it to you.

For a moment I picture how he could prove it to me. How I want him to prove it to me. And then I force myself to take a breath. I'm a married woman, a mother.

> No thanks

> Not like that. Meet me for a drink.

He knows that if I see him, he's got a chance. He also knows I'm going to say yes, eventually. I always do. And I have no reason to say no to him now. I should say no, it's the better option. I do say no. We always go through this charade.

> Why not?

> You know why.

> Aren't you curious? Or are you scared? Don't you want to be treated the way you deserve to be? He can't be giving you what you want.

I tell him no again, even as I plan what I might wear, if I have time for a wax, a blow-dry. Things wasted on Pete. Billie would tell me to do it. Sarah would tell me to speak to Pete – or, the old Sarah would have. The devil and the angel on my shoulders.

> What are you worried about? Can't two old friends go for a drink?

Pete wouldn't like it one bit. He hated Liam for what he did to me. How he had to pick up the pieces. Also, he has a jealous streak when it comes to him. Knowing that Liam got me in ways he never could. But now he has Sarah.

> Why should I? You said enough last time. You gave me bruises.

> Let me kiss them better.

> Liam...

I type, I want answers, I want to claw back some control here.

> You still haven't told me how you found me.

The dots move for a minute or two, erasing and rewriting, creating a narrative that best suits him, and then his reply comes through.

> I told you, I'd find you one day. That I'd come for you. Don't you remember?

Suddenly, I'm desperate to throw myself back into his abyss, let his darkness consume me, obliterate the way Pete is making me feel.

> You said a lot of things back then.

I didn't make it easy for him then, why should I now?

> I know you're not happy, you wouldn't be messaging me otherwise.

He's not wrong. But I don't want to give him the satisfaction of knowing he's right.

> Please give me one more chance. Let me apologise properly. If you're still not happy, I promise I'll leave you alone.

I know I shouldn't do this. It's pointless. It's a bad idea. It was always going to happen, from the second I saw him in that coffee shop.

> One drink, that's it. Then I'm leaving.

He types for a couple of minutes, the grey dots starting and stopping. All the things we leave unsaid.

> I promise you won't regret it. Can you do tomorrow night?

Might as well get it over with. He knows I can't wait. He knows what I'll be thinking, what I'll be feeling. Except this time, I'm not a little girl, his good girl. I'm my own woman and can make my own choices.

Liam sends me through a time and a location, tells me he'll see me tomorrow. Pete can watch Anouk, he owes me.

I don't reply after that. Instead, I make my way up to bed. Some women are scared in the dark, the silence, afraid of the bad guys lurking, waiting to take them. But Liam knows, sometimes I want to be grabbed in the dark.

I lie in bed and think of him. About how one time, he did just that. I touch myself at the memory of that night, and all the other times. But at the end, Anna's face appears in my mind instead – breaking me, putting me back together again, in a way no one else ever could.

NINE

By the time 7pm comes around I am exhausted. I've worn myself out overthinking and catastrophising and remembering. If it was anyone else I'd cancel. But Liam has always made me feel like I'm crawling over hot coals to get to him. Despite myself, nothing has changed.

I shouldn't spend time alone. It gives me too much time to think about the past. About him. About the parties. About a time where I had control... or so I thought.

I know it's really obvious what I'm doing. That it's revenge because of Pete and Sarah. And I shouldn't bother. I'm better than this, or thought I was. And yet like every other time with Liam, I am compelled to think about him, to see him. A switch in me has been flicked and I can't switch it back.

I scroll through Facebook. I didn't post much before I got together with Pete. But I was tagged in a few pictures. Liam wasn't, obviously. But every picture of back then, no matter where I am – dancing on a speaker, in little more than a sequinned bikini, with a flower headdress and glitter eye make-up, or cuddled into a booth in a black bandage dress and cage platform heels, bottles of Grey Goose tipped over on the tables,

I know he was there, just out of shot. The hand on my butt, the arm around my shoulders, the chest against my back. It's all very noughties, the clothes, the music, the drugs. I wonder what we were thinking, but then I remember we weren't thinking; that was the point.

The life of a strategy consultant wasn't all sex on MDMA and parties in private members clubs – plus, I'm allowed a few cool stories to horrify Anouk when she's a teenager. To remind myself I wasn't always this boring. Sometimes I still have nightmares about those parties though. The ones where Liam didn't show. The ones where he left me alone for hours. Sometimes I wake myself – and Pete – screaming, as I run down a corridor of closed doors. When I open my eyes, I can still feel the plush carpet under my feet, a bitter tang in the back of my throat, the unease lurching in my belly, the burns on my wrists. Liam told me we were free birds – living a better life than everyone else. And I believed him. I felt like that. Sometimes. I bet he doesn't have nightmares.

I think about what Anna would say if she were here; if she knew I was seeing him again. She'd tell me to stay home, that I'm making a big mistake if I think this will make me feel better after Pete and Sarah. I can almost feel her tugging on my arm, telling me we can order pizza and watch movies and drink warm Lambrini instead, like she did back then.

But also, she knew me well – too well, even. *You're going to that party anyway aren't you,* she'd say. *Please just be careful. Remember, I love you.* And then I'd disappear into the night, leaving her at home, awaiting blurry photos, drunk texts, and filthy secrets in the morning.

This time though, she's not here. And she hasn't been for a long time. At university someone called her my sister, but she was never that to me. Either way though, I'm alone. And any mistakes I make tonight are mine to own.

. . .

The restaurant we're meeting in is very Liam. I didn't even know there was one like this in Surrey. When he texted the address I didn't look it up, only put it straight into Uber when it was time to go. Not that Pete knows what I'm up to – he's taken Anouk to his mum's for the weekend, so I'm free to come and go as I please. Although I'm not planning to stay long tonight, I don't want Liam getting the wrong idea.

It's all booths and heavy worn leather. The bar is full of a million types of whisky. The lights are low and each table has a flickering candle. The tablecloths are heavy linen and weighed down crystal and silver.

He has his back to me when I arrive but I'd recognise his shape anywhere. The cut of his jacket, the line across his back and shoulders. The way his hair touches his collar. It was longer when we first met. I can imagine the smell of his skin, the prickle of his stubble just under his jaw, the way he breathes in sharply when I kiss him there.

He hasn't seen me yet. I could still leave. I could go home, get into PJs, unmake this mistake. I don't want to, though.

As I walk towards him, the music changes, and though I don't know the name of the band or the name of the song, I know this is something Liam likes and used to play. He loved to try and educate me about music, claiming that nineties pop was pathetic and that they owed everything to New Order and Depeche Mode and The Jesus and Mary Chain.

'Can I help you?'

A waitress approaches me; she's young, wide cheekbones, a piercing in her septum, hair parted in the middle and clipped back from her face in a vaguely seventies style.

Then it's too late. He's seen me.

'Em!' He nods at me and then at the waitress. 'She's with me.'

Just like I always was. A spiral of memories, his arm around my back, holding my hand, leading me behind him, obedient, small, following. The way it made me feel. That I had a place in the world. Even if it was a harsh world, with him, we owned it, however briefly.

The waitress ushers me forward, her skin and hair golden in the candlelight. As I sit down I wait for Liam's eyes to track her across the room. But he doesn't.

'So...' he says, leaning forward across the table.

'So...?'

'You came.'

'I did.'

'Are you expecting me to apologise?'

'Are you going to apologise?' I say this because the Liam I knew would never apologise, his mantra was 'never explain, never complain'.

'What do you think?'

'Are we just going to talk in questions the entire evening?'

He smiles, but when his eyes meet mine, there's nothing soft or kind about them. They say something else indeed. They remind me of the other man that Liam can be, that I loved and feared in equal measures. He replies to me in a predictable fashion.

'I hope not. But let's order some wine while you think about that.' He hands me the wine list. 'We're having steak.'

'Are we indeed? I thought I was just coming for a drink.'

'I thought we weren't talking in questions all evening?'

'I didn't realise I needed someone to order for me.'

'I was hoping we wouldn't have to continue this charade where we pretend I don't know exactly what you want and what you like, and we could simply cut to the chase.'

'Liam. I'm not some little associate consultant in her twenties anymore. I've dealt with my daddy issues.'

'Have you? That's a shame.'

But he laughs all the same. I forgot how exhausting it can be at times, sparring with him. Sometimes all I wanted was softness – and Pete gave me that, or at least he used to. I'm not ready to go back to who I was with Liam. I've changed. I'm not so sure he has.

'Fine. Order whatever. I don't care. Let's get this over with.'

'Don't be like that, I'm sorry. It's hard not to fall back into bad habits with you. You're so easy to be around, so familiar. I miss you so much. Sure you won't stay for dinner?'

'I said I'd come for one drink.'

'If I recall correctly, you used to come for me anytime.'

'Liam!' It's too soon. He knows it's too soon.

'I'm sorry. Force of habit.' He takes my hand across the table. 'Look, I didn't mean for it to be like this. It's hard for me too, you know, seeing you.'

The hand covering mine has a pale indentation around the ring finger on his left hand.

'Yes, I'm divorced, it's messy. I finally left her.'

'So, if I decode that correctly, she caught you, she left you, and now she's screwing you for all your money, just as she should do?'

Any fondness I felt for him when we arranged this has dissipated. But I'm not really angry with him, I'm angry with myself. For showing up, for the way my body responds to the sound of his voice. And I'm angry with Pete – and Sarah. If they hadn't done what they did, I wouldn't be here.

'Yes.' He takes a big gulp of red wine which somehow he has managed to order in between my conversational barbs. I hope it stains his teeth and lips, I hope it takes the edge off his looks.

He removes his jacket and his black T-shirt underneath shows that, despite the years, despite the softening around the edges, he's still big enough to take up too much space. He never looked like the other directors. The only man to ever make me feel small, smaller, doll-like, tiny, shrinking inside myself.

The scar in his ear is from a piercing at school, the blurred tattoo on his bicep – a drunken mishap at university. The way I can read the map of his body, his history on his skin. And he knows me the same way. It's killing me remembering all this, but somehow I'm still here.

'Are you done watching me yet?'

I blush at his words, He's loving it. Does Sarah look at Pete like this? Or does he look at her like this? How can he? What does she have that I don't? Maybe it was never me in the first place, maybe I was always second best.

'My husband is cheating on me.'

'Ah...'

He tops up my wine glass even though I've barely had a sip.

'Why did you cheat on your wife?'

He tips his head to one side, rubs his stubble.

'Because I was an idiot. Because I couldn't help myself. And your husband is an idiot too.'

His face softens as he looks at me. I remember the way it felt, to be tucked under his arm, safe and warm in his embrace.

'So... do you regret what we did back then?' I ask.

As he thinks about his reply, I give in and drink in his every move. I should never have come tonight but, most people walk into their mistakes with their eyes wide open no matter what they might say.

'Not for a second.'

The way he looks at me. The good and the bad caught up so tight. We did terrible things. He did terrible things. He is – he says it himself – a terrible person. But sometimes, when we lay in bed, after, it was the only time I could stop trying, stop running to find myself.

'Do you ever wish we'd met before you got married?'

'We've talked about this.'

We did. We imagined a life where we met at a different time, a better time. But better for who?

Still Anna's voice in my head, warning me.

'I'm all over the place tonight, Liam. I'm sorry.'

'It's okay. You can be however you want. You know that.'

The problem with Liam is his kindness – it's unreliable. He can switch it off and on at will. It's not a facade or a mask, but I should tread carefully. If I couldn't trust him before, how can I trust him now?

The waitress brings over a starter I don't remember ordering. Some fish with bright green and orange sauces smeared across the plate, artfully placed edible flowers, perfectly placed drops of a crimson oil. It looks like blood. I have a sudden flashback to bathroom tiles, drops the same colour on them. I blink and it's gone.

We eat in silence. But he looks at me and I look at him.

After the plates are cleared he speaks.

'Why are you here, Em, really?'

He knows why, but he wants to hear me say it first. Watch me slip straight into past bad habits, behaviours.

'I was never not going to come.' The words are out before I can take them back. It's the truth though, deep down I know it. It's not just about Pete and Sarah. It's about Liam and me, our unfinished business.

'I'm ready to make this work. I wasn't ready before. Like I said. I had some growing up to do.'

'But you're ready now that it's good for you, but not for me.'

Somehow, we are sitting closer in the booth. His thigh is touching mine. It's like he's taking in all the oxygen and leaving none for me.

'Now is good for you too. You said it yourself. Your husband's cheating on you. And he's a twat, by the way. Only an idiot would cheat on you.'

'You cheated on me.'

'I didn't say I wasn't an idiot. But I'm not now. You weren't the only one learning lessons back then.'

He brushes a strand of hair away from my face, but I catch his hand in mine and deposit it in his lap.

'Stop it, with all this... this niceness. This charm. Where's the real Liam, that I know and love?'

'That you love, hey?' He doesn't let go of my hand though, instead moving our hands further up his thigh.

'Liam...'

He looks at me and then lets go.

'Steak – medium rare?'

The waitress is back, this time with our mains. As we cut into them, blood pools on our plates and we mop it up with potato dauphinoise. Liam eats like he hasn't been fed in weeks. I can't stop looking at him. I've lost all sense of myself. My phone bleeps.

> Anouk wants to know if she's allowed to watch Jaws.

Shit! Anouk! I am brought back to the present with a jolt. I have responsibilities, I'm a grown up, a mother. I shouldn't be here, treading thin ice with a man I know is dangerous. Liam looks at me, puzzled, I explain the message.

'I have a son, you know. He's in year six, I do get it,' Liam says, as I bash out a response on WhatsApp.

> No. It's too scary.

WTF is Pete thinking, even considering *Jaws* for Anouk.

'God, please don't suggest playdates.'

'Why not?'

'Why not? Are you insane?'

He puts his hand on mine again. His eyes are dark, he

doesn't smile. But I know he's happy. He's got me exactly where he wants me. I don't know what he's waiting for, why he's dragging all this out. I hate myself for wanting him. Not because of Pete. Because I thought I was better than this.

We've finished our steaks and the waitress comes by to ask if we want pudding or coffee or...

'Sure, we'll take a look, won't we, Ems?'

The waitress, immune to Liam's charms, dumps the menus on our table and stomps off.

'I don't want dessert.'

'Why not? You said yourself, you've got nothing to rush back to. No one expecting you at home.'

He's managed to slink his arm around the back of us and his fingers are tangled up in the back of my hair, massaging my neck, playing with the long dark strands.

'Please don't do that,' I ask him, but he doesn't stop – and I shiver under his touch.

'I like this colour on you. It suits you better than that dark blonde, mousey colour.'

'You mean my natural colour.'

The way he's sitting, it's forcing me to look up at him slightly. We are inches apart.

He takes a deep breath and leans in, whispers in my ear.

'You're killing me here.'

And he puts my hand on his lap.

'Liam—'

'It's all you. And I haven't even laid a hand on you yet.'

I remember all the times he said this to me. In boardrooms and bedrooms and in receptions and kitchens and offices full of people. All the times he acted like the victim, that I held the power, made him do things, made him respond, made me the bad guy.

'You can't manipulate me so easily this time.'

'Emily, no one in the history of the world has even been able to manipulate you. You're the most intelligent person I know.'

'Your lips are moving and words are coming out and you're lying even as you're telling me you're not.'

I want him more than ever now. I'm so far gone, I don't think I'm ever coming back.

'Your husband's the liar. Not me.'

'Don't talk about Pete.'

'Pete...' he squints at me. 'That insipid little consultant we had on the petrochem project? The one who creamed himself every time you walked into the room? Oh, Emily, how very basic of you.'

'Oh, I'm sorry, was I supposed to settle for being your afterthought? Once you were done with Sabine and the kids? Be grateful for you coming crawling into my bed at all hours? Like a puppy with a new toy.'

'You didn't complain at the time.'

We're hissing at each other like snakes, oblivious almost to the waitress hovering by the table wondering if we want dessert. I can tell she's itching to comment. Her face says it all.

Her job must suck. Dealing with middle-aged idiots on clandestine reunions, pawing at each other indiscreetly like we are. I sicken myself. I can't stop this though, even if I wanted to.

'No... no dessert, thank you, just the bill.'

Liam lifts his face from mine, long enough to ask her to put it on the room he's booked upstairs.

The waitress brings some paper for him to sign, his usually scribbly nonsense. He always did have terrible writing, being a left hander.

'Let's go.'

Somehow he has managed to get up from the table and put his jacket on. He's wearing Converse with Carhartt jeans.

'Liam, the nineties called, they want their clothes back.'

He holds out his hand to me.

'Fuck off, you love it.'

And I reach for his hand, feel his fingers entwine with mine. Follow him out of the restaurant, into the lift, up to his room. Like I always was going to.

We do it twice.

The first time, straight after dinner. The way we hold each other like drowning people. I am disgusted with us. The clumsy way we pull at each other's clothes, the way desire has degraded both of us. Was I this pathetic all those years ago? Giving in so easily? So out of control. So ugly.

The second time is different.

In the half light, we do it again. It's different from all the other times before, even with other men, not just him. And it makes me wonder if a different future is possible, for us both. To have the softness and the bite with him, is something I'd forgotten about. Something I didn't know was an option.

We fall asleep after and this time I dream of Anna. But not the usual nightmares. This time we're back where we were, getting ready for the party – eyeliner, mascara, eye shadow, powder. I watch her do her face in the mirror. She doesn't say a word, just keeps going, even as I call her name, even as I beg her to speak to me. When she's finally finished, she turns to look at me, and I see my own face. When I wake, there are tears on my pillow.

In the morning, we shower together and dress slowly. When I look at my phone I have a couple of missed calls from Pete, text messages asking where I am. He's lost any right to know, after what he did. And even so, he won't be worried for my safety – he just wants me home to watch Anouk so he can go and play golf.

Liam orders room service for breakfast and I feel like Julia Roberts in *Pretty Woman*. I remember the first time he ordered room service for me. I'd like to think I'm less easy to impress now, that some fancy scrambled eggs and orange juice in a wine glass are the norm. But part of me relishes the way he's looking after me. A feeling I realise is long missing from me and Pete. The way everything always falls to me, that there is no safety net under me.

That even as I give, I can take with Liam.

'How are you getting home, Em?'

'Uber.'

'Want to share?'

It's unnerving, this side of Liam. I keep waiting for the other shoe to drop, I know it will, eventually.

'Why are you being like this?'

'Like what?'

He tucks his phone and keys into his pocket, runs his hands through his hair, it's still ruffled and messy. Flashes of last night come back to me, my fingers in his hair, the way he looked up at me from between my thighs. The way I tugged him closer, further up my body, the heat of his skin against mine, the ripple of muscle on his back, his legs wound round mine. I blink the memories away.

'We can't pretend there's a happy ever after. This was a one-off.'

'If you say so.'

But the way he looks at me. I know this is far from the end. It's just the start.

'This was a mistake.'

'So you keep saying.'

'I'm married.'

'I don't know who you're trying to persuade of that. He's cheating on you. You said it yourself. Why would you deny yourself happiness?'

'And that's what you're offering, is it? Happiness? Because I didn't hear you say that. I heard you want me, loud and clear.

But you've never wanted – offered – me any more than that. So don't even pretend like you're the good guy here.'

The thing that's killing me about the whole evening, last night, this morning, is that we fell straight back into the same shorthand we had before. We didn't pretend that we gave a shit about what's happened in the last eight years. I don't want to know about his son or his wife or what finally ended his marriage. And he hasn't asked me about Anouk or Pete. He hasn't even mentioned Anna and that last party.

He hasn't asked me anything that didn't relate to us. Because as much as I'm trying to convince myself otherwise, there's still an us.

'Look, I'm saying let's not make this out to be a big deal. We fucked. That's it. I'm going back home now and you're going home and we don't need to talk about this again.'

'Right. But you know, Emily, you always do this. You always back off as soon as there's any chance for you to be happy. I don't know why I expected you to be different. I thought maybe you'd grown up a little?'

In between the words, I do hear what Liam is saying. But I don't care. I've been here before and I was the one left hanging.

'You do not get to do this, Liam. You know how fucked up it all was back then. And you were the one who ended it. You didn't even end it properly, you ghosted me. I had to find out from your secretary that you'd moved away. So don't come crying to me now.'

I walk over to the door of the suite; of course it's a suite – he's a partner now. Taking home millions no doubt. But before I can open it, he's crossed the room and is holding it closed, one arm across the frame.

I hate him then. The way he's looming over me, the way I'm up against the wall, in the corner. The way he's in charge again.

Then, he simply unlocks the door and opens it.

'Em, I promise you, it's different this time. Trust me. I love you.'

And it's those three little words that unlock me, undo me.

He reaches over to kiss me goodbye. Despite myself, I turn my mouth to his. I feel him smile and, as he pulls me back into the room and kicks the door shut, I remember something he said to me all those years ago.

It's not over until I say it's over.

TEN

When I get home I take another shower. Pete and Anouk have gone out; I know because he left me a huffy voice note eventually, mentioning he'd cancelled his golf and they'd gone to the cinema and for pizza. I spend the afternoon online, buying new items of school uniform that Anouk has mislaid, and planning for Christmas. Or pretending to. Mostly I am staring at the TV, whilst the insipid housewives of wherever fight over each other's husbands and slosh Sauvignon Blanc around in red wine glasses.

If Pete finds out about this, we are definitely over. Even given what he did with Sarah. This would make it so easy for him to leave me. Do I want that? I'm not sure.

All afternoon I flip flop between the two, thinking about how Liam told me he loves me, he's changed. But how can I believe a word he says? And how I can believe Pete is telling me the truth about it being really over with Sarah?

The doorbell goes mid-afternoon and it's a bouquet of roses, but there's no card. So that's no help either.

> Did you get the flowers?

Liam messages me a little later on.

> I can't stop thinking about last night. And this morning. When can I see you again?

I don't think I can do this right now.

> It was a mistake. We shouldn't have done that.

> Really?

> Yes.

> Are you feeling guilty? Didn't you have fun?

> No and Yes.

> So what's the problem?

He's got a point. Because the problem is, there is no problem. And that's not a good sign. What's wrong with me? I want to call Sarah and get her advice, and then remember I can't. I don't want to tell Billie. I love her, but I can't tell her this. I can't tell anyone. Anna used to say that keeping secrets never ends well.

> I'm married

I remind Liam.

> I'm not leaving him.

> I'm not asking you to. Not yet.

From anyone else this conversation would be insane, but with our years of history, it's like we're picking up where we left off, midway through a relationship.

But what if it was always meant to be Liam, not Pete?
What if I hadn't gotten pregnant with Anouk?

What if I hadn't taken Anna to that last party?

Either way, I don't reply to his message, it's too much, too soon. He shouldn't make promises he can't – or won't – keep. He needs to prove himself to me, and that doesn't happen overnight. Maybe then I'll reconsider. And then, only if Pete and I haven't reconciled.

That night I prepare dinner, welcome Anouk home with open arms, and tolerate Pete. He's still in the spare room. We're at an impasse. Or so he thinks. We're in the sitting room after dinner.

'Em, the ball is in your court. We can't go on like this. Please—'

'Shhhhh.' I frown and point at Anouk, but she's engrossed in *Frozen*.

'I mean it. You need to decide what you want.'

'What do you want?' I ask.

He flushes and in that instant I know the truth.

'Are you in love with her?' I hiss at him.

'I... I don't know to be honest.'

'And I'm the one that needs to decide?' This time it's me that needs to lower my voice.

But I know Pete, he always takes the easy option. If I don't mention the d-word – divorce – he won't either. He wants to have his cake and eat it. It's like we're playing chicken. It's ridiculous.

'Oh fuck this, I'm going to bed. Let me know when you've deigned to let us mere mortals know what you're thinking.' He glares at me and stomps off upstairs. His anger stings – I know it's justified – even though he doesn't. How did I get this lost? How can he be in love with Sarah?

My heart hurts in my chest, despite my own bad behaviour, and I know tears aren't far behind. I'm tired and hungover and so overwhelmed by everything that's happened in the last twenty-four hours.

'Where's Daddy going?'

Anouk turns to me, the movie credits coming up on screen, her sweet little face making me smile despite everything.

'He's tired so he's having an early night.' He'll be in the spare room, watching God knows what on Netflix, probably messaging Sarah. He'll be making me the bad guy, and whilst I am, he doesn't know that so it feels unfair.

Anouk yawns and stretches out on the sofa.

'Come on, you, I think you need an early night too.' I take her upstairs, supervise tooth-brushing and help her change into her cosy flannel pyjamas.

'Will you read to me, Mummy?'

I look at Anouk, delicious in her little bed, her faded bunny next to her. Part of me wants to pick her up and run far away from Pete and Liam. All I've ever wanted for her was everything I didn't have. I've done all of this for her really. Thinking of the girls before her who didn't have the choice and security she will.

I read until her eyelids droop and she drops off to sleep. When I look at my watch it's only 7:30. This time yesterday I was arriving at the restaurant to see Liam. And now it's like the world has tilted on its axis.

Pete and I go on like this for a week. Barely talking, communicating through Anouk. I'm not proud of myself. I consider couples counselling, I consider leaving, I consider staying.

Liam messages me most days. Tells me about the useless interns working for him, the conference he has to speak at, the funny memes his son showed him. He doesn't mention our night together – or when we were together, all those years ago.

He doesn't send me any more flowers, but instead I receive

beautiful notebooks, a leather wallet, a bottle of my favourite perfume, lingerie. I have to hide it all from Pete.

I tell Liam that Pete's in love with Sarah, but he doesn't use that as leverage, only says that he's here for me, he's sorry, he can imagine how much it all hurts, to let him know if I need anything.

Pete and I suffer through another weekend of painful faux-happy family socialising for Anouk's sake. Take her to a party – the parents are all invited, no doubt so that the birthday boy's family can show off their relative wealth in their hideous neo-Georgian new-build mansion. Of course, as soon as we arrive we bump into Greg and Sarah and we exchange stilted greetings, none of us sure how much the respective cuckolded partner knows about the situation. I didn't want to ask Pete – or Sarah – but I hope Greg's getting the support he needs. To be honest, I'm surprised he's here, but I guess they're putting on a show of being a happy family, just like we're trying to.

Sarah points Anouk in the direction of Beckie, who is in an Elsa dress and fake blonde wig and then the four of us stand there in an awkward silence.

'So, Ems, have you seen your old friend again?'

I knew she was going to do this. I semaphore with my eyebrows for Sarah to stop, but it's too late.

'What old friend?' Pete looks at me.

'Her old friend from work – tall? Dark hair?'

Greg has the grace to blush and tries to give Sarah a surreptitious nudge. I wonder if she's still sleeping with my husband. She's not even tried to get in touch, to ask me for coffee or try to rebuild bridges. Which I can only take as a sign of her complicity.

'Em doesn't have any old friends from work.' Pete gives me a thin-lipped smile. 'Well, unless you mean… Liam?' And his eyes widen at me.

'Liam! That was his name. He seemed very happy to see her.'

'Was he?' Pete looks at me.

'Sarah – I think Beckie wants you.' Greg tugs on her sleeve, but she doesn't move. I'm amazed Sarah hasn't brought popcorn and a chair along to watch the results of the bombshell she's dropped, her head swivelling between me and Pete, trying to read our expressions.

'She's fine, Greg. Also, she's got two parents, you sort her out. I know our first born being at university means you've gotten used to not being needed, but don't worry there's still plenty to do.'

I'm left wincing at Sarah's words to Greg. When I look at her, I can't see any trace of the friend I once trusted. Now I only see someone who views me as the enemy. I wonder if we were ever friends at all, or if it was all in my head, that this was always her endgame.

'I don't know why this is so interesting.' Pete glares at me and stalks off to get a beer, calling over his shoulder that I can drive us home later.

'Emily, I hope I didn't get you in trouble there.'

'Really, Sarah. I'll get you a wooden spoon for Christmas, to help with all your shit stirring.' And then I walk off also.

Before the party finishes, Greg finds me, tries to apologise for Sarah. Every time he looks at me he blushes – he can barely get a word out. It's all very odd, but I lay a hand on his arm and tell him the apology is appreciated.

When we get home, Pete tells Anouk he's taking her to his mum's for supper and that I shouldn't wait up. I slowly feel the tilt as the high ground that was mine sinks back down.

Pete knows exactly who Liam is, but he doesn't know what we did, then or now. Not about the parties, or Anna, or anything else. But he knew we were more than work colleagues. His reaction to Sarah's words also confirms my suspicion that

Pete has considered there may have been an... overlap, between him and Liam.

I know I don't have a leg to stand on here. Not after what I've done. But stirring the pot still seems very out of character for the woman who was my friend and hasn't exactly been truthful about her relationship with my husband. I go to bed and fret for a bit, wondering about Pete's reaction in the morning – if he's going to want to talk – and also the possibility of seeing Sarah or Liam on the school run. I toss and turn in the sheets, but eventually drop off.

When I get to the school, I don't notice the stares at first. I'm too busy making sure Anouk has her hat and mittens. She keeps losing them – some other kid stealing them no doubt. But when I look up from her bag, I see groups of mums glancing at me and each other's phones – and muttering to each other.

'Bye bye, Mummy!'

Anouk reaches up to give me a kiss goodbye. I press my lips to her soft cold cheek and watch as she hurtles into her classroom, calling to Beckie. I wave to her teacher, but she also looks at me blankly. Normally she's quite chatty. We've even shared a joke or two.

As I walk out of the playground, more parents look and stare and point, and now I'm jumpy. Something is up. *Shit.*

As I reach the gate, one mum musters up all her courage, the bitterness in the twist of her lips, as if she's eaten a lemon, and spits at me, 'You should be ashamed of yourself.'

And I don't know if I imagine it or not, but around me I hear whispers, the word shame and disgust.

I run all the way home. Not ashamed, not guilty, only confused.

There's only one person I can message.

> I don't understand, what's going on? Why is everyone staring at me at school?

I gasp at Sarah's reply.

> They found out it was you, in those photos.

My whole body stills. She must be revelling in my downfall. And how easy it will be for her to mop up Pete's tears.

> Why didn't you tell me? I had to find out from Anne-Marie.

Sarah doesn't like Anne-Marie for reasons she hasn't specified, but I think it's something to do with the PTA and a baking competition.

> I don't see why it's anyone's business.

> Are you serious? Everyone has seen it, everyone. All the dads – Greg! My husband has been looking at pictures of you half naked!

Well, that explains his odd behaviour yesterday.

> Why is that my fault? It's your husband looking at the photos. Take it up with him.

> I just don't understand why you always have this need for… for attention! Not everything is about you.

> I didn't do it for attention.

> Why did you do it then?

> Money.

> But you don't need any!

> Pete was at risk of redundancy, we needed another source of income.

So you thought nude photos were the solution?

> They're not nude! Have you even seen them?

A couple. And they were nude enough!

> Are you seriously judging me? I know you're sleeping with Pete!

I wait for her to respond and the grey dots flicker for a while and then stop – but no message appears. I wonder what she lacked the guts to say to me.

I also realise that it's not even ten o'clock and somehow I have to get through the rest of the day. I don't even know what to do with myself. Is it too late not to expect that Pete will find out? Or worse, Anouk?

Out of everything, I worry about the fallout for her most of all. I can bear the anger from Pete, the shaming from the school parents, but I can't bear to see the disappointment on Anouk's face. She's my world, my baby. After the childhood I had, I did everything I could to make hers the opposite. But she'll never understand something like this. She's too young to learn that your parents are only human and fallible too. That we have needs and wants of our own.

To keep myself busy, away from disturbing thoughts, I go into damage control mode. It's like being back at work. I tell myself not to think about Anouk or Liam or anything else and only focus on what I can control; I need to find out how they discovered it was me and even how they're so sure. By the time Pete gets home I'll be on top of this, I have to be. Because heaven knows what will happen when he finds out.

I pick up my phone again.

> My secret is out. Can you find out how they know it's me?

Well hello stranger.

Typical Liam.

> I don't have time for flirting. Can you help?

Blimey. Hello to you too.

> It's not funny.

How do you know I'm laughing?

> Aren't you?

I'm not actually. I told you, I care about you.

> Liam...

I thought you said you didn't have time for flirting.

> Are you going to help me or not?

Only if you ask nicely.

> Fuck you Liam. Fuck you very much.

Oh, we already did that, as I recall.

> Liam! I can't ask anyone else.

Ok ok. I'll do some digging. I'll let you know what I find.

> Have you seen the pictures?

Of course I've seen the pictures!

> Not on instagram, you dick. The ones that they're sharing on WhatsApp or whatever.

> Yeah. I'll see if I can work out who first shared them, let you know.

> Thanks.

He sends me a kiss in return, but I don't reply. I can't right now. It's like my brain is compartmentalising everything – Pete and Sarah, me and Liam, and now this photo debacle. How did my life get so complicated suddenly?

I take myself off to the gym to run some mindless miles on the treadmill, try to burn off some of this nebulous anxiety. But by the time I get back, my phone is hot from notifications. I have many missed calls from Pete. And several messages.

> What is this about you and some photos?

> Are they nude?

> What the fuck – is this what you've been doing to make money?

> Em! You need to call me now!

> Emily, it's everywhere! It's all over Twitter!

> Fuck this. I'm coming home. We need to talk asap!

And when I look, I see he's right. Someone has shared it online, all 'School Mum Shares Raunchy Snaps For Money'. When I go on Instagram, I have hundreds of notifications and DMs. Some are from the press – the *Sun*, the *Daily Mail*, no one I would consider talking to in a million years. And some are from people wanting more photos – ironically I could make more money out of this. I don't want to though. Not now everyone knows, now everyone can point and laugh.

It seemed like such a simple idea to start with. I never thought it would blow up like this. More fool me. I don't cry though, I can't let myself. This isn't only my fault. Someone leaked those pictures, and I'm going to find out who. To be honest, I have my suspicions.

When Pete gets in, he's calmer than he seemed on his texts.

'I'll get Anouk from school.'

'Oh. Thanks, I appreciate that.'

'I'm not doing it for you, I'm doing it for our daughter. The world doesn't revolve around you, believe it or not.'

And for the first time, I blush, being called out like this.

'I don't think the world revolves around me, Pete.'

'Funny way of showing it.'

I don't care about many things, but I do care about Anouk. And what impact this might have on her. From day one I've been devoted to her – I breastfed, I co-slept, I did baby-led weaning, I still cut up her grapes and cherry tomatoes so she didn't choke. I read all the books about child development and psychology, I have done everything possible to try to create a happy, balanced child, ready to conquer the world.

And now, I realise that in a single thoughtless act, a silly plan to make a bit of extra money, I've messed it all up.

I busy myself making lunch.

'Do you want anything?'

'No. I ate on the train. Oh, and just so you know, I could lose my job because of you.'

I roll my eyes. 'Now who's making it all about them?'

'Emily, I could get fired for bringing the company into disrepute! Wasn't I enough for you – did you need to know that lots of men, any men, were cracking one off over you? And while we're on those photos – maybe if you spent a bit less time obsessed with how you look and bit more time working on your personality, you might be a bit fucking happier and nicer to be around! No wonder you don't have any friends. All those people online – they don't actually like you, you know. They're just using you.'

I wince at his comments. But those things are really not why

I did the pictures, or at least, I don't think they are. Maybe that's why it hurts though. Maybe he knows me better than I think, maybe he's right?

'Are you quite finished? Do you feel better now? Got it all off your chest?'

'And you wonder why I cheated! Who wouldn't when they're married to an ice queen like you.'

Wow, okay.

'Oh yes, poor you, Pete. Married to a bitch. Slaving away for his family, with no one to love him or cook or clean or skivvy for him. It's such a tough life you lead, playing the big man in London in your office.

'Were we not enough for you, that you needed a bit on the side? If you weren't happy, you could have said something. You were the one at risk of redundancy, you were the one that said I needed a job. So, I got one. And it works around school hours.'

I know it's a weak defence now I say it out loud. But it really made sense at the time. And it wasn't meant to be forever.

'You know that's not what I meant! And trust you to make it all about money. You know, Sarah always warned me about you, never liked you from the start.'

'Yeah, Pete, you think I didn't know that? And you seem to forget I had a job when we met, I was the same level as you, and earned the same as you. But then I had your daughter and we decided we could manage on one income and I should stay at home with Anouk, it was better for her. We chose this together!'

We go round and round, hurling words at each other, trying to find new ways to make each other bleed and bruise.

By the time it's school pick-up time, I've stormed upstairs to have a shower – a very satisfying slam of our bedroom door on the way – and Pete is sitting in his study, no doubt messaging Sarah about how awful I am.

How's things?

It's Liam.

> Pete knows about the photos.

Ah.

> Yes.

You okay?

> We may have exchanged words.

I can only imagine.

> It's not pretty.

Wish I was there with you.

> I wish you were too.

The words are out before I can take them back.

Wow, things must be bad!

> Don't think this changes anything.

I did some snooping btw. Like you asked.

> And?

Nothing. I'm sorry. It's all screenshots from someone else, another class.

> But how do they know it's me?

I can't work that out either.

> I was so fucking careful. I checked every single picture for identifying details.

> Maybe they did a reverse Google image search. Maybe there was a reflection of you in something. Honestly, people are so sneaky with these things, they'll zoom in on any detail.

> Maybe...

> Are you going to shut the account down?

> Why do you ask?

> That's basically what all the gossip is about. How can you keep going, their precious husbands, lots and lots of pearl-clutching.

> I stopped sending the photos ages ago, though. There's nothing really on my main account. But I guess I should close it.

> Makes sense.

> Yeah

Footsteps thud upstairs, 'Mummy! Mummy!'

> Gotta go. A is home.

> Cool x

More kisses from him, but still I don't return them. Not with Anouk here.

'Baby girl!'

I turn to her as she flings the door open, ready to scoop her into my arms. But the cuddle I'm expecting doesn't come.

'How could you, Mummy! Beckie said you put pictures of you WITH NO CLOTHES ON on Instagram and her daddy saw your MINNIE!'

Her arms are folded, one sock droops around her ankle and her bob is all rumpled. When I look closer I see her eyes are red and her cheeks are blotchy. My heart squeezes at the sight of her. I want to scoop her up in my arms and run with her, far from here. But I know I am the last person she wants right now. And the one thing I know about parenting, is that you have to do what *they* need, not what you need. Which is harder than you might think.

'Have you been crying, sweetie?'

'Everyone laughed at me and said my mummy was a... a SLUT!'

'Do you even know what that is, baby?'

'No! But I know it's not good!' And she bursts into noisy tears and hurls herself at me. I pull her tight against me, fighting tears myself, knowing I am both the person who hurt her and the person who can comfort her. It's a dynamic I've experienced before for myself, and would never wish on someone, let alone my own daughter.

Pete comes into the room.

'The teacher had to take me aside at pick-up because of your shenanigans. Said the other kids were picking on her and maybe to keep her home tomorrow until things have calmed down. Are you proud of yourself? Look what you've done to our daughter.'

Anouk is making a hot snotty mess on the front of my top. To be honest, I'm not far off doing the same thing myself, but unfortunately my options for people to cry on are rather limited.

'Of course I'm not proud. I'm not a complete sociopath!' I hiss. 'I never thought this would happen.'

It's killing me, seeing Anouk like this.

'That's your problem though, isn't it, Ems? You didn't bloody think. You never do. You just do what you want, when you want, and expect the rest of us to pick up the pieces.'

'You're right, Pete. Anouk, I am so sorry sweetheart, I never meant for this to happen.'

I know no amount of movie nights or pizzas are enough to

make up for this. In fact, I don't think there is a way to fix this. Not for Anouk. I mean yes, the parents will stop gossiping after a while and I can take down my account. And Pete isn't exactly the innocent victim here either. But kids don't forget shit like this. People bear the scars of things from school, well into adulthood.

Pete crosses his arms. 'It's too late, Ems. I know I'm not perfect, I know I've made mistakes – but this, this is something else. I don't think I can get past this, I'm sorry.'

Anouk has stopped sobbing and is sitting on my lap perfectly still, watching Pete and me with wide open eyes.

'What do you mean, Daddy?' Her lip wobbles, and I'm finding it hard to stop mine doing the same, even though I knew this was coming, even though I'd even considered being the one to say it, before all this. But he's beaten me to the punch.

'Pete... come on. Let's not do this now. Everyone's had a nasty shock and needs a bit of time to process things. Let's not make any hasty decisions.'

He looks at me, his expression neutral, and shakes his head.

'It's too little, too late, Ems. You and I both know it, let's be real.'

He turns and walks away, closing the door behind him. Even though I know he's only going downstairs, it feels like he might never come back.

'What's Daddy had enough of? Has he had enough of me?'

Anouk's eyes fill with tears again and her expression skewers me. Although I know Pete's right, I would do anything to change the way it's happened, the pain it's causing Anouk – the pain *my actions* have caused her.

I like to think that if the photos hadn't happened, we could have parted amicably – Anouk thrilled that she and Beckie would be stepsisters.

It's too hard though, to explain all this to an eight-year-old, so instead, I tell her a small white lie and hope it'll hold for long enough for us to get some closure on everything.

'Of course not, sweetheart. Daddy had a bad day and he doesn't like seeing you upset. He's a bit cross with Mummy about something, that's all. He still loves you very, very much.'

'Is he cross about the minnie picture?'

'Darling, how many times, it's vulva, not a minnie.'

She waves her hands at me. 'Mummy!!'

'Yes, sweetie, it's about the picture.'

Inside, I'm dying. This is so far from what I wanted Anouk to learn about being a woman, that it's not all about how you look. My own hypocrisy disgusts me. How did I not see this coming?

'So, it's true?'

'Noodle, I don't want to talk about it right now, okay. It's making me feel sad too. Can we go downstairs and I'll make you a special snack, and a bit later on we'll talk about it. Is that okay?'

She folds her arms again and looks at me, her nose almost touching mine, as if performing some sort of mental lie detection.

She's not stupid, my daughter. She knows when she's being distracted. But she tolerates being taken downstairs, given a sundae and allowed to watch TV – normally it's homework and reading first, before device time, but today all rules are made to be broken.

I message Sarah again.

> Beckie told Anouk that her daddy saw a photo of my minnie. Do you think you could have a word with your daughter please? Anouk is in bits thanks to you and your big mouth.

The reply comes almost immediately.

> Are you for real? You took the pictures. And somehow it's my family's fault your daughter is upset. Jesus Christ Em, have a little self-awareness. Don't message me again please. I need some space.

Well, that's that then. As if she hadn't tried to sleep with my husband.

A bit later Pete comes into the sitting room, I'm helping Anouk with a jigsaw puzzle – I've decided it was better to try and attempt some sensible parenting.

'Have you got dinner plans?'

It's so tempting to bite back, but I don't.

'Nothing really, feel free to make something.'

He frowns but makes a swift recovery.

'Pizza for three is it then?'

We seem to be living on junk food at the moment, but I'm actually losing weight. I pick at my pizza, drink a glass of wine as Pete frowns at me.

'Finishing the bottle already, are we?'

I bite my tongue again. There will be time later to lay into each other again, but I refuse to do it in front of Anouk again. She deserves better.

It seems Pete is riding the emotional rollercoaster as much as I am.

We finish the pizza and then Pete takes Anouk up for a shower and puts her to bed, the subtext being that she needs a parent who is responsible and mature. I want to throw my wine glass at him, but I don't. Instead, I idly watch some nonsense on Netflix, and wait to finish the argument we put on ice earlier.

But it doesn't come.

Instead, Pete texts me from upstairs.

> I want a divorce.

> I'm moving out tomorrow.

> You should get a lawyer.

I reply back with one word.

> Fine.

I sit on the sofa in silence for a little while, as if the earth has stopped spinning. That's it then. We're over. I should feel sadness... or even happiness? But I don't. I feel nothing, only numb and still. Nine years, three houses, two jobs and one child. All ended in the blink of an eye.

Except it's not really. It's funny how it's actually happened really slowly – but also all at once.

I think about when we'll tell people – Anouk first, my mum, Pete's family. Our friends. How we unpick our lives together. Should we sell the house? I can't afford to buy Pete out. Shit, will he and Sarah move in together? Are she and Greg having the same discussion right now in their house? And what about Anouk? I can't bear to think about how we'll share custody, how Pete'll make me out to be the worst mum ever. I can't imagine the holidays without her, Christmas, Easter, all those milestones yet to come.

I start to drive myself crazy with all the thoughts of what will need to be done and when. I go round and round, wondering how I could have done things differently, if I'd change anything. But I know there's no point, we are where we are.

I know at some point the tears will come – and the anger; I'm probably in shock.

So, I do what I was always going to do.

I text Liam. Ask him if I can come over.

Somewhere in the back of my mind, Anna's voice whispers to me, asking me if I'm sure, if this is the right thing to do. But all I can think is that maybe this was all meant to be. That this is our chance to be together again.

ELEVEN

March 2023
Naomi

Brigham seems to occupy a strange limbo, where she is both a victim, and not a victim. Her legal team played it very carefully in court, maintaining that the power imbalance of the relationship and the grooming that took place meant that she never consented, properly. They argued that everything happened as a result of this – the last party, the deaths.

And that she had a history of being groomed, that she was vulnerable due to her upbringing. The single mother, the housing estate she lived on, all the usual clichés and assumptions about the working class.

Mum told me, when she first met Brigham, that she always seemed a little closed off, reserved. But otherwise, she fitted in, she seemed just like everyone else, even down to the refined accent. Brigham told me afterwards that her mother paid for elocution lessons, saying that *if it was good enough for Margaret Thatcher it's good enough for you*. She paid for them using money from an inheritance apparently, seeing it as an investment in her daughter's future.

As Mum said, Brigham passed for being one of them, to a degree, even if she was always vague about her past. I never thought of Mum as being snobby, but the way she sometimes talked about Brigham, made me wonder.

Some of the original media coverage had interviews with Brigham's mother, and she certainly didn't seem snobby. Hardworking, yes. Ambitious and driven, for her daughter to have everything she didn't. And maybe that translated into a certain way of thinking, a certain way of trying to ensure Brigham had financial security.

And some of it was generational, Mum acknowledged that herself. *You don't understand sweetheart, the nineties were nowhere near as advanced as you think. Women were still very much the underclass. I know you think it's tough now, with all this about the gender pay gap and so on but it's nothing compared to how it was back in my day. Women were only tolerated in offices if we knew our place – as secretaries, administrative assistants, there to look pretty and take the coffee orders. Woe betide a woman if someone thought she was getting ideas about her station like, say, I don't know – coming back to work after having a baby, or wanting a promotion – or anything that threatened the status quo.*

The interviews with Brigham's mum didn't reveal much I didn't know, but it contextualised so much of her obsession with wealth and money and security, no matter how much she tried to mask it. When you come from a home where it was a choice between heating and eating, when you are the only kid at school in clothes that haven't been washed enough – or washed too much and are hand me downs several times over. Brigham's mum scrimped and saved to try to give her what she could, but I sense from what she doesn't say, that it was never enough.

Not that Brigham was demanding as a child, not at all, but

children are expensive, keeping a roof over their head and food in their mouths is hard enough, let alone extras for school trips or stationery or the right clothes and books.

Brigham's mum herself came from a family in Sheffield, just her and her brother and her mum and dad. But her father was severely injured in the war and couldn't work. Brigham's mum didn't even finish school, had to go out to work when she was fourteen. *Generational poverty, trauma, society, are all to blame for where we find ourselves,* says my supervisor, *nothing happens in a vacuum.*

So Brigham's upbringing and moral values were understandable to a degree. But as Mum said, and I had to agree with her, the chameleon way that Brigham changed, adapted, to get where she wanted to be, was all hers alone.

Every time I read my interview notes, or meet Brigham, I see something different, she's kaleidoscopic.

Recording #3 – March 2023 – Emily Brigham

The first time I let a man take photos of me topless, I was seventeen and it was with a Polaroid camera, to avoid collecting the pictures in Boots the Chemist, alongside the pensioners collecting prescriptions for piles ointment and constipation.

I'd never seen any porn or even any top shelf magazines, as they were known then. All I knew is that fashion designers wanted women to look like heroin addicts and men wanted women to look like inflatable dolls – according to the editors of *FHM* and *The Sun*. Somewhere I could see a link, but it didn't stop me wanting to look like them or to be like them.

My legs were long, my hips were narrow and my stomach was flat – but I spent my allowance on every Wonderbra I could get my hands on, to funnel my breasts into Eva's va-va-voom dreams.

I wonder what happened to those grubby Polaroids. I let him take three. I kept one – the close up of my face, in case a model scout needed it – and he kept two.

Of course he promised me he wouldn't show the pictures to anyone, but he kept them in his wallet – close to his heart he said, despite his wallet living in his hip pocket not his jacket.

He – Jamie – was twenty-five. He had a degree in business management from Nottingham Trent and was a sales rep for a big pharmaceutical company. He had a bottle green Ford Mondeo and was always being sent off to places like Coventry or Doncaster – grey, dreary towns. I sometimes accompanied him on the trips, he was often put up in dusty five-star hotels, former manor houses and listed properties – where we rattled around half empty dining rooms and clumsily fucked on creaky divans.

In hindsight, it said a lot that Jamie couldn't manage to get a girlfriend his own age and was stuck with a schoolgirl, a friend of the younger sibling of another friend. He was obsessed with acting out heavily staged fantasies. I dated him for two years, thinking I had made it – an older boyfriend who had money to burn, or so I thought.

I broke up with him before I was due to leave for Oxford University, despatched him on his tearful way with a quick hand-job by way of apology, and a cup of tea after. I remember watching from my window as he climbed into his car, head drooping, much like his penis often did. When he turned to look up at me and wave, I simply walked away and let the curtain close behind me. Mum was ready with a hug, telling me I'd done the right thing, that the boys at Oxford would be a different calibre entirely, that I didn't need any ties to home. I was the first person in my family to go to university. I knew she wanted me to focus on having a better life than we did now.

<Pause and rustle, clink of a glass>

My mother was a post war baby – a boomer through and through, and born with her red lipstick and nails applied, the knowledge of how to make a perfect martini and dress for any occasion innate in her.

Her sole aim in life was, as early as possible, to find a man, settle down, pop out babies and then when they were old enough to have babies themselves, to spend every weekend and afternoon sozzled on gin whilst gardening and shopping with her best friends. Unfortunately that didn't quite go as planned because my dad turned out to be a habitual gambler who left us when I was nine for the mum of one of my school friends.

It's a cliché but Mum was always on a diet – I blame my father, who would constantly tell her she needed to lose a bit of weight, that she was turning into a fat pig. She had all the Jane Fonda workout videos and the spandex outfits. She took me for a makeover when I was thirteen, weighed us both before and after every holiday season and if she felt either of us were gaining weight, out came the cabbage soup recipes and halved grapefruits. She'd say, 'Do you really think you should?' if I ever reached for chocolate or carbs. She taught me to take care of myself.

I don't think she was ever happier than on my wedding day.

When I had all the things she wanted. Behind the scenes was a different story though. She refused to speak to me on the day itself because I didn't buy the shoes and veil she wanted me to have. Her only daughter, after all she did for me. It's a complex relationship I know. But it doesn't matter now.

After the session, Brigham's guard tells me that her mother never visited her, she died quite soon after Brigham was incarcerated, from Covid-19. When I get home and look at the court reports, I also note that Brigham had several boyfriends as a teenager, all at least five years older than her.

What does it all mean? I ask my boyfriend Max.

But he doesn't answer, only sighs and fetches me a cup of tea, leaving me to it.

PART 2

THEN

TWELVE

2005

The first time I go to one of Liam's parties I am unprepared. It is not a date. None of our dates are dates, but this one definitely isn't. I know it's good to be invited. I know he hasn't asked the girls before me. I know this means he's serious about me, about us, about whatever we are. That he trusts me.

He tells me he'll see me there. Tells me to bring some friends. He doesn't tell me which ones, but I know who to ask – and who not to ask. I haven't gotten this far with him by being stupid. I know I should be careful, I shouldn't be doing this. But it's too late. I think I love him. I think he's the one. And I think maybe he loves me too.

After all, he wouldn't risk it all if he didn't.

Lilly and Noush have drinks at ours beforehand. Cheap vodka and mixers, rosé, Prosecco – whatever we have really. I warn them to go slow, but they wave me away, knocking back full glasses and singing along to MGMT in the kitchen.

I redo my hair twice, my make-up three times, fret over which shoes, which bag, which earrings. I remember Coco

Chanel's advice about removing one thing before I leave the house, but as Noush reminds me, she was also a Nazi sympathiser so *fuck that shit, babe, more is more*. Still, when she's not looking I swap my hoop earrings for the diamond studs Liam gave me. He'll be happy I'm wearing them, even if they aren't really my style; besides, I tell myself, diamonds go with everything.

On the train, with leftover wine in plastic water bottles, I watch our reflections in the windows as we zoom under houses and rivers and shops. We look like a Benetton advert: one white, one black, one brown. I kind of hate myself right now. Blonde, freckles, milk bottle skin – 'alabaster', Liam calls it – but that only makes me think of friezes of the ancient Greeks in battle, frozen in time, stolen treasures in a museum.

We are all in bandage dresses from Reiss or Topshop or Warehouse because we can't afford anything better. I don't know what I expected when I graduated, but I expected more than this. High-street labels on champagne tastes, Liam says, promising he'll someday buy me the real deal. When you grow up with nothing, and then you see what everyone else has, you want it too. Mum drummed it into me: work hard, go to university, get a good job, meet a good man, settle down, pop the kids out. Don't turn out like her, was the subtext. I'm on track, sort of.

Noush is loud and giggly, wrapping herself around the central pole in the carriage, flipping herself around, the way she's learned in her classes. In her four-inch cage sandals, it's impressive. But the only people looking interested are old men with grey hair, in grey suits, sweating in the clammy heat. Everyone else is turned away.

'Can you do that upside down splits thing yet?'

Lilly is fumbling around for her digital camera, trying to remain upright despite the wine and the motion of the train.

'Not yet; soon though. But I can do this.' Noush grips the

pole with one hand and raises her leg smoothly up in a perfect standing split, her ankle by her ear.

'It's not fair. Must be all those years of ballet.'

'You bet, babe.' She smoothly brings her leg back down, unconcerned that half the carriage on this part of the Northern Line have seen her thong.

Noush is so beautiful, so sexy. She always gets hit on, wherever we are. Sometimes I worry Liam might prefer if I was more like her, but he tells me it's tacky, what she does. Tells me I have other talents and, '*If I wanted a stripper, I'd go to a club.*'

Although he does go to clubs, but a different sort he tells me. And that I might enjoy them, but he's not sure yet. I told him that it was fine and I didn't want to go anyway. And then he laughed and mentioned Groucho Marx. I didn't laugh though and he wasn't happy, and I had to use some of those talents he mentioned to cheer him up again. I love making him happy.

'Is Alastair going tonight?'

Noush has a crush on one of Liam's friends. I don't rate him personally.

'I don't know, maybe. Liam didn't say much.'

'Where exactly is it we're going?'

'I'm not sure. I think it's like a private room at one of their members clubs?'

Lilly laughs when I say members and I wonder if she really was the right choice for tonight. She can be unpredictable. I love that she doesn't take any shit, but I'm not so sure what she'll make of Liam's friends. Or what they'll make of her. I just want everyone to have a good time, and I want to prove to Liam that I'm worthy of his trust.

'Behave, babe.'

'Boooooring.'

But she winks at me all the same and then swigs from her bottle and grimaces.

I've been sleeping with Liam for six months. The girls know but they won't tell anyone, I told Liam; they don't know anyone to tell.

He's come out drinking a couple of times and that's how Noush met Alastair. Needless to say, all his friends are from work. Either from Detner & Vinci or places he's worked before. I haven't told them Liam's married. They can be a bit funny about things like that. It's a good thing he doesn't wear a ring.

'Girls, sit down okay. Stop showing off.'

They're both dancing around the pole now, grinding on each other and giggling. I have a horrible feeling they've taken something. Liam won't like it.

Not that he's anti-drugs. Far from it.

But they're acting up already. This must be how parents feel, the ones I see sometimes on the bus or in McDonalds, their faces drawn tight with telling their kids to behave, without shouting at them.

I go over and drag them down beside me.

The train is busier now and some French tourists get on and sit opposite us. One of them winks at us. He's cute. All dark hair and dark eyes. I can't remember much from French class but I know when a guy is talking about us. I ignore him though. I don't need boys like him anymore.

Lilly flings an arm around me, her breath scented with pineapple and malibu as she talks at me. 'How come you're out tonight anyway? What happened to the crazy hours project you were working on?'

'Finished it yesterday. Hence the party tonight. Everyone got their bonus.'

Noush wriggles in her seat. 'I hope they need help spending it.'

She can't even begin to imagine how much money these guys have. She's just your regular grammar school, suburbs, redbrick, party girl. She's never travelled first class, never stayed in five-star luxury. She wears branded designer stuff, ready to wear, thinks that's haute couture. Still richer than me though, still had so much more than I did.

I'm not jealous of my friends and their upbringings though. I know I'll get mine. Besides, it's not that Liam doesn't buy me things. I don't tell anyone about them, even though Mum would love it.

'Yo! Ems, is this our stop?'

We're at Green Park already, after hopping off at Leicester Square and rushing across to the Piccadilly line. We wind our way out of the complex maze of exits and find ourselves in the hustle and bustle of Mayfair.

'It's not too far, is it? I can't walk in these fucking shoes.'

But Lilly giggles all the same and drains the rest of her water bottle.

'Nah, it's just behind here,' and I lead them through the entryway of the park, before we cut through a Victorian covered passageway with a door and a bell.

'Well, this is all kinda shades of Jack the Ripper.'

One thing I love about living in London now, is how beautiful it is, especially in the centre. All the incredible buildings, the streets like something out of a movie. I play it cool but secretly I'm so happy to be here, living this life. Well-paid job, shared flat with the girls, out every weekend, hot man. It's what Mum and I dreamt of, back when I lived at home, dating a series of losers, killing time until I went to uni.

'Jack the stripper more like.' Noush and Lilly giggle together but I ignore them and say the password into the cut-out in the door.

Liam told me about the speakeasy vibe, but I didn't really get it. I mean, I've seen *The Great Gatsby* and the aesthetic was cute, but I wasn't wild about it otherwise. Plus, Leo Di Caprio is getting on a bit. Though I definitely did not say that to Liam.

The door creaks open for us, and a man in black tie greets us.

'Ladies. Can I take your coats?'

The girls clatter around on their heels, acting as if this is a complete novelty, but I slip out of the wool overcoat Liam bought me and act as if this is a standard Saturday night for me.

We're in a long, dark, wood-panelled hallway. There are stairs up to the right, behind the reception desk, and lit candles in sconces up the walls. The air smells of lavender and wood polish.

'Blimey, this is a bit old-school, isn't it?'

'Shhhhh.'

We follow the receptionist down what seems like endless corridors, three Alices tumbling down the rabbit hole. Behind me the girls are silenced. We stop short in front of a pair of double doors.

The receptionist raps on them smartly.

'We're not in Kansas anymore,' mutters Noush, but her eyes shine in the dim light and I know she's intrigued. This is very different from their usual Friday nights at Revolution and then the sticky carpets of Infernos, snogging boys who went to uni with us.

And I did this. I got them here. For a moment I'm light-headed with the knowledge.

The double doors are opened with a flourish and in front of me is a room like I've never seen before. Well, I have, but only behind velvet ropes on school trips. Or on TV.

But now we are behind the velvet rope it seems.

The walls are decorated with what I later find out is actual watered silk, in a pale mint green shade. The ceiling is double height, with sets of French windows leading out onto a marble terrace. Scattered across the room are plush sofas and chaise longues in various shades of green, moss, fern, emerald, strewn with cushions and throws with flecks of golden thread.

On the walls hang various pre-Raphaelite paintings I recognise from my Art History A-level, and at the opposite end, above a gaping, lit fireplace, is a huge painting of a naked cherub with black feathered wings. I'm pretty sure it's an original Caravaggio.

'Oi, art wanker,' hisses Noush, watching me, 'Liam's coming over.'

I close my mouth and remember to accept a coupe of champagne from the black clad waiter that has materialised to my right. Liam told me that champagne coupes were based on the shape of Marie Antoinette's breasts. Either way I sip the golden bubbles, crisp and perfectly chilled.

There are, perhaps, a total of thirty people in the room. And we are the only women so far, I note.

When Liam told me about the parties he threw with his friends, he described them as a sort of *salon*. But I think he may have omitted some key details. It doesn't matter though, because I'm not here to make more friends.

Liam greets Noush and Lilly with a kiss on the cheek, as if we are all of equal importance. He leaves them giggling and unsteady on their feet. He has that way about him. But I hide it better and I can tell from the way he looks at me, he's noticed.

'Lovely to see you again, Lillian and Anoushka. Did you find it okay?'

'Ems.' He reaches down and his lips brush my cheek, I catch the scent of Chanel Bleu Pour Homme, and something inside of me squeezes and swells. The way he's looking at me, I can tell he feels it too. But we both hide it.

He praised me early on, for my control. The way I wasn't like the other girls. Even though I've heard that before, a fair few times, somehow it means more from him. It's the first time I've really felt different, wanted to be different.

He ushers us past groups of men in jeans and jackets, heavy silver and leather watches, winking signet rings, and out to the terrace, where Alastair and another man that I don't recognise, wait. As we sit, there is the slightest brush of his hand against my back, in the slit where my skin is exposed. It's like I've been branded.

'So... where are the other girls?' Lilly giggles up at Alastair.

'Why would we need anyone else, when we have you?' He inches closer to her, but flashes a look up at Liam.

The girls settle down, chat amongst themselves, flag down a waiter and nab a full bottle of champagne. I pretend to listen in, they're mostly gossiping about other people from university – someone has recently come out, someone else has cheated on their long-term boyfriend. They debate the merits of Ibiza over Sicily for a girls' holiday. I nod and smile in the right places, but I don't care about the people from university, and I won't be going on holiday with them – not that they know this. Mostly I think about Liam and I wait my turn.

The party drifts on. I have more champagne. Liam comes and goes. When I go to the toilet, there are suddenly new girls in there, heavy accents, sniffing coke from the countertops. They offer to share but I decline. Sitting in a cubicle, I hear what sounds like a sob from the person next door. I don't get involved though. It's none of my business. Sometimes this happens when we go out with Liam's friends. It's why I was careful who I chose to come with tonight. I didn't want anyone who didn't know how to have a good time.

I find Liam on my way back out to the terrace.

'It's got busy.'

He raises an eyebrow at me and snags some canapés from a passing waiter.

'Try these.' He feeds me a morsel of rare beef, a flash of horseradish.

'Where did all those girls come from?'

He pulls me close to him, and I wind my arms around his neck, watch his mouth and then his eyes as he talks. This close to him, I can feel how much he wants me. The knowledge is more intoxicating than all the champagne I've had so far.

'I'm sorry. You know how these things can be.'

I don't though, but I am in no hurry to remind him it's my first time at a party like this. It doesn't work though.

'Aren't you having a good time?'

I smile – I've often accused him of being a mind-reader. He always seems to know what I want, what I'm feeling. No one else has ever been able to read me like him.

'I am, I promise.' I press myself against him, notice his sharp intake of breath, the flicker of a smile at the corner of his mouth. 'Don't worry about me.' I'm not needy, I'm the cool girl. And all men want the cool girl.

He turns us around so we are in a corner, his body sheltering me from sight, and kisses me, the taste of his mouth, hot and bitter like strong liquor. I wonder if he knows I'm wet already. I wonder how long he's going to make me wait.

One time he sent me a hotel room key with a message that told me to strip naked, put on a silk blindfold, lie face down on the bed – and he'd be there in forty-five minutes, maybe.

The truth is though, I am bored at this party. I don't want to spend any more time talking to men old enough to be my father, their hands with sweaty sausage-like fingers on my thighs as they tell me about their house in Antibes, their new boat – read, yacht – and did I go to Ascot this year? How did I find Henley? And Wimbledon?

Liam pulls away from me, his gaze heavy on me as he speaks.

'I like watching you with my friends. You're so charming, everyone loves you.'

'Of course they do. I'm delightful!'

'You are indeed.' And there's that crooked half smile I love again. I trace it with a finger. I want to trace it with my tongue. His smile fades and I feel the intensity of his gaze between my legs. He pulls my hand away, entwines his fingers with mine behind his back and turns us back around to face the room.

'Go and play some more. I'll come and find you in a while. I need to catch up with a couple of people.'

And he disengages me with a little nudge toward Lilly and Noush, who are dancing in front of the fireplace. Before I can turn and say goodbye, he's gone.

I dance. I drink more champagne. I hug my girls. We give each other affected lip kisses to a cheering audience. More people arrive, more girls in short, tight black dresses. More people start dancing. The music is a mess: EDM, funk, Motown, eighties. It doesn't matter. It seems like I blink and each time I see something new.

The men in the corner, girls on their laps. Blink again and they are gone.

Blink again and Lilly and Noush are the ones on men's laps.

Blink again and they too are gone.

I keep dancing and I keep drinking. Enough until I forget about the hands on my waist, on my legs, on my hands, in my hair. The hands that I want on me, aren't here.

Eventually I take a break. I ask for water and the barman looks dubious. But when I ask again, he gives it to me.

'You must be tired. You've been working hard, all evening,' I say.

He nods at me, but continues mixing drinks for someone else. I watch the blurry tattoos on his hands move from the heavy liquor bottles, the ice, the lemon. I want to reach over and touch his fingers, with their intricate markings, I wonder how different they'd feel from Liam's, inside of me. He seems nice, he must be, to put up with us all night. I wonder what he's like in bed. I never used to think about these things before I met Liam. He asks me questions like this all the time, asks me to guess about other people, their needs, wants, desires.

'Can I get you anything else, miss? A cab?'

His eyes bore into mine and I wonder what else he's seeing as he looks at me. Disgust and desire can be very similar.

I twirl the straw that I stole from his side of the bar, take a sip of my water and look at him longer. He's got another tattoo flicking around the nape of his neck and dipping into his white shirt. Maybe not such a nice boy. He's not that tall, but stocky. I imagine him pinning me down in a bed of white sheets, his hands around my neck, his tattoos shadows against me.

He's watching me too, even as he works. But then his expression changes, and he steps away from the bar as a hand lands on my back, again in the slit of my dress where the skin is exposed.

'She doesn't need a cab. Do you, Ems?'

Liam knows I love tattoos.

'Nope! All good.' And when he looks at me, a full smile this time, turning me on my bar stool to face him, I know what's coming.

'Good night, mate? Busy yeah? Got time to grab me a whisky?'

And just like that the barman is nothing, is no one.

Liam's stubble is scratchy under my palm as I draw his face close to mine, revelling in his happiness. I don't know where he's been or what's going on, but this side of him, this boyish, playful side, I don't see all that often. I want to keep it close to me. I forget to be wary.

'Hey, gorgeous.'

'Hey, gorgeous to you too. Come here often, do you?'

I know the script. I know how this ends.

'Nah. Not often.'

We keep playing with the script. I make him laugh, he makes me laugh. He asks me where my friends are and I say I don't know. Which is true. Noush and Lilly disappeared down that long corridor I don't even know when. It's almost like Liam and I are a real couple. Well, a normal couple. He likes to pretend that way sometimes. As if I could just leave when I wanted, as if he could.

He picks my hand up, pulls me off my seat, pulls me onto the dance floor, and twirls me and honestly, I am so, so, so very happy. He brings me into his chest and then spins me out again. I don't know what the music is, and I don't care. There's no one left really in the room now, but to be honest it could be crowded with thousands of people and he'd find me.

Later on, much later, I lie in the dark with him.

He moves over me, inside me, whispers to me. And I feel found when I'm lost; I feel seen when I'm invisible. Even when he shatters me over and over again, it hurts so much, better than I ever imagined possible.

And when I say his name after, a breath, a sigh, an incantation, a spell, I hope it's enough to bind him to me for good – this time.

The parties became a regular thing after that. Sometimes I'd bring the girls, sometimes I wouldn't. And the men changed too. I started to recognise faces from papers, in the financial press, online, but I pretended I hadn't. Liam never spoke about the parties when we weren't there.

We were still careful at work. As I'd moved on to a new client, it made things easier in some ways and harder in others. I had to tell people Liam was mentoring me if they saw us having lunch together. Which we rarely did. When we saw each other it was in splinters of time. Maybe Wednesday or Thursday nights. Whenever he could tell his wife he was entertaining clients – and he'd book a hotel room.

Even when we weren't together, he'd send me gifts, not only the usual things, but old books – first editions of Jane Austen, Emily Dickinson, or framed monographs of artists he thought

I'd like. I'd hang them in the flat, tell the girls I found them in the charity shop.

The parties happened every few weeks. Sometimes Liam would message me the day before, tell me what to wear – or send me what to wear. Couriers would arrive with full outfits in a suit carrier, silk, satin, crepe du chine, often full length. Sometimes with buckles or straps. High necked or long sleeved. And underneath it, lingerie. Lace in shades of clotted blood, ink blue, peacock green, old ivory. And always a letter with instructions. How to walk, how to talk. What to say and not say. Which rules he wanted me to break.

The girls loved him, of course.

You're so lucky. Can he buy some for me?

They called him my sugar daddy. Which annoyed me. Because it was never like that. Transactional. I couldn't tell them it was love though – I didn't want to see their faces. They laughed about the parties, laughed at the creepy old men, sometimes they didn't want to go. I couldn't believe they actually preferred being pawed at by consulting grads in a sticky-floored club.

Even their requests to do something different annoyed me – *babe, can't we have a girls' night out, no boys? Just once.*

But I didn't want to. I was getting somewhere, even as I knew that the higher I got, the further I had to fall. But I didn't look down once, I kept climbing. Because maybe this time no one had to get hurt.

I knew not to question the parameters of my relationship with Liam. I'd never been like this before – not in the driving seat. Though Liam would deny that.

We'd barely speak. He'd talk nicely to room service or the hotel receptionist but then we'd walk upstairs in silence and he'd rush me into a bedroom, a meeting room, a cupboard, and turn me around, pin me against the wall, the only sound the clink of his belt and the rasp of his zipper, his palm dry against my mouth.

People talk about how it feels the first time someone you trust hits you, hurts you. But I can't define a before and an after with Liam. I can't remember the first time he told me I couldn't leave until he said so, the first time he shamed me into covering up. But then again, I can't remember the first time I put a lit cigarette out on him when he asked me to. The look in his eyes. The way I felt after, yoked to him in ways I couldn't explain.

That was the real reason why I didn't want girls' nights out. I didn't want to talk about my sex life, or who Lilly and Noush were sleeping with. I didn't want to explain how Liam showed me that no sometimes meant yes. I knew they wouldn't get it. And besides, it was private, for us only.

The parties got busier. There were more women, but different women. Some of them barely spoke English. So slender and young, baby gazelles in their Manolos.

I'm not sure when the mood of the parties started to change. When people were openly taking coke off the lounge tables. When hands disappeared up skirts and down tops and in trousers, without waiting for a closed door. When girls crying in the toilets became a regular occurrence. When girls stuffed wads of notes in their couture clutches and no one asked what they'd been paid for. When some girls stopped showing up altogether.

Even so, I kept going. For Liam.

THIRTEEN

2006

I don't mention the upcoming party to Anna, when she calls for a catch up. It's not her scene and I don't think she'll like Liam. It feels weird, thinking about them meeting. The two people in my life that mean the most to me.

Anna and I haven't seen each other for a few months. She's been away, digging wells or something for a non-profit in Africa, something very worthy, whilst I've been a slave to capitalism. It still baffles me, our friendship, but somehow it works.

We don't spend long on the phone before I'm summoned back to the office for yet another client briefing, but we arrange to meet the following week near St Paul's. She lives in North London – God knows why – so we don't see each other that often, and even less so recently.

I'm nervous in the run-up to seeing her. It's not like I haven't had boyfriends before, heaven knows she's seen everything on nights out at uni. But Anna is very protective of me. Wants the best for me. Sometimes she doesn't realise that you have to let people make mistakes; it's the only way they learn.

Not that Liam is a mistake, I just don't think she'll understand. And I don't know how to tell her.

Lilly and Noush don't understand either, not anymore. They don't like coming to the parties that much now. They think it's all a bit weird, don't get why I'm hung up on what they're wearing, how they act; can't they just have a laugh? They tell me that I need to fucking relax. They don't get it though. I need Liam. It's not some fling. I need the parties, I need his trust, I need his love. And he needs mine.

He tells me I can do better than them, that I shouldn't spend time with people who don't want the best for me, like he does. And I believe him – even when it doesn't always feel like he does. Even when it's hard – when he's cruel, when his love is suffocating, when he needs to know where I am, who I'm with, what I'm doing, what I'm wearing, when I need his permission to exist, it seems like – I know it's better than the alternative. It's better than working the supermarket checkout for the rest of my life, marrying the first boy who knocks me up, never moving five minutes away from where I was born, my whole life in the tightest orbit possible to where I grew up.

How boring is that? he says to me. *How small, how ordinary. That's not the life you should live, that's not the life you could live.* And I listen to him, and I believe him.

And everyone else falls away.

When I see Anna, I'm reminded of the first time we met. The wide blue eyes, the long red hair, the wide smile, the gap between her teeth. I can tell she still uses the same cherry-flavoured ChapStick she had at university. Waxy and thick, her lips shine prettily.

'So, what's new, Ems? You've been super sketchy recently!'

'Just working so much at the moment, really. You know how it is.'

'I do indeed. But, Ems, you can't fool me. I know you finished a project the other week because you posted about it, and I saw those pics from a party at the weekend. So, spill, who's the new guy?'

The thing I loved – love – most about Anna is how direct she is. Not insensitive, but forthright. She doesn't play games or mess around. If she wants to know something, she'll ask.

'Anna... I can't tell you, you won't like it.'

She drinks her wine.

'Is he making you happy?'

'Yes.'

'Is he making you come?'

'Anna!'

'Is he? I can tell he is!'

'Well, yes.'

'Does he treat you well?'

Anna's idea of being treated well and my idea of being treated well differ drastically but I say yes all the same.

'Well, then I'm happy for you.' And she chinks her glass to mine. 'Cheers!'

'What about you? Anyone I need to know about?'

Her face colours slightly and she has a sly little smile.

'Anna!'

Anna doesn't give her heart away lightly. In the time I've known her, she's had maybe one or two proper relationships, and a couple of flings. I get the feeling there was someone she really liked at university, but she never told me much about them.

'Who is it? Tell me!'

All I can prise out of her is that it's not someone at work and she met them in a bar. But she, too, is happy. And I'm glad. She deserves someone who sees how lovely she is and treats her well. Anna is one of those people I feel the need to protect, and there's not many people I feel that way about. I know it's been frustrating for other people, boyfriends who complained I wouldn't let them get too close. But Anna is different. She's my ride or die. She gets me like no one else ever has – well, until Liam. But that's different. Amongst my friends, Anna is special.

We spend the rest of the evening drinking wine and eating pizza and whinging about the various dickheads we have to work with. I don't mention Liam. I don't talk about the parties. And if she notices the bruising on my forearms, she doesn't say anything. Anna also knows when to keep her mouth shut. It's one of the things I love about her. She knows that if she probes too much, I'll clam up. That I'll tell her when I'm ready. But I'm not ready to share Liam with her yet. And I'm not ready to share her with Liam.

When it's time to leave she walks me to the train station by the cathedral; she's getting a bus, she says. I tell her to text me when she's home safe.

'It's sad we have to have these conversations, isn't it?' she replies.

I agree that it is. I don't think about how I will hold my keys in my hands all the way home, and so will she.

When she leans in to kiss me, her lips are cool on my cheek. Part of me wants to stay there, safe in her arms, and it shocks me to realise that I now feel about Liam the way I've always felt about her. The thought is not entirely comfortable.

As she pulls back, the image is in my head of another night, long ago, with her.

'Miss you, lovely, let's not leave it so long next time.'

And with that, she is gone, striding into the night, sure about the world and her place in it.

We're in bed, when Liam asks me.

'I've got a friend coming to the next party. He's a good mate. He won't know anyone though. Would you be an angel and look after him for me? I know you'll like him. He studied Classics too.'

Liam likes to tease me about my degree, calling me a bluestocking, making me indulge his bizarre middle-class fantasies of fucking me in a library. He likes to pretend he studied at Oxford too. Sometimes he makes me wear little wire-framed glasses, the lenses made of clear glass. And call him my professor. I have to bite my lip then. It's like he's forgotten where I came from, how far I am from this image.

I haven't told him everything about where I grew up, what it was like. I don't want to see the pity on his face. I don't want him to think differently of me, to think of me as weak, needy. I know he respects my drive, but I don't want to become a little adventure into the dark side for him, vicariously experiencing poverty like some reality show.

'Sure.' *Ugh, I don't want to babysit some middle-aged classics bore. The things I do for love.*

'I've got you a new outfit just for the occasion. I think you'll like it – and he will too.'

'Why can't someone else entertain him? After all, he's only going to be annoyed when I go home with you.'

I'm tucked up in the crook of Liam's arm like some lovestruck idiot, as I say this. He smiles as I mention going home with him. He likes watching me with other men – nothing inappropriate. Just the knowledge he has something they all want. With other boyfriends, this was such a turn off. I'm not a possession or a toy. But with Liam, it's different. I don't know why. I'm like a precious object, a piece of art. Others can borrow me, but no one else can own me.

He rolls on top of me.

'I don't want to talk about my friend anymore. Let's talk about what we'll do when we get home.'

'Looks like you're about to give me a live demo.'

'I love it when you talk dirty to me. Say *Powerpoint*.'

I start laughing and so does he, I push him off and then climb on top him.

'What if I went home with him though. How would you feel? What if he's offended if I say no?'

His eyes darken, the laughter gone.

'Would you want to?'

'No... I don't know.'

'Could he do this to you?'

He sits up but keeps me on his lap and kisses my neck, his lips hot on my skin, watching as my nipples harden.

I look at him.

'Or this.'

He puts his hands between us, between my legs. Moves his fingers. I gasp.

'Or this.'

And he pushes me back towards the foot of the bed so that I'm sprawled out in front of him, wide open. And he trails his mouth down my belly until his tongue replaces his fingers. I twist my fingers in his hair, as he makes my back arch off the sheets, makes me scream his name.

Afterwards, he turns me over so I face the wall away from him, pushes himself into me.

'Do you,' he breathes into my ear in time with how we move, 'want to go home with him... now?'

He pulls me by my hair back onto him, so hard I know my scalp will ache tomorrow.

Without words, my body gives him my answer, that I'm his. And only his. And no one else's.

Always.

Liam's friend is called Drew. He does something in tech I think, or maybe hedge funds or, well he could be an astronaut, I wasn't really listening when Liam introduced us. I'm not interested. I don't really know why I have to do this. But as Liam was so... persuasive, I could hardly say no.

I am in a cream silk slip dress that hangs like the drapery on the sculpture of the Parthenon, Drew tells me, a gleam in his eye.

Drew is one of the strawberry blonde types with eyelashes and eyebrows so fair, you can barely see them. He is not married, he tells me. He's very single. He spends too much time at work to have time for anything else. He doesn't really like parties either, but he came because he doesn't see Liam often. He's based in New York but, as anyone with multiple properties is always eager to let you know, he has places in Miami, London, Paris and Geneva also. And he's considering getting somewhere in Shanghai. I really couldn't give two shits.

I know I need to buck up my ideas though because Liam comes back over and asks how we're getting on.

'Well, I was just boring Emily here with tales of the nomad lifestyle.'

I force a laugh. 'Not at all, Drew, it sounds fabulous!' I put my hand on his arm. I'm surprised to feel muscle under his sleeve, he doesn't look the type – tall, wiry. He's not unattractive. He's no Liam, but he's better looking than ninety per cent of the men in this room. He's definitely catching a few eyes. I wonder when he last got laid.

'With all that travelling it gets hard to meet people though. So, I'm lucky enough that I know Liam, who wangled me an invite to this party.'

'We don't let just any rando in,' Liam quips.

'Are you sure? You let me in.' And they both laugh and do that clapping each other on the back thing that blokes do.

'Well, Em knows all the best people, I'm sure she can introduce you to a few.'

'Of course!' Except I don't know where Noush and Lilly are

– they came but said they didn't want to stay long – and I can't imagine Drew with one of the Russian girls.

At the look on my face Drew laughs and chinks his glass against mine.

'Don't worry, I'm quite capable of finding my own amusement, you won't be stuck with me all evening.'

But there's something about how he says it that intrigues me. I wonder if he pays for sex. A lot of wealthy men do, Liam tells me, though they don't think of it like that, so transactional.

I wonder if Liam would pay to sleep with me? And if so, how much. But I'd never do that.

Drew tells me about his job, but I don't really listen. Instead, I think of who to introduce him to. But draw a blank.

Despite myself, I keep catching Drew's eye as he's talking and he shifts closer to me until I am leaning against a wall. I can't do this with him, I know. But I haven't felt a pull to anyone else in a long time now. I wish Liam was here, I need him to rescue me from myself.

Drew is so close I can smell him, the scent of something light and citrusy. His skin is fair and freckled like mine. When he puts his hand out to steady me, I realise I've stumbled. I'm drunker than I realise and excuse myself to the bathroom.

In the stall, alone, I listen to the chatter at the sink.

'Apparently he's the richest man here.'

'Have you spoken to him yet?'

'I don't know which one he is.'

'Someone must know.'

They're talking about Drew.

Back out at the party, I try to drag him onto the dance floor but he refuses, only waves me off. I dance, and drink some more. But every time I turn around, Drew is watching me, even as he chats to Liam. And then both of them are watching me. I spin around and around, until all I see, and all I feel, is their eyes on me. And it feels like power.

. . .

When I wake up the next morning, I'm sore. Everywhere. I'm in a hotel room. That's nothing special. There's a shower running and then it's switched off and the bathroom door opens.

'Hey.'

I roll over, wincing, at the sound of the voice.

It's Drew, with a white towel wrapped around his waist. He's rubbing his hair dry with another.

'Hi...'

'You okay?'

He sits on the bed and reaches down for me.

'Yeah... I...'

'I've ordered up breakfast, you look like you need coffee.'

He doesn't get dressed but lies next to me and scrolls his phone.

There are scratches on his back and a vicious bite on his neck. When he notices me looking he smiles.

'You were a little wildcat last night. Not surprised, though.'

I open my mouth to say something, but I don't know what, so I close it again, and instead go to the bathroom.

I look like shit. My hair is wild down my back, there are bruises – fresh ones, on my forearms and on my thighs. When I swallow it hurts, when I pee it burns, there's blood when I wipe. What the fuck? I can't remember the last time I got blackout drunk before last night. Liam always tells me to be careful, he doesn't like it when I'm messy, out of control.

I remember leaning against Drew, asking him where Liam was. We kissed. There was kissing. I think we were in a lift.

I call out to Drew that I'm having a quick shower, hoping he doesn't offer to join me. I want to lock the door, but I don't want him to ask why.

I do my best to wash my hair with the tiny bottle of shampoo, use body lotion to finger comb out the knots and tangles.

When I wash my body, the water is pink tinged. There are teeth marks on my belly, something that looks like a burn on my hip.

I remember being on a bed, Drew... and Liam – *Liam?* – standing up still in their suits, backs to me, talking. I still had my clothes on then.

I step out of the shower, dry off and then tie a robe tightly around myself, brush my teeth with my finger and a blob of Drew's expensive toothpaste. When I spit, I retch and gag.

'I need to get home.'

'Sure. Want me to order you a cab?'

'That would be great.'

I'm acting like this is simply the morning after a regular date. *It's all good. It's going to be fine. I'll get home and see the girls and go to the gym and message Liam and it'll be just fine. I'm fine*, I tell myself, *it's all good, it's a bad hangover, that's all. There's nothing to stress about.*

But when I get dressed there's a tremor in my hands.

'What's your address?'

I pretend I haven't heard at first, try to buy time, try to think of a different address to give him, because how would he even know? But then I'll be stuck somewhere else. So, I tell him.

He calls down to reception and I gather my things up. My phone has messages from the girls, but nothing from Liam. I don't know how he'll react to knowing where I've woken up. Maybe I don't need to tell him.

God I want to be at home, eating a sausage sandwich. Or better, a Big Mac. But when I picture the food, my stomach roils.

'Are you okay? You look very pale.'

'I'm fine. All good.'

Before I leave, Drew kisses me on the cheek, tells me not to worry, he won't say a word about last night, that it'll be our little secret. I only just make it to the lift before I'm sick in my bag, but all that comes up is bile; there's another woman in the lift and she glares at me in disgust.

When I get home the girls are on the sofa in their duvets, watching *Sex and the City* reruns.

'Ems! What happened to you last night?'

For a minute I consider telling them the truth. But what is the truth anyway? And seen from different angles, is my version the right version? I can't remember most of it, I'm only guessing from this morning. I don't even have the words to say anything, so it's better to say nothing.

'All good!'

'Did you stay in The Stafford *again,* you lucky bitch?' Lilly says.

It's safer to let them think I was with Liam. Why would they think otherwise? I just have to hope they don't mention it when they see him next. Although it's not like he asked where I went. He hasn't even messaged me this morning to check I'm okay.

'What time did you leave?' I ask.

'Oh, I dunno... about eleven? Didn't we?'

Lilly prods Noush who appears comatose in her duvet.

'What's up with her?'

'No idea. She's been like this all morning. I didn't think she drank that much.'

'Hmmm... any sausages left?'

'Yeah I think so.'

Lilly clambers out of her nest on the sofa and follows me into the kitchen.

'Listen... I wanted to say, like, I'm worried about her.' Lilly cuts her eyes across to the sofa and back to me, continues whispering. 'I think maybe something weird happened last night at the party? You've not heard anything have you?'

'Weird like what?' My voice rises at the end and Lilly

gestures at me to keep my voice down. As if Noush wouldn't know we were talking about her.

'I don't know. Like... funny stuff happening? Some of those guys can be a bit... pushy? And like, you know I don't care about them offering us coke or whatever, but some of the girls seemed well out of it yesterday. Like there were hands *everywhere*.'

I turn and flick the kettle and try to think about last night, but everything is still a blur.

'I mean, I haven't noticed anything like that, but if you want I can, like, say something to Liam? If you want? Though... what do you want me to tell him, it's a party so people are gonna... party?'

'Yeah, no they are, I'm not saying they're not. It's just... look, Noush is our friend, and I'm worried about her, okay? That's all.'

The kettle clicks and something flares in me. I'm already in enough trouble, and if I complain to Liam about this... does she really want to go back to warm chardonnay in the Slug & Lettuce and being pawed at by entry-level management consultants in navy suits with brown shoes?

'You don't have to come to the parties, if you don't like them. No one's asking you to do anything you're not comfortable with. And you always look like you're having a good time.'

'That's not what I mean, and you know it. I'm just saying... not everyone wants what you do.'

I think about what Liam said to me a few weeks ago, as he watched Lilly and Noush on the dance floor, his mouth close to my ear.

The thing about you, Emily, is that no one knows what you're thinking, what you want. No one except me. You're a closed book and you're all mine. Look at them – he gestured in front of us – *they're so... messy, so obvious. But you hold it all inside you, locked up tight, you save it all for me.*

'Look, why don't you guys skip the next party? Maybe I can drag a different friend along instead.'

Lilly snorted. 'Like who? Don't worry. We're still up for it. Let's just keep an eye on Noush. Maybe you can get Liam to introduce her to someone nicer? What about that guy you were with last night?'

'I wasn't *with* anyone last night.'

She looks at me funny.

'The guy you were talking to? The ginger one?'

I put a hand to my neck, the skin by my ear is so tender. I put my hand away, fiddle with my hair instead.

'You mean Drew? Yeah, sure. I mean, he travels a lot, but I'll let Liam know.'

'What are you bitches cooking up over there?' There's movement from the sofa as Noush fumbles her way over to us in the kitchen.

'Nothing, babe, just talking about last night.'

'Right.'

'Everything okay?'

'Yeah, fine. Just the hangover from hell. Where's the coffee? I need intravenous caffeine, stat.'

'Are you sure you're okay?' Lilly asks.

'I said I'm fine. I don't want to talk about it.'

She takes the water and makes herself the strongest Nescafe I've ever seen, then stomps back to the sofa. Lilly looks at me and widens her eyes.

'She says it's fine, Lil. So leave her alone. I don't know what you're making a fuss about.'

'Okay...' But Lilly didn't train as a journalist for nothing. If she thinks there's a thread to pull, she'll tug until everything unravels.

. . .

About a week later, I get home from work to find Noush in the kitchen ordering takeaway and crying. But when I ask her what's wrong, she tells me it's only PMT and not to worry. I do though. Doesn't she get how lucky we are? Why does she have to be so uptight?

When Lilly gets home an hour later, I can tell right away that something has changed, that they've been talking about the parties behind my back.

'I'm only saying though, some of those men are really old. Like it's disgusting. Why would we ever want them?' Lilly says.

'You're so ageist. Like some of them are really interesting – have you even spoken to them?' I reply.

'Why would I bother? As soon as I get near them, they tell me how *exotic* I look and ask me where I'm from. And when I tell them west London they look at me as if it's the wrong answer.'

'She's not wrong, babe,' Noush adds. 'You don't get it. I mean, why would you? No one's ever kept on with the whole *but no really, where are you from* shit.'

'But there's other guys there, like Alastair. I thought you were having a good time?'

Lilly and Noush look at each other and then me.

'What?'

They shake their heads.

'Seriously, spit it out. Or just deal with it.'

Liam is in London tonight. I could text him and stay with him.

'You're okay. You've got Liam. But because of that, sometimes you don't see what's going on? I heard that one of those guys keeps bare-backing that girl Jessy when she told him no.'

I pull a face.

'You know what that is, right?' Noush says.

'Yes!'

'So, don't you think that's rough?'

'Look, how do you know it's even true?' Even as I say it, I hate myself.

'Seriously, Emily, are you for real?' Lilly's pissed off, her jaw all tight, she's chewing her lip.

'No, Lilly, what's your problem? It's none of our business? If Jessy has a problem then she doesn't need to keep coming to the parties, does she? And besides, she's always making snarky comments about you guys.'

I'm lying, but I need to get out of this. They're so ungrateful.

'Ladies! Let's chill,' Noush interjects. 'How about next time you hook us up with Drew and one of his mates, and we'll hang with them instead? And maybe have our own parties? Imagine Drew at Infernos!'

Lilly laughs at this and the two of them start sniggering away and dancing in the kitchen.

I don't want to think about Drew. I don't want to see him.

But Liam says he's back in town next month. I don't know what I have to do to avoid him, but I will. I still don't know what happened. My mind probes the memories that flash up every so often, like a tongue touching a sore spot in a mouth.

I remind myself that Drew was hot. I wanted him. I probably went with him willingly. And I spent time at the party, talking up close, our mouths inches apart, our body language saying all the things our words didn't. So, I have no right to think that the night was anything but what it was. Even if I can't remember any of it. Even if the bruises took weeks to heal.

'Look, I'm going to Liam's tonight. I need some space.'

'Oh, don't be like that. We love Liam, you know that. He's a babe.'

'And super hot for an older dude!' Noush waggles her eyebrows at me, her tears long gone. I know I probably shouldn't leave them alone. That I'm starting to take sides, if there are sides to be taken. But Liam gives me something no one else does.

'It's fine, we're fine. I just promised I'd see him tonight, that's all.'

I'm lying. Again. But I know Liam has a work event tonight – and a hotel room. He gave me a key, *just in case*.

It feels very cliché, leaving for his hotel in just a coat and lingerie. But I do it anyway.

> Hey, I'm on my way. See you soon.

> Cool, awards do all done, well timed.

When I get to the hotel, he tells me he's still five minutes away and he'll meet me in the bar.

Before I met Liam, I never went to hotels like this, where a drink at the bar wouldn't leave you change from a tenner. Where you had to be a resident to drink, where you needed to be a member to dine in the restaurant. I thought that happy-hour margaritas and the odd fancy dinner were enough. That, a bit like a scratch card, if I dated enough boys from Nottingham or Durham or Warwick or Exeter, eventually one of them would stick. And certainly Mum would be happy.

I order a Diet Coke at the bar. Specify a slice of lime and ice. The barman looks at me. He knows what's under this coat. I think.

I don't want to drink tonight. I just want to be in the dark with Liam. Cut out all the other thoughts, the things that are meaningless and pointless.

'Is this seat taken?'

He's here. The way he smiles and the way I'm ready for him – and the way he knows it.

'Hey.'

The barman comes over but Liam waves him away. 'We're heading off, put her drink on my room.'

Although the bar is brightly lit, it's not that late yet, but all I see is him.

We walk to the lift and he doesn't say a word, just a hand on my back. The way he has control, if anyone else had tried it I would have laughed and despised them for daring.

As the last person leaves the lift he turns to me.

Runs a hand down me, splits me open like a ripe peach. Looking at me the whole time he's touching me, without saying a word. My legs shake and then he lifts me up like I'm nothing.

Pinned against the wall of the lift, he has one hand around my neck, one hand holding me up, I undo his belt, and make us one. Just like that, I'm gone again.

It's a rainy Monday when Liam next texts, asking to meet him for lunch. This is unusual for him. Our relationship exists in the cracks and shards of time we don't give to others. When we're apart I try not to think about his wife and children and his big house. And I know he doesn't think about me, and the gaps between our lives.

When I get to lunch, some steak place in Paternoster Square, I'm surprised to see we're at a table for three.

'Who...?'

'Drew's in town.'

I never told him about that night. He never asked.

'Sure.'

'He was very complimentary about you.'

'Well of course. I'm a delight.'

His mouth curves in a smile – it's an old joke between us. I know Liam's thinking about exactly how delightful I am, for him. And him alone, he assumes.

'Hi, both! Liam, mate, good to see you.' Manly back slaps take place. 'Emily, an absolute pleasure, as ever.'

Drew kisses my cheek, his lips brushing the corner of my mouth. When I look up, he's watching my reaction. Liam is distracted with the wine menu.

They chat about stuff that is meaningless to me – cars, golf, people they know, work stuff. I don't care. I order red wine that's £125 a bottle and drink it whilst looking out at people walking past, try to remember what happened that night with Drew.

He's lost weight in the last couple of months, he's rangier than ever, with a scruffy red beard and rumpled hair. And no suit like Liam today, only a shirt and jeans, battered black Converse. It takes a lot of money to look that poor.

Liam doesn't pay me the slightest bit of attention. But Drew's eyes flicker back and forth between us. And when I feel a foot nudge mine, I know it's him.

I get up to go to the ladies' and he follows me. My skin prickles as we walk down a winding corridor, into the basement. When I come out of the toilet, he's waiting for me. One arm against the wall.

'It's really good to see you again, Emily.' He rubs his nose and sniffs.

'You too.' I plaster on a smile. I want Liam.

Drew leans in closer.

'I had a good time at the party. Are you going again this weekend?'

I don't know how to play this. Drew was Liam's best man at his wedding, his oldest friend.

'Probably. If Liam's going, then yes.'

'Excellent!'

'I'll bring a friend for you, so you don't get stuck with me all night.' I have no idea who to invite, but I can't go through this again.

He looks at me.

'If you want – but not one of the girls you came with last time. Someone new. Someone like you.'

My phone bleeps and shatters the weird tension. It's Anna. I'm definitely not inviting her.

When we get back to the table, Liam laughs at us.

'What have you two been up to down there? Ems, you're blushing!' Liam's smile doesn't reach his eyes.

'I was only telling Em how fun the last party was, and how she was excellent company.'

'Ah of course. Well, I hope you're coming this Saturday, D?'

'Definitely!'

'Excellent, Em will be there of course.'

I don't understand why he's pushing us together like this.

'I was thinking I might bring someone else this time, Liam. Instead of Lilly and Noush?' I don't know who. I can't bring someone knowing they might wake up next to Drew with black spots in their memory. My eyes sting at the thought.

Liam doesn't answer. Drew reaches under the table, handing Liam a yellow Selfridge's bag.

'Oh, mate, I've got something for you – it's a replacement for the sweater you lent me last time.'

'Cheers!'

'How very grown up of you –' I feel compelled to comment – 'sharing nicely.'

'Well, you know what they say, sharing is caring.'

And they look at each other.

'We've always shared things.'

The hair crawls on the back of my neck. What am I not remembering here?

After lunch, Liam sticks me in a taxi, tells me I look tired, to take the rest of the afternoon off. All the way home, tears crawl down my face and I don't know how to stop them, so when Anna calls, everything comes out.

Not about Drew – never about Drew – but about Liam, and the upcoming party, and wanting to impress him, and needing to bring someone. I don't mean her, I never mean her.

'I don't understand,' she says, 'it's just a party, why can't your flatmates go?' She knows Lilly and Noush through me, they're not super close, but she likes them.

'They are going.' I can't explain without telling her the truth – and I can't even face the truth.

'I don't know what to do,' I sob down the line.

'Ems, I'm worried about you, this isn't right. I don't get it. Look, when is the party?'

I can hear a noise like flapping paper and I realise she's checking an actual diary. The thought that she still has one makes my heart squeeze and I cry harder.

'It doesn't matter, please, it's nothing, I'm being silly. I've got my period.'

'Emily, just tell me when the fucking party is. It's about time I met Liam anyway, especially if he makes you cry like this.'

'It's not him – it's not. It's just work stress. Oh my God, he'd never want me if he knew I was being like this.'

I know I've had too much wine at lunch, I'm a mess.

'I was joking, honey. I would never tell him. Let me come to the party, please. Even if it's to see you. If I'm bored, I'll make friends – you know me!'

She won't let me go until I tell her the date and the venue. Until I stop crying. Until she makes me laugh, reminding me of the night she stole a traffic cone at university and named it Norbert.

When I hang up the phone, I'm smiling. Maybe Anna's right. Maybe it'll all be okay. Maybe I'm worrying about nothing.

FOURTEEN

2001

It's Michaelmas term in our second year at university when it happens. Anna and I stride through the quads and libraries ignoring flustered freshers who are constantly in the way, dropping books. It's good to have the confidence now, to know what we're doing. When I'm with her, I don't have to pretend about my background, make up stories about where I 'winter' or where I 'summer'. She doesn't ask me if my daddy has a house in the country, or who I played lacrosse against in the upper sixth. Because she didn't do any of these things either. The class divide at Oxford is both a gaping chasm, and a narrow crack, depending on who you talk to – and who you are able to become.

I learned fast, in my first year, to disguise where my clothes came from, to call my outfits vintage and retro, instead of second hand, to make out they came from Portabello or Camden, rather than cheap rip-offs from Kingston market. I toned down my make-up, learned the art of looking expensively undone, rather than cheaply overdone. And somehow it has worked. I manage to pass as one of them, one of the Roedean and Bedales types, who shop on the Kings Road and party in Mayfair. And that way I am allowed access to the boys, the rugby players and the rowers.

We are in the smooth glide down from Halloween to Christmas, after reading week. Or at least, that's how I see it. I'm enjoying myself, at last, instead of feeling like I'm going to be made at any moment. I've found my place, in a way that I never have before. And none of it would be possible without Anna. We met in a tutorial in our first term of first year, we were partnered on a project about Emily Dickinson. I knew I'd made a true friend when Anna suggested writing a paper comparing her work to 1990s female grunge artists. We spent all night staying up listening to Hole and PJ Harvey and Tori Amos and Verruca Salt and Bikini Kill. We compared the lyrics written by Shirley Manson and Kathryn Hanna and Dolores O'Riordan. It's the best paper I've ever written. Our tutor – middle-aged, white, male, thought great literature ended in the 1960s – hated it, but still gave us a first after the one female professor got wind of what we were doing and asked us to present to her postgraduates.

Anna is at her desk in her shared room. I'm lucky enough to have a single this year, but Anna shares with some jolly hockey sticks type. Luckily her roommate is a med student so she's pretty much never around. It means I get to flounce into their study whenever I like and have Anna all to myself.

'Come on, just one drink, Anna, pleeeeeease.'

I tell her it's only us, no one else. It's only the pub, only a quiet one. Just some wine and chips.

'Have you even pulled this term?'

Anna pulls a face at me as she closes her textbook, recaps her highlighter. In front of her on the desk are pages of lined A4 covered in her tidy scrawl.

'Yes, of course I have!'

'Who?'

'Someone in my medieval literature class, you don't know him. We had a formal event and I got really drunk. Really bad kisser too. Like a plunger.'

She mimics slurping noises and I giggle.

'And like a washing machine!'

'Noooooo!'

'At one point we were pressed up against a wall and he was like, bunny hopping against me, like with his pelvis like this.'

And she demonstrates against the side of her desk.

'So that definitely means you need to come out for a drink!'

We deserve it, I tell her. We've earned our right to relax, we're both on track for firsts this year – and hopefully in our final year also. Sometimes though, I think Anna works *too* hard. Maybe it's the only difference between us, my need for external stimulation, the desire, every so often to go out and just... let my hair down. Dance, and drink – and show the world who I really might be.

We meet in the Kings Arms. She's resistant at first – *It'll be rammed, full of rugby twats* – but I persuade her that if we get there early, we can get a table at the back and hide away from the rabble.

I clink my glass against hers.

'I've missed this – missed you – stop working so hard!'

'Ems, we're not all like you!'

I'm the only one who notices when she's falling too far down the rabbit hole. When I've decided she's done enough, she needs a break, I rock up at her door and beg to hang out, try to drag her away from dusty law textbooks at her desk. I lie on her bed or braid her hair or play music on her CD player. Talk about boys. She doesn't want to talk about boys, but she laughs at me, tells me to go find one of those boys, burn off my energy. I don't though, I stay with her, read the latest Marian Keyes lying on her bed as she studies, reading aloud the good bits, trying to make her smile.

Anna is a private person. She makes friends easily, everywhere, but she also doesn't trust easily. I don't know why she's picked me to be her bestie, why she lets me occasionally drag her out for tequila shots and dancing on bars.

In the pub we talk about what if we'd met at school.

'I bet you were a proper bitch,' she teases.

'No *was* about it, I am a bitch.'

She smiles.

'You love it,' I say, 'I'm your bitch.'

'You'd have hated me back then, with my nerdy glasses and my addiction to the library.'

'I love your nerdy glasses!' I wind a strand of her hair around my finger. She smells of coconut.

'Well, you're the only one.'

Anna isn't perfect, of course, but... compared to me? She's never kissed someone else's boyfriend, didn't sleep with anyone until she was eighteen, doesn't seem to have a dark side.

'Am I ugly, Ems?'

'No? What the hell? Why would you ask me that?'

'Don't give me the friend answer. Give me the real answer.'

'That is the real answer.'

'Come on...' She looks at me.

'It's the truth!'

'I just... you have it so easy. Looking like you do.'

She gestures at me.

'What? It's all hair and make-up – you know that, you know my mum. She'd love to do the same for you given half the chance.'

'Sometimes it feels like, what am I trying so hard for? Should I just wear miniskirts all the time and flirt with my professors and sleep with the right people to get funding for my masters? Am I kidding myself?'

'No! Don't do that. Why would you even think that?' What I'm really saying though is, *don't be like me*.

'Oh come on, you totally have the pretty privilege, even tonight. How quick did you get served?' She rolls her eyes at me and makes quotation marks in the air as she says the words pretty privilege.

Ouch, I think. I mean, I'm aware that how I look earns me things, but it's not everything. And hearing Anna say it like this, so bluntly, stings. I know she doesn't mean to be unkind though.

'You're smart though, Anna, really smart. Smart enough to change things. Do you really want to be like me? I'm just a notch on someone's bedpost.'

We never talk about the nights I disappear from the pub. When I knock on Anna's door the next morning, laddered tights and bedhead, stinking of booze and cigarettes – and other things. She just welcomes me in, makes me coffee, runs me a bath and lends me clean clothes. It doesn't happen often, but it's enough that it's a thing.

Anna looks at me.

'Don't you enjoy it?'

'Sort of... yes.' I don't tell her how validating it is, knowing the power I have over men. Much as I hate myself, I know I'm doing exactly what my mother did, but better. I'm practising for real life. For how I build security for myself.

'So, why do it? Why not stop?'

'What else am I going to do? Don't you want to find someone, Anna?'

'Well, yes, eventually. But not yet.'

'Oh no, not yet. But there's no harm in trying out a few wrong ones, on the way to the right one, is there?'

'If you don't enjoy it though, what's the point?'

'I do sometimes. And I have other ways to entertain myself. Like tonight! Drink up, bitch! This is all getting a bit heavy!'

And I order another round, put it on my credit card, try not to think about how much I owe.

The conversation moves on to which professor is being suspended for sleeping with students and then on to rumours of an essay-writing factory in one of the other colleges and who is taking Ritalin and pulling all-nighters to finish coursework.

Anna is tipsy enough to agree to move to another bar, where we find people from her course. Her face lights up when she sees one of the girls and goes off to talk to her. I'm left with some rugby-playing bore called Rupert, who insists on regaling me with stories from today's match. I tune out, nod and smile as needed, think about what Anna said about herself, wonder how I can help, how I can make her feel good, feel valued for everything she is.

Eventually I go outside, feigning the need for fresh air, but he follows me. When we get there he offers me a cigarette. I let him light mine and then watch him cough as I blow smoke in his face. He pulls the usual move of putting his hand on the wall behind me, leaning over me. He's big, I'll give him that. But tonight I'm not interested. Tonight is for Anna.

Still, I let him kiss me, put a hand down my top. Get a thrill from knowing he wants me.

It's only when he starts undoing his jeans and my jeans, pushing them down, wrestling my flesh as if it's clay to mould around him, that I come back to life. I don't want this tonight, not like this.

'Hey... no, can you not?'

But he doesn't stop. I try to push him away, but he's big and heavy – and focused.

'Stop, goddamnit.' I bite his tongue next time he goes to kiss me.

'Bitch!' Desire and anger read the same on his face, the flare of his nostrils as he determines what his right is, over me. 'Fucking keep still.'

I'm still pinned against the wall when, by some absolute miracle, Anna walks out.

'Here you are!'

'Emily's busy right now.' He speaks over his shoulder at her, but my eyes meet hers.

'Are you okay, Em?'

It's not like she hasn't caught me like this before. But those times, I wanted it.

I take advantage of his distraction to wriggle my jeans up.

'Fuck off, you dyke bitch,' he says to Anna, still pinning me to the wall. The pain in Anna's face strikes a match in me then and I bring my knee into his groin. He collapses like a burst balloon, there's an audible thud as his head hits the cobblestones.

'Don't call my friend that!' I scream at him and I leg it over to Anna.

'Are you okay, Em?'

'I'm fine. Let's go.'

I take her hand in mine, but she shakes it off and marches over to Rupert, all five feet nothing of her.

'That's Dr Dyke Bitch to you, you absolute cock. At least I don't have to resort to violence to fuck a girl.' And she spits at him, lying there, jeans around his ankles, stunned.

I look at her open mouthed and then start laughing as we run off. When we pause to catch our breath several minutes later, she asks me if I'm okay, if I want to go home.

'Asshole,' she pants.

'I can't believe you, back there! You were amazing.'

'Why thank you.' She takes a mock bow.

'Wonder how long it'll take him to go back into the pub. Pretend to his friends. Though I expect they all do it too.'

Of course there were other times things like that had happened to me, when Anna wasn't there to rescue me. No one was there to rescue me.

'What now then?' she asks. I don't know if she can handle my answer, but I say it anyway.

'I want to get fucked up. Really fucked up.' My voice trembles as I reply.

She looks at me and reaches out her arms.

'Don't...' I say, struggling not to cry.

She nods once. 'Okay. Let's go then.'

I've not seen this side of Anna before. Where she's leading and I'm following.

We find a bar, we pick up where we left off. But instead of slow pints, Anna brings me shots. I forget that anyone put their hands on me.

There is another bar, more tequila, more friends of friends, dancing and still more shots. There are guys, of course there are. But none of them register. All I see is Anna.

When the bar staff are on the bar with us, when we're screaming out the words to Rage Against the Machine, when we've drunk the bar dry of tequila. When I don't recognise a single face, except Anna's, but I love them all. When Anna takes my hand, I know it's time to go home.

In the cab, we don't speak. But we haven't let go of each others' hands. Outside the streets are a rain-slicked darkness with splashes of neon.

The music in the cab is something I think I remember from childhood, synthy and dark. Something about my personal Jesus.

When we arrive back at college, Anna pays and we tumble out onto the street, she pulls me in through the little gate and then we are in the darkness of the cloisters.

Somehow Anna finds my hand again and this time our fingers entwine. The air crackles and spits around us. We walk together in the velvet of the night, blind to everything around us.

I've always known there is something else about Anna that she doesn't tell me. When she too disappears on nights out, when she is glowing the next morning, but I don't ask and she doesn't tell me.

When she stops by her door, I can only make out the shape of her face in the darkness, the gleam of her eyes.

'Emily...'

Her voice is so quiet and yet it's so easy to hear the question she's asking me.

My heart is beating so loud and so fast, I wonder if she can feel it in our entwined hands.

There is a fraction of moonlight in the quad; the world is dimmed for us. I can't breathe properly. But Anna is still. She is my calm, my home, my anchor. And she pulls me closer to her until we are inches apart. I can smell her coconut shampoo again. I lift my other hand and tuck a strand of her red curls behind her ear.

The darkness hides her expression. And mine. I don't want to think too much about this. Normally I tell Anna she's thinking too much. But something has shifted.

The gap between us seems too big.

I step forward and close it.

When I wake up it's to the sound of rain on the windowpane. It's gloomy outside but warm in Anna's bed. She's asleep next to me, her hair flung across the pillow between us.

Pieces of the night come back to me – dancing, tequila, music. It's not unusual for me to go home with someone but at this point I'd normally get up and leave. Or chuck them out of my room. But I can't do that to Anna.

I creep out of bed and into the bathroom. My hair is a snarled tangle and mascara clots smear under my eyes. On my neck there's a red bruise the size of a ten pence piece. I suddenly remember everything that happened last night. The pub, the attack, the drinking. The kiss. Anna's bed...

I wash my face in cold water and brush my teeth with a blob of toothpaste on my finger.

When I come back out, I pull on last night's clothes in silence, trying not to wake Anna.

The room smells of us – coconut, cigarettes, alcohol – and underneath it all, the bitter tang of my shame. Walking home, remember how we made our way slowly from the cloisters, to her room, to her bed. The way she held my face between her hands.

Other images come back like photo negatives. Our skin peachy in the half light, our legs tangled together. She felt so different beneath me and then on top of me. No roughness, only softness. Her private face, turned only to me.

I can't do this though. It won't end well. We'll only end up hurt. It's not worth it. I've always been the person who rips a plaster off. So, I know this morning I was cruel – that she'll be feeling confused and alone when she wakes up. But sometimes you have to be cruel to be kind.

It's not until a few days later, I hear about Rupert the rugby player. He spent a week in hospital after he was found unconscious in an alleyway. Apparently he fell over when he was drunk. There's the usual flurry of op-ed pieces about students drinking, but nothing changes. The pubs continue to fill with drunk students all the way to the end of term. What isn't reported, what's never talked about, is how many girls are pinned up against walls or in beds, or anywhere, and where saying yes is safer than saying no.

FIFTEEN

2006

'Where's Anna?'

Liam shrugs, slumped in an armchair with a tumbler. He's drunk, drunker than I've ever seen him before. The party is emptying out, but the music is so loud, I still struggle to hear his response.

'Dunno... with Drew probably?'

'Well, I want to go home, I need to find her. Say goodbye.'

'Babes, Anna's a big girl, you're not joined at the hip.'

'No, I know, but I... I want to make sure she's okay. Like bro code, but for girls.'

How do I explain without revealing anything? About Drew or Anna. Why I'm worried. I think about cobbles gleaming in the moonlight. About what happens when girls can't save themselves.

'You don't normally give a shit, when it's Lilly and Noush.' The whisky in his glass sloshes gold in the light as he manoeuvres it to his mouth. Liam has a nasty side, but he very rarely takes it out on me – in public at least.

'Anna hasn't been to a party before—'

'Ems, you're making a fuss about nothing. She's probably gone back to Drew's and he's balls deep in her right now.' He smirks at me.

'Liam!' I don't know what's got into him this evening. And I don't want to think about Anna like that.

'Fuck this, let's go. I can't be bothered with your nonsense. Look I'll message Drew, will that make you happy?'

He gets out his phone and taps it with effort, as if to prove a point.

It's okay for him, he's not the one with memories of waking up with Drew, the morning after. The necklace of bruises. His smile, his sharp, white, even teeth. Making me think of how sharks keep moving, even in their sleep.

I imagine her in that room right now. Is she drunk? She wasn't when I last saw her. Just happy. With a glass of champagne. Talking to a man who amazingly enough wasn't staring into her cleavage. I know she offered to come here, but still, she wouldn't know about the party if it wasn't for me. If anything happens to her, it's my fault.

I need to be there for her, to protect her, like she did for me.

'Ems, baby. Let's get out of here.'

Liam seems to be channelling his inner Vince Chase from *Entourage*. He'll be getting out the cigars next. Sometimes, when I look at him at work, I see the wrinkles in the corners of his eyes, the grey hair poking out of the top of his shirt. I picture his face when I'm tied up and hurting. Even though I wanted it. And amongst the desire and love, there's a slimy feeling of disgust.

But I don't know whether I'm disgusted by him, or by me.

Once, I heard two girls talking about him in the toilet in the office –

'—and he looked straight at my tits. Ugh, he's old enough to

be my dad. Did you know he's seeing an associate? Isn't he married? You couldn't pay me enough.'

I waited until they'd left before I came out of the cubicle.

We're kidding ourselves that no one knows. But he doesn't care. He says himself, he's got a watertight prenup, his wife will never leave him. But if he leaves, he goes with all his money.

I'm not the first girl – I hoped to be the last. I really thought maybe I could be enough.

The trouble is though, tonight, in the dark, in his room, I'll forget the girls at work. Because when he touches me, when he whispers into my ear, when he sees the most secret part of me, the way he reaches my soul, I burst into flames. And I don't know if I'll ever get that again.

All the way to the hotel, in the taxi, I text Anna, fretting – Drew hasn't replied to Liam's texts.

> Hey, looked for you to say goodbye but couldn't find you, all ok?
>
> Text me when you get this, let me know you got home safe.
>
> Anna, where are you?
>
> I'm worried about you.
>
> Anna?

Liam works his hand up my thigh and under the edge of my knickers. He meets my eyes but I remove his hand, close my legs and turn away. I'll pay for that later. And inside me something shudders in anticipation. Fear and excitement – two sides of the same coin.

Sometimes I think about spiders and webs. And the fly. And I'm not sure if the fly didn't deserve to be eaten. *I'm so fucking stupid*, I think. *So fucking stupid.*

But I'm still here, in this cab with Liam. And soon I'll be in his hotel room. He'll order drinks. And he'll take some coke.

He'll call me a dirty bitch and I'll let him. He'll tell me I'm worthless and I'll let him. And then when he's finished with that, he'll take my clothes off and then he'll fuck me. And even when I'm coming he'll tell me I'm disgusting and dirty. And the worst thing is, I want it, I want him to tell me all of those things and do all of those things. Because I know it's the truth. And I won't be thinking of Anna anymore.

In the morning, Liam wakes me and tells me he needs to get home, he's ordering me room service. He tells me I'm beautiful and sorry if he was a grump last night. To please forgive him and he'll make it up to me.

I think about the new weals on my wrists and my ankles. And how I woke in the night to the shower running and his side of the bed empty and cold.

I let him kiss me with morning breath and then he leaves money on the side.

It's the first time he's ever done that. When I count the notes – all twenties – I barely make it to the toilet to be sick. When I come back, he's gone, but the room service has been wheeled in. Sausages glistening in pools of congealed fat, orange juice viscous in a glass, a hair coiled on its surface. My stomach turns again.

> Anna, can you please let me know you're okay?

I send several messages along the same lines on my way home. But still no reply.

'She's probably asleep.'

'Or having her brains fucked out by that rich dude.'

Lilly and Noush try to make light of the situation, but I see the way they glance at each other when they think I'm not looking.

'What?' I finally ask, annoyed.

Again with the glances.

'Are you going to tell me?'

'Just... don't freak out okay?'

'Why would I freak out?'

'Well, you are kind of weird about Anna sometimes.'

'What's that supposed to mean?'

'Jesus, nothing. Only that we know she's like, one of your long-term besties, okay? And you're protective.'

'What is it you want to tell me then?'

'So... I bumped into Saskia in the loo last night – you know, the one with the super long hair?' Lilly gestures to her hips and I have a vague recollection of some bleached blonde with extensions down to her bum. I nod for her to continue.

'She said she saw Anna crying in the corridor – the one with the doors that lead to the... the other rooms. The ones we're not supposed to know about.'

Everyone knows what the rooms are for. But Lilly, Noush and me, we don't use those. We sleep with people in hotel rooms. We're not escorts. Though with the wad of notes burning a hole in my pocket, I'm not so sure what I am anymore.

'She's wrong. that couldn't have been Anna.'

'Well yeah, that's what I said. She got it wrong. But she was adamant. And you know, Anna is pretty distinctive with her red hair and everything. She specifically said the posh English girl – and she didn't mean you.'

Thing is, Anna isn't posh. She's not even middle-class really. Her mum is a receptionist, her dad is a cabbie. She's from Basingstoke. She lived in a boxy 1960s semi – she showed me the pictures. I know I'm missing the point.

'Well, whatever. She's wrong. Anna was fine... is fine.'

'Have you heard from her since last night?' Lilly looks at me. 'You haven't, have you?'

'Why do you care anyway?'

'Because we remember what you were like the last time Drew went to a party!'

'What are you talking about?'

'Come on, you were a wreck for days after that. And you didn't speak to anyone. We know you went home with him. Does Liam even know?' She slurps her coffee loudly, but doesn't let me escape.

'You're imagining things. I don't want to talk about it.'

My hand goes up to my neck, the way my body remembers, even as my mind avoids it.

'Whatever. But Saskia said she's heard things about Drew. She's got some friends in Ibiza that went to a party with him last summer—'

'Yeah? So what, he's allowed to go to a party.' I don't know why I'm standing here defending him, but I am. It's not their business, judging me for who I hang around with.

'Are you going to let me finish? He went to a party and one of the girls came home the next day and said he'd attacked her. That it was, you know...' Lilly mouths the word at me. It makes me flinch.

'Bullshit. She's making it up. You know what Saskia's friends are like. They're total cokeheads – and worse. They'll take anything. She was probably off her tits, can't remember and now she's blaming Drew because she regrets sleeping with him. Girls like that make me sick.'

I hate myself. Every word is a lie but they're still coming out of my mouth. I need to not be here. I need Liam. I need to be alone.

'Emily, are you for real?' Lilly glares and steps towards me, but Noush pulls her back. 'How can you even say that? Where are you getting this shit from? Do you even hear yourself?'

'Leave her, babes, it's not worth it.' Noush folds her arms at me, and shakes her head. 'This isn't like you, Ems. I don't know what's going on with you, but it's not good. We're going out, but let us know if you hear from Anna, yeah?'

'I'm sure she's probably on the tube as we speak. And you'll regret saying any of that shit about Drew.'

'I don't understand why you're defending him.'

'Because you're attacking him! With no evidence!'

Again my hand creeps up to my neck. Noush notices.

'I hope you're right about Anna. I really do. That's all I'm saying.'

But I was wrong.

Anna's father calls me two days later to ask if I'd heard from her. She was due to meet them at a family lunch on the Sunday after the party. And when they went to her flat – because he has a spare key – she hadn't been home either. Did I know where she was?

I had to tell him I didn't. And then as soon as he hung up the phone, I ran to the bathroom to be sick, but nothing came out except bile. I think about what Drew said to me at the party, when I told him he wasn't Anna's type. My stomach roils and I message her again, but she doesn't answer.

I lie in bed all day after that, in the dark, crying into my pillow. Outside my door Lilly and Noush whisper and knock for me, but I don't answer.

Instead, there's only one thing I'm thinking, only one question I need an answer to.

What have you done? I ask myself.

Although really I know I'm asking someone else entirely, and that's what scares me.

The police found Anna's body the next day.

There was an investigation, an inquest, but it was ruled as misadventure – an accidental drowning in the bath. There were drugs in her system – it was a tragic accident. I pictured her wet bronze hair, creamy marble skin, the light in her eyes dulled and gone. But none of it made sense.

There was no mention of Drew, or the party. Just a young girl who wanted to have a little too much fun.

> They always blame the victim

Noush texted me when it hit the headlines – a nice white girl, a glittering legal career destroyed.

And when I asked Liam about it, he told me Drew had escorted her to a hotel room. And they had some fun. But in the end he'd fallen asleep. She'd been fine in the morning, he said. And that was that.

Drew moved back to LA, his tech business skyrocketing across the pond. I'm sure there were parties there though, and girls – always girls. I wonder how many of them ended up dead in baths too, after a night with him.

The parties stopped, rumours about journalists infiltrating, everyone had too much to lose, Liam told me. But more likely his wife finally found out about us. Either way, he stopped calling. He didn't even say goodbye, just disappeared from my life so slowly that by the time I realised what was happening, it was all too late.

SIXTEEN

2006

I wasn't looking for a boyfriend. I wasn't looking for anything. In fact, it was the opposite. After Anna's funeral, after Liam decided his wife was what he wanted after all – that he hadn't loved me, that he'd never said that, that I was imagining it – I threw myself into work. I took on any project people would give me. I did side projects, I did extra hours, I took on the clients no one wanted, because then I could travel and I didn't have to stare at the four walls of my bedroom.

Instead, I stayed in anonymous hotels and had sex with anonymous men. And I cried afterwards, every time, in the dark, by myself. Not because of what I'd done, but because of what they didn't do. In the dark I said Liam's name. And then I cried some more.

When I wasn't travelling, I lived on a diet of sleeping pills, Red Bull and vodka. With the odd cigarette and McDonalds for protein.

I ignored the looks on Lilly and Noush's faces when I was home, the way they whispered about me when I walked in or out of the sitting room. The way my clothes slipped off me, waistbands loose, straps falling off me, dresses baggy and voluminous.

I met Pete when I was on a work trip. He was just thirty. A level above me at work, all his friends were in steady relationships – hence no more shared flats. We'd been to three engagement parties in the first few weeks of us dating. Stiff white wedding invites were on the kitchen worktop, waiting for us to respond, buy gifts. And we were a 'we'. We were Emily-and-Pete. All one word.

Timing is everything in life. That whole sliding doors thing, or the way the ancient Greeks and Romans believed the gods played chess with our lives.

If I'd not gone to that university, joined that company, worked on that team, led that project. If I'd arrived in a pub a bit later or a bit earlier, looked to my right, not my left. All the chances, all the potential opportunities. But we only see what we want to see.

When the two lines came up on the pregnancy test, we'd been together for three months. Pete knelt down on the bathroom tiles in his tiny flat in Balham, took my hand in his, fashioned a ring out of a piece of toilet roll.

'Marry me, please?'

'Are you sure?'

'I'm sure that I love you. I know it's not been long. But when it's right, it's right. Like they say in the movie, I want to spend my life with you – and I want that life to start now. Why waste time?'

Like I say, timing is everything. Even if I hadn't gotten pregnant, it was inevitable. Moving in together after six months. Buying a property after a year. And then the 1.5-carat princess-cut diamond and platinum solitaire from de Beers, the proposal on holiday. The hippy-chic wedding at Babington House. The honeymoon in the Maldives, the John Lewis gift list. The lace and silk 1920s hand beaded dress from Jenny Packham.

It was a well-trodden path and one that we followed, only slightly out of order.

A year to the day that we buried Anna, I gave birth to Anouk.

Eighteen months later, in a size eight, I walked down the aisle.

And by the time we moved to Surrey, everything from the past – Liam, Drew, Lilly, Noush – I packaged away in my head, taped up brown boxes and stored them in the attic along with my school reports and university dissertation and clothes long out of fashion.

That's not to say I didn't think of them sometimes.

Not long after I got married, I received friend requests from Lilly and Noush on Facebook. They looked happy, both of them – Lilly in an ivory silk, strapless Vera Wang wedding dress in her profile picture, Noush with full 'fro and face glitter, on a beach in hers. I accepted them both but didn't bother replying to their sporadic messages. Why mess with the past? What did we have to talk about now? It's not like I could go out partying with a toddler attached to my ankles, knee-deep in potty training and trips to soft play and the park.

Sometimes I would see Drew in the news. A billionaire now, by all accounts. Untouchable.

I wondered if he ever thought about Anna – or me. I wished I'd taken photos, kept some evidence, something to prove... to prove I didn't imagine things. But equally, then I'd have evidence to prove I had been shameful, sick, disgusting.

After the last time, with Liam, I asked to switch teams. I said something about development, career paths, growth. And because I did so well, they didn't question it, I got what I wanted. But once Anouk came along – and Pete's career took off at the same time, I stopped working anyway.

Liam and the parties were just a blip, a pothole in the road to success. This was where I was meant to be. After all, how else would I have met Pete? I needed to refocus, to see what was best for me. And that was at home, changing nappies, pureeing vegetables, going to Monkey Music, teaching a tiny human how to exist in the world. I couldn't argue with the importance of the role. Or how much I loved Anouk, and wanted the best for her.

But somewhere along the way, I worried I'd lost a part of myself.

When I handed my notice in, towards the end of my extended maternity leave, Frankie, one of the female partners, asked me for a coffee.

'Emily, lovely to see you!'

I parked Anouk's pushchair to the side of the table in the canteen and hugged Frankie. She smelt of Chanel No.5, cigarettes and coffee. There were no lines around her eyes and her mouth, her forehead smooth except for the central vein, the telltale sign of Botox. She had shadows under her eyes though and grey roots peeked through her expensive chestnut blow dry. Pete would consider her a perfect case study for why I'd left, no time for herself or anyone else, trying to juggle everything. *Having it all is a con,* he'd said to me.

'You too. You look great, Frankie.'

'Ah thank you – but I know that's a lie! Though you do look amazing, I can't believe you have a one-year-old already– and she's so gorgeous.'

Anouk slept in the buggy, all soft ringlets and rosebud pursed lips.

'Don't be fooled. She's a little terror when she's awake.'

'I bet she is – she's got you for a mother, so she'll be a very smart cookie indeed.'

'Oh, don't ever start me. The sass is outrageous already!'

'I can imagine. I remember when mine were the same age. But look, Emily, how are you really? Anouk is an absolute credit to you, but what's this I hear about you trying to leave us?'

I was unsure how to play it. There weren't many female partners. Frankie led the whole of London and the Southeast region. She was well respected, but she'd always made time for me. I'd worked on a project for her, very early on. I'd stayed late when a client messed things up, worked my weekends, got us over the line. And she'd told me she was impressed, that she saw potential in me. So, in some ways I wasn't surprised that we were having this discussion.

'I know I should have come to you first...'

'Yes, you should have. Tell me what we have to do to keep you.'

My gaze darted to Anouk. And then to Frankie, who I knew was flying to Frankfurt that evening for a client dinner. And then giving a keynote speech at a conference in Boston next week. She didn't take holidays often, but she did work from her second home somewhere in the Dordogne sometimes. She and her husband – and their teenage kids – lived in one of those white stucco-ed villas in St John's Wood. I visited her there once, to drop off some work files. She had a swimming pool.

She told me *all this can be yours, Emily, follow my path*. But I didn't. I met Liam.

'I'll be honest with you – Anouk wasn't planned. It's all been a bit of a shock. And now with the move to Surrey and the wedding and – well, everything – it doesn't make any sense for me to work. I don't need to work.'

Frankie nods and then steepled her fingers, pressing them to her lips.

'I see. But what about what you actually want? Why are you throwing away all your hard work?'

'Please don't do this, Frankie.'

'You had – *have* – such potential. Senior manager already,

on track to make director within a year. Partner before you're thirty-five. That's unheard of for a woman!'

'Apart from you.'

'Well, yes, apart from me. But I was thirty-six. And I had my daughters after. You're missing the point. You can do this. We can help you. Is it money? Name a figure. We'll pay it.'

She looked like she was about to pull out a cheque book.

'It's not the money. Well, not just the money.'

I was intrigued though. Wondering what I could ask for. 'It's everything. The travel, the childcare, all the logistics of it. I couldn't bear the look on some people's faces when I say I have to leave because Anouk is sick or the nursery is closed or—'

'Get a nanny then. We had one. She was a delight and the girls loved her. Ugly as sin though, didn't want Albert getting any ideas.'

'Frankie—'

'Seriously. You can't leave me here to fight the good fight alone. Come on. We'd have so much fun. You can have any client you want. Equity partner role guaranteed.'

I opened my mouth, closed it again. Anouk stirred.

'Look, don't decide anything now. Go home, think it over, talk to Pete. Do some sums and come back to me.'

'But I've already emailed HR…'

'Don't worry about that.'

I realised she'd already intercepted my resignation. Frankie always was the best at outmanoeuvring people. It's why she got so senior so fast.

'I'll think about it.'

'You do that.' She put her hand on my wrist. 'You've got until the end of the week to let me know what you decide.'

And that's when I knew how much she wanted me to stay. Frankie was the kind of manager who wanted your work yesterday, or preferably before she'd even given you any direction or asked for anything. To have four days to decide was unheard of.

She looked at her watch.

'You've got to go in a minute, don't you? I get it. Would you just watch Anouk while I pop to the loo?' Anouk had woken up while we were talking and stared up at me, rubbing her eyes in confusion – last time she'd been awake we were on the train!

'Of course – we'll have a lovely time, won't we, poppet?' Frankie smiled down at my daughter, unsnapped her clips and lifted her out and onto her lap, offering her a bit of croissant.

'Your suit—'

'We'll be fine. You go. Enjoy the solitude!'

She wasn't wrong. It was nice to not feel like there was a ticking bomb waiting whilst I peed. When I walked out, I spotted Liam straight away. He was sitting directly opposite the window, drinking coffee with another woman. Young – maybe even a fresh graduate. He leant towards her, smiling that smile. The one with all his teeth. She mirrored his body language. No doubt thrilled someone as important as Liam had paid attention to her.

He showed her something on his laptop and they both tried to tap the same key, I saw their fingers brush, watching them catch each other's eye. If I squinted, time fell away and the girl could have been me. And I knew what came next for her. I still had the scars. Still woke in the night with his name on my lips, the memory of him inside me.

'Emily!'

Frankie walked over to me, holding Anouk on one hip, wheeling the stroller in the other.

'There's your mama! Yes, baby girl, your mama is here! Oh, you're so gorgeous, yes!'

Frankie looked at me and at then over at Liam, narrowed her eyes.

'Everything okay?'

Her voice snapped me out of my reverie.

'Fine, all fine. Hello, sweetie!'

Anouk held her little arms out to me, babbling, drooling, and showing off her gummy little smile. I took her from Frankie and settled her back in the buggy with a board book and some rice cakes and kissed her cheeks.

I hugged Frankie, told her I'd be in touch.

I made it out of the building and down the next alley before the panic attack hit. As Anouk screamed at the unfairness of being left in the buggy, tears pricked the back of my eyes.

I drank some water, wiped my mouth with a baby wipe, careful not to remove my make-up. I found a piece of chewing gum and breathed minty air in and out for five.

'Right, baby girl, let's get you home.'

Anouk scowled, but accepted a beaker of water and a rattle, banging it against the side of the buggy as we emerged from the alley.

'I thought it was you.'

The sun was in my eyes, but I knew the voice anyway.

'Hello, Liam.'

'What are you doing here?'

'Well, I am an employee.'

'That's not what I meant.'

'I came to hand my notice in.'

'You're not coming back?'

We'd not seen each other in person for almost two years. And the last time, in Swindon, I didn't like to think about.

'Are you surprised?' I hissed at him, and he stepped back. 'There's nothing left for me here.'

'I'm sorry you feel that way.'

'Always the politician, Liam.'

'Don't be like that.'

'Like what?'

'Look, I'm sorry.'

'For what? For ghosting me? For using me?'

'All of that, more. I've behaved atrociously, I know. But you shouldn't leave because of me.'

'Don't flatter yourself. In case you hadn't noticed, I've got more important things in my life than you now.'

'That's not what I meant – God... I miss you, Ems. I know I made mistakes. I'd do anything to go back and change things, but I can't.'

'All in the past now. I've moved on. Shame you haven't.' I'm saying the words, but even then I'm not sure how true they are. When he looks at me, I feel it inside but where a spark would lead to flickers, nothing burns now.

'I've got to go, but don't be a stranger, Emily. If you ever look to come back, let me know.' Fat chance, he'd block my every move no doubt. He waved and turned away.

'Say hi to Drew!' I called to his back as he hurried back into the building.

Pathetic creep, I muttered to Anouk, as I hustled her home, *still married I see. Still perving over other girls.*

But the tears threatened again and I lifted Anouk into my arms on the train, snuggling into her sweet-smelling warmth as she fell asleep on me. Transferring her to the buggy, I typed out a quick email on my phone.

Hi Frankie,

I've thought about your offer and even though it's very generous, I'm afraid I'm going to have to decline it. I need to put my family first now. I'm a mother. I'm sure you understand.

All best,

Emily

PART 3

AFTER

SEVENTEEN

April 2023
Naomi

Most of the time, as Brigham tells each part of her story, she narrates the action with the detached intonation of a schoolteacher reading to a group of rowdy seven-year-olds. None of it really seems to get to her.

'It's on you, Naomi, to bring it to life, to give the readers what they want. I trust you. Besides, if you're anything like your mother, you'll know when to reveal the truth, bit by bit.'

It's not the first time she's mentioned my mother. I don't know how she found out who I am. My surname is pretty common.

'You have your mother's eyes. That's what gave it away, even before she visited me. I knew you were hers. Don't forget, I knew your mother for years, long before she stole my husband. I even met you, a few times – you won't remember, it was only in passing. You were busy being a teenager – and then of course, you were at uni when Pete moved in.'

Max finds it very weird that I'm pretending we don't have

this other connection – that my mother isn't married to Brigham's ex-husband. It's not like Mum was an innocent party in all this. Sometimes I wonder if we'd even be here, talking like this, if Mum hadn't had an affair with Pete. Would Brigham have done what she did? She'd have no need to leave Pete, to remarry.

But in a way, creating that separation has helped me do my research, ask the questions I need to. None of it takes away from the fact that Brigham was groomed, abused, and is a survivor. Her story is still important.

Max and I argue about the concept of the perfect victim. I tell him that she doesn't exist. That it's all part of the societal construct we live in, where a woman's value is always tied to her looks and her fertility, consciously or not. He argues with me that it's not that simple and not all men think like that. And I say I know it's not all men, but we also don't know which men.

I feel bad though. I don't want to shade all men. But I also know how many women have been reduced to less than the sum of their parts, purely for male gratification. How it happens without anyone realising it.

Max and I go round and round on this point. He argues that I can't believe in feminism if I don't believe in equality for all. And am I giving Brigham a free pass because of what she's been through when, regardless, she killed someone. I question myself too, but I can't take away what I know about her, what it feels like to live as a woman in man's world. But then Max reminds me she's rumoured to be a sociopath, that she could be manipulating me. I tell him we're never going to agree on this, and that's okay, that I value his input.

But secretly I imagine an uprising of women like Brigham, unleashing holy hell on the men who created them. Is it possible to be the victim and the villain in your own story?

I'm at the stage now with Brigham where she'll answer any question, no matter how insignificant – 'what was the name of your first boyfriend?' – or how gruesome – 'what did you do with the body after?' And despite the colour in her narrative, and her honesty, in some ways her story becomes murkier when we explore all the things she did and said.

We get stuck on the photos she took and sent to strange men. How the press had a field day, printing them double spread and full colour, with headings like 'MILF – Murderer I'd Like to F***'. The way she explains it all makes sense, but it just adds to the idea that any of us could end up in an unexpected situation, our actions used against us in ways we don't expect. As she says herself, *until you've been in that situation, experienced those things, you don't know what you'd do.*

Sometimes I wonder if her trust in me is because she sees me as a second chance with Mum, but on her terms, without all the messy stuff with Pete. Mum misses her, despite everything. Female friendships are so unique – that loyalty. I know Brigham would never forgive Mum for what she did, taking Pete, but I also think that connection to her past means I've become a combination of therapist, friend, and priest for her.

Max tells me not to be stupid, that she's in prison for a reason. But that doesn't mean she doesn't deserve kindness, empathy. After all, she didn't do anything to Mum, even if the fallout from her affair with Pete affected Anouk. Maybe I am walking into a trap, maybe I am a fool for believing her, but what's the alternative? There's no one else like Brigham. And although she went about things in a way no one could condone, it takes a heart harder than mine not to relate to how she was treated.

EIGHTEEN

Spring 2017
Emily

It seems unreal to be planning a wedding – my wedding – when I'm not even divorced yet. And it's very different the second time around.

A white dress – who am I kidding here? And God knows who'll show up on the day. Acrimonious is not the word when it comes to how Pete and I ended things. More like he hoped I burned in hell and some other unpleasant things I believe were in his messages. I don't know, because I stopped reading them. I figured he'd be okay. After all, he was having an affair with Sarah. I had only slept with Liam in a moment of weakness, after I discovered what Pete had been up to... surely it was a blow to his ego, rather than true betrayal? Why was it okay for him to do it, but not me? If he was that in love with me in the first place, then why cheat? Why not try to make it work? I know there's more to it than that – the photos I took of myself, the harm it did Anouk – but it's not like he was the innocent victim in all of this. It's a mess, is what it is... what it *was*, with neither of us taking accountability for the breakdown of our marriage. Not that it even matters anymore. It's been a tough journey to get to this point – to some new measure of happiness.

Detangling our financial lives together was an experience I'd rather not repeat. He fought me on everything. House, cars, savings, Anouk. As if she was ever better off with him. I'm waiting for the final paperwork. It should come through any day now. How we've avoided court I'll never know, but somehow despite the arbitration we've made it through. He's with Sarah now, and I'm with Liam. We've split custody of Anouk, just like Greg and Sarah did with their two girls. Maybe this was the way things were supposed to be all along – *bechert* as my grandmother would say.

I wasn't expecting Liam to propose so soon. I wasn't sure, if I'm really honest – was it too much too soon? Still that nagging feeling that it was all too good to be true. But he said he'd wasted time before, he wasn't going to waste it now. And to be fair to him, I've never felt as loved and safe as I do now, with him. There's loyalty and trust, implicit in everything we do together. Even when Pete was awful during the divorce negotiations, even when I cried every night, the only place of comfort was Liam, in his bed, in his arms. It's more than pure chemistry this time, it's something deeper, richer. That feeling that we are a true partnership. I don't feel like I have to be someone else with him, someone good, someone perfect. And neither does he.

To be honest, I didn't think he'd ever remarry, not after everything with his ex. So it means even more that he's proposed, that he's so sure, that this is it.

Maybe it was risky, but I moved in with Liam as soon as I could. I know they say not to leave the marital home, especially if you're the mother, but I didn't see the point in waiting, because I knew we would never live together there. I worried about Anouk, about the change for her, but Liam reassured me there was really very little upheaval for her. We were in the same town, she'd be at the same school, it was okay. And it was.

We didn't stay in Liam's cottage for long. It was a bit cosy for all four of us, even if Nicolas was with Sabine most of the time – though Liam is keen to get Sabine to consider upping his custody allowance. We moved to a lovely Edwardian double-fronted villa in the next town about two months ago. It needs work of course, to put our stamp on it. But for now, it'll do – and the location means Anouk didn't need to move schools. After all, I have time now. I don't need to work, Liam tells me, and I've stopped my Instagram entirely – in fact, I stopped it as soon as I was caught. The house keeps me busy, and the wedding planning – and, of course, Anouk too. Liam's job means I don't need to worry about the day to day, life admin type stuff. We have a housekeeper and a cleaner and a nanny. Liam wants to make sure I am never too tired for him, never feigning a headache, never dealing with the mundane. He's brought back the rules we had before, when we first started. But back then I was only his girlfriend, and now I am his fiancée, soon to be wife. And it's a big job, one I'm finally ready for.

Sabine messages me sometimes, Liam doesn't know about it – but of course we need to have each other's numbers because of the children.

> Are you okay, Emily?
>
> You can trust me you know.

I never reply, but still, she persists.

> It's not just you.
>
> I'm here anytime you want to talk.

I don't know what she thinks I'd want to talk to her about. I mean, no relationship is perfect, we all have our secrets, but her time with Liam is over.

> I know he's doing it to you also.

I'm currently sorting out the guest list for the wedding. Apparently we have to invite her for the sake of the kids, but there's no way on earth Pete would ever want to come, so I'm not inviting him. Liam tells me I can invite as many people as I want. It's nice, not to have to worry about anything. Not that we didn't have money when I was with Pete – it's just different with Liam, a whole other level of wealth. Something Mum could only dream of when I was little. In her eyes, I've made it – she loves Liam, maybe more than Pete.

With my first wedding Anouk was a toddler, it was nice, but it wasn't anything extravagant for that reason. This time round though, I'm having the full luxe treatment. Not a big wedding, but special, boutique, unique. We're flying everyone to Sorrento in early September for it. I've got a bespoke Marchesa gown. Paulina Pryke flowers. Sucre D'Anges cake. Sometimes I look at the invoices, think about what the money would have bought when I was a child. The time we lived on beans for months. When there was frost on the windows, or the black mould in the bathroom. Whenever I can, I take Mum out for lunch, or for spa days. I don't enjoy the time with her, exactly, but I remember how hard she worked, and what she did. I want her to see what her parenting has brought us both, how she benefits too. No matter the cost.

I've not invited many people, but I got back in touch with Lilly and Noush – after all, they were there when it all first started. *Blast from the past*, Noush said when I messaged her. *When's the hen?* from Lilly. Some things don't change at all. They were both quite surprised to hear from me. Liam wasn't so sure at first, but I pointed out my side might look a bit empty otherwise. So many people who I considered friends that Pete now has custody of. Our whole friendship circle turns out to have been his. Liam tells me I don't need friends, asks me if he's not enough for me. I tell him he's rubbish on spa days and hates shopping, so he acquiesces.

I didn't really want a hen, but as the girls pointed out, I didn't have one the first time round. *Fine, I said, but there are some ground rules. Nothing with blow-up cocks, nothing with excessive drinking, nothing too silly.*

They only posted laughing face emojis and told me to trust them. It's only Lilly, Noush, Mum and me on the hen; I did think about inviting Billie, or some of the others, but they're just reminders of a past I don't want any more.

Mum was a bit worried. I think she remembered some of what we got up to, before.

It will be classy, won't it, darling?

And Liam only told me to be discreet. This from the man going to Dubai for a boys' weekend with Drew. Much like many things with Liam, the don't-ask-don't-tell rule applies to both of us.

The bulk of wedding prep is done by the planner, but I'm sorting the last few bits now so that I can focus on myself in the next couple of months, on the run-up to the wedding. It's why the hen do is now – we're combining it with a girls' reunion – then I can go on my diet and exercise regimen ahead of September. Plus, I might have a few tweaks at the aesthetician and those will take time to settle. I was anti-Botox and fillers for so long, but now I'm Liam's wife – or will be soon – I know there's a level of maintenance that comes with that. And I enjoy it, to a degree, looking the best. If it's done well enough, no one can tell.

Lilly and Noush, true to their word, have organised everything. It's a bit odd, relinquishing control, trusting them, but it's also nice. I've missed my female friendships, much as I love Liam. I've been told to pack for two nights away. I've not been told what we're doing, only that passports, bathing suits, vintage and black-tie outfits are required.

Sarah collected Anouk yesterday – we didn't say much during the handover, as Anouk was itching to get going because Naomi was home from university. As much as Anouk loves Beckie, she idolises her big stepsister. I wasn't happy with Pete's behaviour though and messaged him after to say I was disappointed he'd not even bothered to collect her in person, leaving everything to the women again. And as much as I may have a certain amount of animosity towards Sarah, she treats Anouk like she's her own. After the disaster last year, and the public reveal of my side hustle on Instagram, I'm so glad Anouk is surrounded by people who love and care for her – not just me, but all of her blended family, as I call it.

Liam's already left for Dubai, so I'm alone in the house – Nicolas is with Sabine. I sit on my Samsonite suitcase to zip it closed and then make sure my passport, phone, keys, and purse are in my vintage Miu Miu satchel. I'm wearing white paper bag tie canvas shorts with an old Missoni zigzag print chiffon blouse, plus orange wedge espadrilles, for that 1950s French Riviera vibe. I'm definitely working on my influencer look today. Even if I've stopped my private photos, I'm enjoying a more fashionista angle to my general Instagram content. And Liam is very happy to support it.

My phone chimes to let me know my Uber to the station is two minutes away. I'm getting the train to St Pancras where I've been told to meet the girls and Mum. When I get there, I spot them immediately. Noush is holding a giant inflatable penis balloon and another, smaller one, saying hen do. I can't help but laugh. Noush always did have a wicked, sharp sense of humour.

'Babes!' They gather me into an embrace, scented with

what I immediately recognise as Tom Ford's Black Orchid. It's not cheap – Noush and Lilly have come up in the world too.

'You look amazing. It's so good to see you, Ems, you haven't changed a bit.'

'Ah... thank you.'

'How long has it been since you girls last saw each other?' Mum asks.

'Wow, I don't know.' Lilly looks at us, a hand to her forehead, her sheet of shiny dark hair held off her face by a pair of bug-eye Bulgari sunglasses.

Neither of them appear to have lost the taste for the finer things in life. Perhaps we have more in common now than we did then.

'Last time must have been... my wedding?' I did actually go to Noush's wedding. Anouk was a toddler and we had no childcare, so we had to bring her with us. I wasn't happy about it, but Pete loved playing the dutiful daddy, letting the photographer take adorable pictures of Anouk in her flower girl outfit and him in his suit.

'Wow. That's like six years ago! Well, let's make up for lost time!'

And they tell me we're checking into the St Pancras Hotel, which even I concede, is pretty cool. Even if they do insist on making us do a photoshoot – penis balloon included – at the Harry Potter platform 9 ¾ sign.

After check-in, I'm told to bring my bikini, and my beach cover up and meet the girls in reception for the first part of our adventure. I'm blindfolded and inserted into a cab.

There's muffled laughter and Mum tells me not to worry. She's been inducted into the secrets of my hen do, it seems. The girls chat and talk about the journey, travelling down High Holborn, spilling out onto the Strand. But I'm lost in nostalgia.

Nights out in private boxes with Liam, drinks after at the Savoy. Getting lost in Soho, visiting private members clubs, the

Groucho on occasion. Being parked at a table with other men in suits and left there whilst Liam went off to talk to someone important, promising he'd be back soon. Wondering how rude it would seem if I pushed wandering hands off my thighs. Making extra trips to the toilet to 'freshen up', the girls in there powdering their noses. And then when Liam came back for me, leading me down labyrinthine corridors, until we could be alone in the dark.

'Here we are!' The taxi lurches to a halt, snapping me out of my reverie.

'Can I take this mask off now?'

There are hands in my hair and then I blink, adjusting to the light. We're outside a stuccoed row of houses off the Strand. I recognise it immediately – the John Adam's club is round the corner. I've been pressed into its deep caverns by Liam many times. Another men-only club.

But here we are outside a luxury spa that looks to replicate the ancient roman baths.

'I've been wanting to go here for ages, thanks!'

We're ushered inside and immediately there is the ozone smell and echo of water. We strip quickly, effectively in individual cubicles. There are seven rooms to explore and we're booked in for massages. Mum's gone for hers first, so it's only me, Lilly and Noush for now.

When I walk out, they're already swaddled in their plush white robes and spa slippers, towels in hand. The last time I saw them in bathing suits was a trip to Ibiza, pre-kids, pre-husbands. Pre-Liam actually. I wonder if Noush still has her back tattoo or if it's been lasered off, like I did mine. Back then our suitcases were crammed with cheap string bikinis from Primark, tiny shorts and cover-ups, wedge flip-flops. The cost of this spa trip would probably cover all of us for that trip to Ibiza.

In the first room, we shed our robes on loungers and walk into water that is amniotic – warm, viscous, scented. The domed ceilings are tiled in a vaguely Moroccan style and the darkness is only broken by pockets of subdued under-arch lighting and tea lights. The flickering flames cast long shadows back into the hallways and the darkness of other rooms.

As it's mid-morning on a Friday, the spa is quiet – we are the only people in this room, though distantly a splash and laughter reminds us we are not alone. But for now the womb-like ambience embraces and relaxes us. Lilly and Noush speak to each other in hushed tones as they wade across the water to a recessed ledge in one arch. I follow behind, in a leisurely crawl, allowing the water to caress my skin.

'This is amazing, thank you so much. I don't think I've been this relaxed in years.'

Lilly laughs. 'Same. In fact, I don't think I've been this relaxed since I had pharmaceutical help.'

Noush splashes her. 'Naughty!'

'Nothing naughty about it. I pulled a muscle in my shoulder and my lovely GP prescribed Valium to relax it, bloody amazing stuff.'

I nod in agreement. 'I distinctly remember us knowing a very non-reputable supplier for pharmaceutical relaxation.'

'Yeah but that was back in the day – can't do anything like that now.'

Well, you can, I want to say. *Nothing stopping you.* We're just supposed to be better behaved now. Being with Liam again though, reminds me of the fun I used to have. When I wasn't so trapped.

'Yeah, a bit too old now.'

'Speak for yourselves!' I laugh.

I can see it, though. The changes time has wrought on their bodies, the looseness of the skin on their bellies and arms. The creeping spread of cellulite. The faint lines around their eyes, the crepey skin appearing on their necks.

'Oh come on, you can't still be partying like you used to, Ems.'

'No, of course not.' But even though I'm not, doesn't mean I don't want to. 'I miss it though, the fun, the freedom. No consequences.'

Even Liam is the same. I don't want to think about what he's getting up to in Dubai. Drew is still single, of course.

There's a pause – Noush and Lilly look at each other. They've stayed close over the years, attended weddings and christenings, godmothers to each other's children. If things had turned out differently, if Anna hadn't died, would I be part of that? Instead of what I have – *had* – with Billie and Sarah, a poor imitation of my friendship with Anna, or these two.

'Do you and Liam talk about back then much? The parties and stuff?' Noush asks.

The water trembles with the weight of so much unsaid.

'Not really. Why would we? I mean, obviously it's how we met, but times have changed... it's the future that counts.'

Liam says it to me all the time, whenever I'm tempted to reminisce, to book trips for us to our old haunts. *Darling, that was then, this is now, let's not miss out on what's right in front of us, by looking back.*

They look at each other again. Lilly speaks this time.

'We were a little surprised, you know, about all this. Leaving Pete and marrying Liam... after everything that happened.'

'What do you mean?'

Noush scrunches her eyebrows and lines form on her forehead.

'Well... those parties were a bit dodgy, weren't they?'

'How?'

Again, they look at each other.

'The guys – they were all really old. And we were so young.

I mean, it's kind of grim when you think about it now. Imagine Anouk dating someone twenty years older than her.'

'Anouk will never need to do what I did.'

'No, I know...'

She doesn't know, though, what I've done, so that Anouk will be provided for.

'All I'm saying is that now, if you talked about those parties in public, questions would be raised. I mean come on, remember how they'd just shove champagne down our necks? We were so drunk! Oh, and the coke too. I'd say yes to anything in that state. In fact, a lot of nights I was barely able to speak.'

'You're making it sound like none of us wanted to be there! I seem to remember you both having a pretty good time.'

They nod at me.

'We did. Sometimes. We're just saying, maybe we remember it differently from you. Don't you remember how you were after Drew? And after Anna?'

Her name is loud in the silence. I look away so the others don't see the tears in my eyes.

The tension is broken by another group of women walking in. They slip off their robes and sliders, like Noush and Lilly, they look a little... shop-worn. It makes me even more determined to keep up what I do, to stay beautiful, desirable. After all, look where it's got me now.

As we climb out of the pool, a younger woman walks in. I look at her concave belly, her thigh gap, the way the skin on her face is taut and pristine.

'I wish I still looked like that,' I say, without thinking.

'Okay, for starters, that is a child – she's like eighteen, max – and second of all, you do pretty much look like that!'

Lilly smiles as she says it, but the sting of 'pretty much' is still there. I haven't ever considered an alternative to not maintaining my looks. And now I'm starting to lose them, it scares me, because where will I be then?

'I feel like I'm holding on to my youth the way Tom Cruise clings on to the rocks in *Mission Impossible*. At some point soon, my fingers will slip and then where will I be?'

'I'm sorry you feel that way.'

'Don't you?'

'No. Not really.' Noush tosses her head. 'I mean yes, my tits look like oranges in socks and I can tuck my belly into my pants, but who really gives a shit? I've got bigger fish to fry. I'm the MD of an award-winning consultancy. I've got three kids. I've got a fucking life. Who cares if I don't look the way I did when I was twenty-five? I didn't have anything to do when I was twenty-five, other than look good.'

Lilly ushers us into the steam room and we recline on benches. Sweat prickles across my brow and between my breasts. I remember having sex with Liam in a hammam once, slick and slippery as eels.

'Do you feel the same, Lilly?'

Lilly shrugs, careful to express an opinion that navigates the middle ground.

'Surely you *want* to look good?' I press on. 'It's about your health. You have to have some standards, no?'

'Well, I've never had a problem with ageing – remember how much I used to get ID'd when we were out? But I get what Noush is saying. You can't stay the way you were in your twenties. It's not realistic. And would you even want to? God knows I was a total fuck up then.'

'Okay, well not twenty-five. But surely it's important to present the right image? You wouldn't pitch in your pyjamas would you? It's no different. People judge you!'

I can hear the screechy tone in my voice.

'Honey, we're all still hot. Quite literally.' Noush fans herself and laughs, and adds more water to the hot coals. 'But I'm just saying, for me, it's not the only thing. But you do you babe, you know. Promise me though, you're doing it for you.

Not because of Liam or some weird patriarchal shit that means you won't leave the house without mascara on.'

Lilly and Noush laugh and high five each other – and me.

I don't say that I haven't worn mascara for a while now. That my lashes are tinted and enhanced with individual mink lashes every six weeks by a Ukrainian woman who Liam booked. So technically I do go out without mascara on.

'Remember the way we used to spend hours getting ready for those parties? And all for those creepy men. Ewww!' Noush makes fake retching noises, but Lilly catches my eye and then hers.

'Oh, sorry, Em, I didn't mean Liam was creepy, obviously.'

There's another awkward pause. Noush looks at Lilly again.

'Okay, enough with the side eyes and eyebrow raises?' I hiss. 'I know I was a shit friend after, but it was a really bad time back then, for me. Anna dying and breaking up with Liam didn't exactly leave me in a good place – none of us were our best selves though, were we?'

They both move closer and Lilly puts her hand on my leg. Noush looks at me, her face softening.

'We're sorry, okay, we didn't mean to make you feel that way. We just want to make sure that you're sure about all this,' Noush says.

I don't know what they mean – am I sure. What would I have to not be sure about? Liam and I love each other, the past is in the past. We've all done things we regret but I'm older and wiser now. I don't have a chance to respond though, because the other women come into the steam room and we move on to the plunge bath, where we have to pause conversation as the shock of the cold cuts out our ability to speak. Instead we walk, teeth chattering and goose bumped, to the last room. Which turns out to be the same as the first – that warm, soothing water. Where my mother is waiting.

'Darling, it's your turn for a massage now.'

I want to continue the discussion though, especially when I turn and see Noush and Lilly, heads close together.

Instead, I head into the private room and lie down on the massage chair, put my face through the hole. I don't understand what they mean – I'm not saying we were perfect back then, or that some of the guys weren't creepy. But none of it was non-consensual. Just because I don't remember saying yes, doesn't mean I didn't want it, I don't think...

I don't like being painted as some silly girl who just went along with it all, because she didn't think she could say no. That's so patronising. As if I didn't have a voice, and didn't use it. And okay, sometimes maybe I did things that now, I'd say no to. But we've all got regrets.

I think back to what I used to wear. How Liam told me he couldn't control himself. Face down, now, with a strange masseuse in the room – a man – I feel myself tighten at the thought, the power I had – and still have – over men, over Liam. How much he still wants me, even now, how much he loves me. How I have all his attention, not like with Pete.

I fall asleep during my massage and dream of endless corridors, endless hands, a voice telling me I'm a good girl and to take it nicely. When I wake, my face is damp, as if I've been crying.

When I come out, the girls are off having their massages, so I shower and change, and go back upstairs to the light to wait for them.

The rest of the day is quiet, I am informed we are getting an early Eurostar to Paris! And also, this is where Mum is going to say goodbye, she didn't want to travel despite the shopping temptations. Whatever is planned, she tells me to enjoy it, but her facial expression implies a certain disapproval.

The surprise is that we're watching Dita von Teese perform at Le Moulin Rouge. Which is both cool and a little tacky.

Which is about right, really. I know we could be somewhere more exclusive, more expensive, but I also know that Lilly and Noush wouldn't enjoy that. There is something about this that is both ordinary and wild. Neither of which my life in Surrey permits.

'We thought you'd like it. You love all that retro stripper stuff – all that lingerie you got. When we heard she was here this weekend, we had to book it!'

I message Liam a picture of us outside the famous building in Montmartre. He sends me back a rolling eyes emoji, but also an eggplant. I wonder where he is, who he's with. But I also don't want to know.

'It's a great idea. Bring on *la champagne*!'

They've booked a VIP package so we're up on the balcony for dinner and the show – and unlimited drinks.

'This could get messy!'

'I knew you'd get bored with just a spa day. I bet you thought we'd gone all sedate and middle-aged, didn't you?'

'Well...'

They both squeal with laughter and fling their arms around me, still girlish despite everything. And I remember the good times. The nights where we got back at dawn, the trips to Glastonbury, the time we went to a trance festival in Spain. Even when we just hung out in the flat, taking the piss out of everything and everyone.

I look at what they're wearing – Lilly in a leather pencil skirt, white shirt and black leather harness and collar, sequin pins in her hair, cherry-bud lips and razor-sharp eyeliner, red-soled black six-inch buckled Mary Janes. Noush in skin-tight burgundy jodhpurs, over the knee black riding boots and a blazer with a single button at hip level, nothing underneath except silver sequin nipple tassels, matching the sequinned horns in her hair.

'You got the memo, I see?' Lilly laughs.

'I did.'

They told me it was black tie. So I'm wearing a floor length black sequin strapless fitted gown, with a split up one thigh and a fine silver chainmail hood. I've styled my hair to fall over one eye and shoulder like Dita – and Veronica Lake.

'You look like a goth Jessica Rabbit.'

'I'll take that.' And my shiny red lips part in a smile.

Inside we're ushered to our seats and champagne is poured.

'Cheers, bitches.'

Lilly whoops and, despite what they said about growing up, growing older, there's something in the air that feels electric, exciting.

When I look around, the tables are filling up – glitter, sequins, leather, satin, silk, heels, corsets. A mix of people, but more women than men. I wonder what Anna would think of all of this? She'd laugh at us probably. She had no time for what she called 'lipstick lesbians', but things were different when we were at university. The women here now, some with men, some with women, some with... well, as Anouk tells me, *it doesn't matter if you're a boy or a girl.*

I wonder if Noush and Lilly are missing their husbands. The harness Lilly has on reminds me of one that Liam bought for me. It came with accessories. But I wouldn't wear them in public.

The one thing I'm surprised at though, is how some of the women here, regardless of their size, are still wearing skimpy outfits. The way they act like they are free to be whoever they want shocks me.

'This reminds me of that party we went to in our twenties where the theme was *Gentlemen Prefer Blondes*.' I'd forgotten actually, but as soon as Noush mentions it, the memories come rushing back, making me laugh.

'Oh my God, yes! And we all tried to dress as Marilyn. With the pink dress and the wigs!' Lilly points at her own head, now in a neat mum cut, but back then she had hair to her waist, a nightmare to pack under a wig.

'Oh, those fucking things, they were so itchy.'

'We looked amazing though,' I say.

'We did.'

'See, it wasn't all bad?'

'It wasn't.' Lilly puts her hand over mine.

'When was that party anyway? Like... mid 2007? 2008?'

'Yeah I think so. Wait, it was after Drew so—'

They look at each other again. I talk a gulp of champagne.

'What?'

'Does Liam still speak to Drew?'

'Yeah – they're in Dubai together for his stag right now.'

'Even after what he did to you?' They both stare at me, wide-eyed.

'What do you mean, what he did to me?'

'Are you serious? The man basically raped you. And your fiancé is BFFs with him!'

'Raped me? Are you serious?'

'Yes! You were a mess when you came back, you couldn't remember anything.'

'That's because I was drunk! Look, I know you all like your vanilla suburban sex, but some of us like it rough, okay? That doesn't make me a victim. It's all consensual.'

'I'm going to ignore that absolute slur on my sex life, true as it might be, to point out that at least my husband's bestie isn't a total creep. And to be honest, Liam back then wasn't much better, how do you know he's changed now?'

'Oh my God, stop making me out to be some helpless little woman. I wanted everything Liam did to me back then. Hell, I did it back to him.'

They're being ridiculous. Also, it's not like he hasn't changed – he left his wife, didn't he? He proposed to me. We're living together and getting married, I have everything I wanted.

I don't appreciate this sudden desire to rake up the past. I've done my best to put it behind me for a reason.

Noush and I glare at each other as Lilly looks on and chews her lip.

'Look, this is not what I meant okay? It's just, have you forgotten the things he put you through?'

'I agreed to it. It was' – I lower my voice – 'a sex thing.'

'Was it though? Or is that what he's told you? Because I distinctly remember you coming home crying several times. Saying it was over and you were so humiliated.'

'I don't know what you're talking about. You must be misremembering. Also, everyone has the occasional fight with their boyfriend. I'm not saying we didn't have a fiery relationship, but it wasn't like that. I'm not some battered woman.'

Lilly looks at her glass. 'Okay. Fine. But what about Anna?'

Noush drains her glass, and then glares at Lilly.

'What? Why are you nudging me? If she won't listen about herself, then maybe remembering Anna will help.'

'Don't even mention Anna. Take her name out of your mouth.' I can feel my lip tremble as I speak, and hear my voice crack. Both their faces soften.

'We didn't mean to upset you. Truly.' Noush pours more champagne for us all. 'But you know she wasn't the first girl who ended up in a bad situation after those parties.'

'She died. That's a bit more than a bad situation.'

'Well... yes, exactly. But there were other girls who went missing. You know, some of them had to go to hospital after? That they got paid to have abortions, but were made to sign NDAs.'

As she says this the stage lights go down and the music starts, so I am reduced to hissing at her across the table.

'I don't see what any of this has to do with Liam... or... or... Drew.'

I never think of that morning, waking up in the hotel room

with him. I don't talk about it. It's like it never happened. That girl I was then, she doesn't exist anymore, and I don't care what Drew does now.

'Come on, Emily, open your eyes. How do you think it all got covered up? How do you think the NDAs happened? We're not saying do anything drastic, but please, go into this marriage with your eyes open. We don't want you to get hurt.'

I sit in the dark, watching any number of beautiful, young women taking their clothes off and dancing and moving in ways that don't seem humanly possible. Dita herself is a goddess in diamanté. I look at how she moves, the way she holds herself. But I also see the work it takes to maintain it all. And for the first time, I feel sad. Her control over her brand and her image is unique and iconic. But when does it stop?

I drink more champagne and wonder again what Anna would say if she were here. Probably tell me to get over myself, to stop overthinking everything.

But then if Anna were still alive, maybe I wouldn't be here in the first place? Maybe I'd be somewhere else, someone else, entirely.

NINETEEN

Spring 2017

It's about a week after I get back from Paris when I receive an email from Anna's mum, Sophie, telling me she's sent me a parcel – and could I call her when I receive it?

It wasn't unusual to hear from her. She called me sometimes – after Anna died, it was weekly, but then it dropped to monthly and then tailed off, until she only called on special dates, like Anna's birthday, the anniversary of her death, sometimes Christmas.

I sent her a picture of Anouk when she was born, and then every birthday after. After all, she was named after Anna – but I used the full version of her name. Anna never liked it. But I thought it was beautiful.

Even so, I was intrigued as to what she'd sent me.

'*Cherie*.' Sophie's accent hasn't faded over the years she'd lived in England, her Parisian style and elegance was something my mother always envied.

'*Tante* Sophie. Anouk sends you *bisous*.'

'*Merci, ma belle* Anouk, *ma p'tite*.'

I hold the phone up so that Anouk can wave at her. She's never met Sophie in person, but she knows who she is, who Anna is – *Mama's friend that died and now she is in heaven with les anges.*

Sophie comments on how she's grown, how beautiful she is, how clever, until Anouk wriggles off my lap and darts away to the sofa and her iPad, her attention waning fast.

'She's so like you, Emily.' Sophie smiles and her eyes crinkle at the edges. 'She has your... how do you say... *charisme*? The way she looks at the camera, that little pixie face. You must love her so much. Daughters are so special.'

Before, even a year or two ago, her voice would crack, and she'd catch herself before it broke. Her control, in the face of loss, is something that I'm not sure I'd ever manage in the same way.

I don't have constant reminders of Anna. I don't live in the house she was born and brought up in. I can forget her, for a while, and never feel the guilt a mother would feel.

I hold up the padded jiffy bag with my name on it, Sophie's address marked on the back in perfect cursive, her name in navy ink crisp and clear – Mme S. Leroi.

'Ah yes, so, I am sorry for the mystery, but I felt I should call you and tell you myself, not put it in an email – or a letter. I'm sorry to tell you, but we've had to sell our house.'

'What? Why?'

Her mouth twists before she replies.

'Michael is ill. Too ill, he needs more care than I can give him. We have no savings – not enough anyway – we used them all when we paid that investigator...' Her voice tails off and her eyes glisten.

She looks away and takes a deep breath before continuing. 'So yes, Michael needs to go to a hospice; he needs specialist care. It's breaking my heart, but it's the only way we can afford it.' She gulps back a sob and something inside me cracks a little.

I remember Anna's dad, a big man, but reserved, but with the blackest sense of humour, just like her. I can't imagine him now, a shell of a man, reduced to an overgrown infant by the slow incessant creep of dementia.

'I'm so sorry, Sophie, truly.'

She sobs and holds the phone away from her so I can't see her face. I give her a moment to compose herself.

'It feels like by moving, we're losing her, we're losing our Anna – our Anouk – all over again.'

I look at her and see how grief has ravaged her. The brackets around her mouth, the lipstick bleeding into rivers around her lips, the wobbly drawn on eyebrows, the parody of beauty. The strength it takes to still put a face on and set your hair. Anna got all her determination – stubbornness, I called it – from her mother. Both taureans, bullish to the core.

'I wish I was with you. Is there anything I can do?'

She only shakes her head.

'That's why I've sent you something. We had to go through Anna's room. All the things you sent back after—'

I packed up her room after the funeral, her brother helping. Carefully, as if she were going on holiday, I wrapped her clothes in tissue paper, her jewellery in soft bags, her shoes in Perspex boxes. Anna would have thought me ridiculous, treating her old band and protest T-shirts like the finest cashmere. But they were special to her, so they were to me. Michael came to collect her things, Sophie hadn't been able to face it. *She's at home in bed, the doctor's given her something.* I remember loading up his beaten estate in the pissing rain, such a bloody cliche.

'—I didn't open any of them, only one to see who they were from,' Sophie continues, 'but I thought you should have them.'

'Sorry?'

'The letters? In the package? Anna kept them, the letters you wrote to each other over the years, during the university holidays, and when you first moved to London.'

Even though we could email, Anna loved writing a letter. She felt there was something more formal, more honest about committing words to ink and paper. That you could channel emotions more effectively. And with no room for error, no backspace key, you had to think about your words before writing them.

'Thank you, Sophie, that's so kind of you, really.'

'Well, I know you miss her too. I feel like everyone else has forgotten. That she's disappearing.'

'I haven't forgotten her. Not for a single minute. And you know, if I could go back, if I could change things, I would.'

'Emily, you mustn't blame yourself. How could you know? It wasn't your fault. It was those men – one of them.'

I haven't told her I'm marrying Liam. I don't think she'd remember him, but either way I know she wouldn't understand. It would be a huge betrayal. I can't explain it to myself, so I can't explain it to her. It's the closest I've come to shame.

'I wish we knew what happened. It'll bother me forever,' I say.

Sophie looks at me, kindness in her eyes.

'Darling, you mustn't let yourself go down that path. It'll only consume you. You must move on, remember the happy times, *non*? How much you loved each other, the great friends you were. And then smile. I hope the letters help you to do that, to remember only the good. To heal. It's been so long now. It's all I want for you. After all, you too, are like a daughter to me.'

'Oh, Sophie—'

There is a crash somewhere distant behind Sophie and any further discussion is stopped as she tells me she needs to get back to Michael, but that she loves me and she wishes me so much happiness – and to call when I've read the letters. I promise her I will and that I will visit soon and to please send me her new address.

As she ends the call I think about how Anouk and I can go

to The White Company – Sophie loves it – and pick out some lovely homeware for her as a moving gift.

In the end I don't open the packet until the weekend even though it arrived midweek – Sophie had sent it to our old house, but I'd had the post redirected. I manage to resist it until Anouk has gone to Pete's and Liam is busy playing golf – with Drew, of course. It's not that I don't think about it during the week, after I speak to Sophie, and I walk past it on the hall table where we dump post and keys and all the usual crap that comes through the letter box. But I want to open it when the time is right.

And that time is mid-morning on Saturday, with sunlight filtering over me in the conservatory and fresh cup of coffee in my sweary bitch mug.

I pull the tear strip gluing down the sealed flap and letters pour out onto the table in front of me, the paper of them soft with age. Some of these letters are nearly twenty years old. And even though they spill out, as I gather them, I see Sophie – or someone – has tied them into bundles by the age of the date stamps on them. They form three separate piles – first year, second year, and after graduation. All with my neat block writing, twee hearts over the letter i, addressed to Anouk Leroi – I used her full name to wind her up.

It seems crazy that we'd write to each other – and we didn't do it with any regularity – but more as a surprise or a joke on important days like Halloween or Valentines. Random pop culture dates – the anniversary of Kurt Cobain's death, or April 25th after we saw *Miss Congeniality*, or Amy Winehouse' birthday.

I don't actually know what happened to all the letters she sent me. I don't normally keep things like that, I'm terrible for forgetting birthdays and anniversaries – Mum used to call me ruthless, how I'd clear away the cards and decorations the day after birthdays, and insist on the Christmas tree coming down on Boxing Day. But I definitely wouldn't have binned her letters. I can only think that they went missing during one of the house moves. They probably got chucked by someone thinking it was a shoebox full of rubbish.

It means a lot though, that Anna kept my letters to her. She always was a softy underneath the black nail polish, the battered DMs, the shouty music, the feminist rants.

One time, after our summer exams in first year, there was a party. She got horribly stoned and I remember her hotly debating the existence of God with some awful pizza-faced kid in the year above. He was so miserable, but I remember her voice, clear as a bell, insisting that she didn't believe in God, but she damn well believed in love. And that love made the world go round. And all you needed was love. We all pissed ourselves laughing, but I knew she meant it.

I stack the piles on the table and consider reading them. Or whether to tuck them away, with the old photo albums and knickknacks from years ago. But that seems disrespectful to Sophie somehow, when she's gone to the trouble – despite everything – to find them and send them.

I check the jiffy bag to make sure I've not missed anything – and lo and behold there is one last envelope in there. But this one is addressed to me – in Anna's scratchy left-handed writing. Nothing like a letter from the dead to make your heart skip a beat.

The envelope is sealed and stamped. And yet for some reason Anna never posted it. I hold it and almost hear her voice in my ear, asking me what I'm waiting for, *bloody open it*. I'm wary though, because surely if she'd wanted me to read it, she'd have sent it?

The first thing I notice is the date. And straight away I can smell the coconut of her shampoo, remember waking up in her bed at university. And how I left while she was still asleep. I'm impressed she's managed to have the last word, well over a decade later.

Ems,

You left this morning before I could say anything – you thought I was asleep, but I wasn't. So, I thought I'd write you a letter instead. Like we always do.

I don't know if I'll send it. Maybe I will, maybe I won't. I probably shouldn't. But even so, I wanted it down on paper, how I feel, how you feel. Because at least here, in one small way, it's real.

I let you leave because I know it was all too much for you. I didn't expect any more.

I know you'll say last night was a mistake – and that you want me to say the same thing.

But it wasn't, you know it and I know it.

I know you're scared. I'm scared too.

Sometimes the labels we're made to wear are so weighty, I feel like I might break beneath them. But with you, I'm so much more – and so are you.

After it all, isn't it just love?

Because that's truth of it, Ems, I love you. Always have, always will. And you love me too, I think. That's what scares you.

I know this isn't the life your mum planned out for you; it's not the life you see in films and TV. But don't you owe yourself a chance to be happy? Don't you wonder what could be?

Life is short, you tell me that all the time. We don't have forever, all we have is now.

The ink then changes colour on the page –

So I took a break from this letter because I had to go to the library and you were there, acting all normal. You called me over and said hi, asked me how my hangover was, all the while wriggling around on the lap of some rugby moron, winding your arms around his neck and batting your lashes at him.

I knew then, that even though you feel it too, you were sending me a message.

I'll never send you this letter now. Maybe it's better to accept what you'll give me, not want for more. How can I be fair to me and fair to you? I don't know. One of us will only end up hurt, and right now, maybe it's better that it's me.

So, I'll sign off now. I need some sleep – some space from all of this, my head's a mess.

Plus, knowing you, you'll show up later, when you're done with your friend in the library. You'll come in, and switch on my music and sing along; you'll probably be drunk, and insist we order pizza.
And despite everything – I haven't even stripped the sheets from my bed yet – I'll let you do all those things.

You'll make me laugh until my stomach hurts. And for those few brief hours with you, I'll be the happiest I'll ever be.

And isn't that all any of us can ask for, really?

The letter stops there.

I can't breathe for a few seconds when I finish reading. I put the letter down on the side next to me, gulp back a shock of tears that threaten. Because I'm right there with her, in her room, with the cheap pizza and the music, and the laughter. Where I was also the happiest I've been – before I had Anouk.

Anna was right, I did love her. Maybe in the way she wanted, maybe not. But, either way, I wasn't ready. Like she said, it wasn't possible, not for a girl like me. And even now, years later, it's not clear cut. I love Liam, I loved Pete – and certainly I was attracted to them both. And even Drew, despite myself. Every man I've slept with, I've wanted to, wanted the power and intimacy, to know I was desired and desirable. Anna is the only woman I've let myself feel like that with.

So maybe it could have been different with Anna… I'll never know. Either way, it makes her death even more upsetting, because she only came to that party for me – because she loved me and wanted me to be happy, with no ulterior motive. She could have pushed her own agenda, and she never did. If that's not love, I don't know what is. It kills me to think what she sacrificed and hid for our friendship. And then, to think how I repaid her…

I think back to Sophie's words of wisdom. About leaving the past behind me. To be happy. But this letter is a call through time, to a person I used to be and to a person I used to know. I barely took a breath without Anna knowing. And somehow I let her death go without question, accepting the party line.,

I want to call Sophie back and say, *I'm sorry, Sophie, I owe it to you, to me, to find out what happened – and most importantly, to your beautiful daughter who loved me when no one else did.*

I tuck the letter back into its envelope and then I go upstairs and put it in the bottom drawer of my bedside table. Next to the strip of photos I have in there. Not even Liam knows about them. I keep them under a notebook.

I look at the faces in the photos. Happy, young, laughing, carefree.

Me and Anna – before everything.

And I know then, I'll do whatever it takes to find out what happened to her. No matter what it costs me.

TWENTY

Spring 2017

One day I unexpectedly get pulled aside at school pick up. Anouk's face is blotchy and the teacher looks serious.

'There's been an incident in class today that has upset Anouk. Another child – an older boy – very unfortunately tried to put their hands inside Anouk's underwear.'

'He did *what?*'

The expression on the teacher's face shows she has underestimated my response to the situation. If there's one thing that's such to get me fired up, it's if Anouk is involved. I'm already seeing red without knowing further detail.

'The headteacher is aware and the child in question has been reprimanded.'

'I'm sorry, did you say that another child sexually assaulted my daughter and that all that's happened is that they've been told off?'

'I'm not sure I'd apply the word sexual assault to this.'

'If I were you, I'd be very careful about what words you use next.'

She twists her hands and looks anywhere but at my face as she then offers to get the headteacher for me.

Anouk looks at me, tears creeping down her cheeks.

'Baby! Are you okay? What happened?'

But she only shakes her head and cuddles into me, as the teacher arrives back, the headteacher in tow, who has clearly been waiting in the wings and goes into crisis management mode, all corporate bullshit.

'We've spoken to the child in question, they've been suspended from school and we're investigating what exactly happened. In the meantime, Anouk is welcome to take a little time away from school if she wants.'

'So my daughter should hide at home, because she's not safe from predators at her primary school? How old was this boy? How could you allow this to happen?'

'She is perfectly safe at school—'

'Well, clearly she isn't or we wouldn't be having this discussion. I mean, do you even know what happens in your school? Has this child done it before?'

'He's a year-six child. We understand this is a game that has come from social media – and we are not responsible for what children watch outside of school. We have banned mobiles and asked parents not to send them to school with their children.'

'So, you were aware of this game as a potential issue?'

'Not as such, no.'

'I'll be making a formal complaint to the governors. I'm very unhappy with how this has been handled – but also how it was allowed to happen.'

'You're within your rights to do that, Mrs…?'

I ignore the attempt to use Pete's surname.

'I'll be taking Anouk home now. I'll also be taking legal advice around contacting the police.'

The headteacher presses her lips together and I see her nudge Anouk's class teacher, as if to prevent her from speaking.

'You must do as you see fit.' She clears her throat and addresses Anouk, 'I'm so sorry this horrible incident happened and I hope you'll come back to school very soon.'

Anouk gazes at her and then cuddles in closer. She's little, for a nine-year-old, and I am reminded of how she'd cling to me at nursery, relying on me to shield her from the world. I may be many things, good and bad, but I would go to war for my daughter.

I hustle her out of the building and into the car. My hands tremble on the steering wheel as I speak to Anouk, offering her any treat I can think of, but she's quiet all the way home. And once we're back she goes straight up to her room and closes her door, no begging for snacks and negotiating for extra YouTube or to FaceTime Beckie.

When she eventually lets me in, she's in her fluffy unicorn onesie and she looks up at me with the saddest expression.

'What can I do, darling? Tell me. Anything. I can't bear to see you like this.'

She murmurs something but I don't catch it.

'Sweetie, say it again, louder.'

She bites her lip and then indicates for us to sit on her bed.

'Tell me what happened, baby.'

'He said he wanted to see if I was like my mummy.'

'What do you mean?'

'You know...' she points at her crotch, then hisses at me, 'with the pictures of you.'

I look at her in horror.

'He made me follow him into the toilet and lift my skirt up so he could check.' Her little face crumples then, but she won't let me hug her. 'And he said he'd tell the teacher it was my idea if I screamed.'

I want to rip this boy apart with my bare hands. I want him strung up on the playground. He's barely eleven, if that. Where do they learn these things? But I know really, where they learn.

It's everywhere, even when they're tiny. He'll have older brothers, he'll watch YouTube. He'll think he knows what girls are for. Ice settles in my stomach. I clench my fists and bury them in Anouk's blanket so she doesn't see. I'm still trembling.

'Oh, my darling. My baby girl.'

This time she lets me gather her into my arms, her little body shaking with sobs. I've always taught Anouk that it's her body and no one has the right to touch it without her consent.

I realise I need to tell Pete. That'll be fun. And he'll blame me, of course, because of my pictures. And for once he'll be right. I did this. I caused this to happen to my daughter, the person I love more than life itself. If I did this, I need to undo it, somehow.

We go downstairs and snuggle on the sofa, watch *Black Widow* at Anouk's request. She's a bit young I think, but she loves it. Especially the sister in it. I make popcorn for her and chocolate milk. Stay like that with her until Liam comes home. He'll know what to do here. He's always calm in a crisis and I can't be calm right now.

As much as I love Liam, he's not perfect and I know if I go full tiger mom, teeth bared, he won't listen to me. Even though he's not Anouk's father on paper, she lives with him, he needs to care about what happens to her. It's strange to be nervous about talking to him. It's not fear, so much as concern that he won't take my worries – Anouk's welfare – seriously. That he won't understand how big this is. He's never had to be afraid walking at night, keys in his hand, or checking every window and door is locked, or making sure no one is in the back seat. He's never had to pay a price simply to exist in this world. And now Anouk is – but how can he understand, if he can't relate?

I lurk in the kitchen when he gets home, faffing around with

Uber Eats on my phone, undecided whether I am better broaching the topic before or after he's eaten – and even the best way to describe what's happened, so he'll listen. I need to be firm, but approachable. I try to channel how I'd approach tricky directors at work. Gently influencing and manipulating until I got what I wanted – but letting them think it was all their idea. Liam's never experienced that side of me, only witnessed it from afar.

'Hello, darling!'

I receive kisses, I receive a bum pat and he uncaps a beer and faffs with his phone.

'How long until dinner?'

I wave my phone at him – 'It's on its way.' I've decided on pizza, even as he complains that we've had it once already that week, but he goes upstairs and I follow, fretting.

He leaves a trail of keys, coins, clothes in his wake and takes a shower. So I take the chance to check on Anouk – he's not even asked about her – and she's hunched over her tablet on her bed, swaddled in her blankets.

I tell her I'm going to sort everything out. That Liam will help. That she's safe. I promise. And then I go back to the bedroom, catch him as he's dressing.

I'm hoping that taking him by surprise, he'll listen without other distractions. But as it turns out, I am the one caught by surprise.

'Oh, Emily, come on, don't you think you're overreacting a little? They were probably messing around. You've said it yourself, she's a little flirt!'

'Well... she's really upset though. She's still crying now.'

'I mean I can't blame the boy for trying – she takes after you, after all.'

'Liam, she's nine years old.' I bite my tongue from adding, *and she's a child*.

'Yeah... don't get me wrong, she's young, of course, but I

remember what I was like back then. Playing spin the bottle on school trips. They start early, that's all.'

'Not that early, surely?'

Why doesn't he get it?

'By the time I left primary school, I knew *exactly* what I wanted to do behind the bike sheds – and with who.' He pulls me over to him on the bed. 'Maybe we should play naughty school kids.'

'Liam, stop, this is important. Don't you care?'

But he doesn't listen. 'Or, even better, teacher and naughty schoolboy...'

'Can you please focus here? I need your support and Anouk needs it too.' It's worrying me that he doesn't care about her.

'Look, I'm sorry she's upset, sweetheart. Let's do something nice this weekend, make it up to her. But I still think you're making a fuss about nothing. Boys will be boys.' And he shakes his head, turns away from me and gets dressed.

I'm stung by his dismissal, but I know I shouldn't be surprised. I guess I expected more support for Anouk. But then it's not like he's her father. *He still wants to help, to do something nice*, I remind myself. *He does care, in his own way.* I tamp down my anger, his defence that it's okay for boys to act like this. And I wonder why I even expected any different really. It's not like I don't know who Liam is, what he's like.

At least Pete will support Anouk – and any action I push for by the school, even if he blames me. Which might sting, but as he'd say, *truth hurts.* He was raging when I told him, called the headteacher despite my conversation. We discuss it and he agrees to leave me to deal with it in the best way I can. We may not be close any longer, but he knows all too well the machinations of my mind when I'm not happy about something.

I don't report the boy or school to the governors. I don't report it to the police either. But I tell one of the other mums in passing when she asks if Anouk is okay; she'd seen her crying that day.

And once I see Sarah post on the class WhatsApp – *Did you hear about a girl in year 3 being s*xually assaulted by a yr6 boy?* – I know what I did worked.

Anouk tells me she is not the first child this has happened to. That this boy has a reputation. And the school has done nothing. So, I let the other mothers in the pride attack. And I sit back and wait. A few weeks later, Anouk comes home, tells me that the boy is leaving, going to another school. That the family is moving away.

Liam laughs when I tell him. 'Clearly babe, there's no messing with you.'

'No,' I say, 'there's more than one way to skin a cat.'

And he smiles and pulls me close into him, but as he touches me in the dark, I think about all the times he's touched me before, how he and others before him, told me I wanted it. For the first time, I think that maybe Liam hasn't changed as much as he claims.

I drop the car at the station car park and head into London. I'm meeting Lilly for a coffee before my first dress fitting – it's early, I know, but they're planning to do some bespoke additions to my gown and wanted to take some measurements.

I wasn't expecting to feel closer to Lilly after all this time, but we've been messaging a bit since Paris and her office isn't far from the shop, so she offered to come. Mum would be champing at the bit to be here too, but I don't need her asking questions about whether Liam and I have plans to have kids, or making comments about how she had a twenty-two-inch waist when she got married – and that she was only married once. She's very supportive, in her own way, but I don't need her in my head right now. Not with four months until the wedding. I still have a lot to do and I need to think clearly.

When I get to the coffee shop, the Weinstein revelations are all Lilly can talk about.

'It makes me think of all those parties we went to. There were loads of famous blokes there – well, famous in business. Like the British version of Jeffrey Epstein. We were just toys for them to play with.'

'What do you mean?'

'That Drew dude, he's been in the papers over a dinner he spoke at recently – where they had hostesses.' And she makes quotation marks in the air with her fingers.

'What's a hostess?'

She looks at me.

'What world do you exist in? Did you time travel from the early 1900s? A hostess is a young attractive woman, hired to serve men and be groped.'

'That last bit is not in the job description, surely? And some men are like that – gropey. We had to deal with it, it's a fact of life.'

'But why should we? I'm not a fucking toy for someone to manhandle. Don't you think it's wrong?'

'Yes it's wrong, but what can you do? Men are like that, they want women. It's a basic thing. Sexuality.' Even as I say it, the incident with Anouk and the boy at school comes to mind. But they're kids, I tell myself, his behaviour was totally inappropriate. With grown men, it's different, not quite so black and white.

'What are you on about? It's total toxic masculinity to assume that men can't control themselves around women. Why do we have to manage their feelings for them – and put ourselves in harm's way? Is that all we're worth?'

She rolls her eyes at me and sips her coffee.

'Look, I know Drew was a creep, okay. Does that make you happy now?'

'It's not about making me happy. It's about wanting creepy guys like him to take accountability and for predatory behaviour to be outlawed. Do you want Anouk to go through what we do? Isn't it time for things to change?'

'Funny you should say that...' And I tell her what happened with Anouk at school, curious to see what she thinks and also keen to steer her away from reminiscing about the past.

'You are definitely not overreacting. And I hate that whole boys-will-be-boys bullshit. I'd take it to the governors personally. Probably not the police. That might not help Anouk – or the boy. He's still a child too. It's more the way the school is trying to brush it all under the carpet. Kids are total sponges, especially at that age. Everything they do and say they learn from elsewhere. So it's more about the kind of environment that fosters that sort of behaviour – that's how you end up with people like Drew or...'

She doesn't say Liam. But I feel like she wants to.

'I think you're right. I'll email the head and the governors, make sure it doesn't happen again.'

'I can't imagine Pete was too thrilled – what did he say about it?'

'Same as me, raging, but he trusts me to deal with it. And it's worked – the boy has moved away. We don't need to worry anymore.'

'Don't you?' Lilly raises an eyebrow at me. I feel judged, lacking, as if I don't love Anouk enough, as if I'm not protecting her well enough.

'What would you have done, Lilly? It's really easy to judge when it's not happening to you or your child. They're kids. It's the parents I don't trust, teaching their boys all sorts of shit.'

'I didn't mean to upset you. I'm just protective of Anouk too, I don't want her going through anything like...'

Like Anna, she means, but she doesn't say it, even though we're both thinking it. I look at my phone, get a shock at the time.

'Shit! We need to go. I'm due at my fitting in ten minutes.'

Lilly hugs me as we leave the café, and I put the discussion to the back of my mind. But on the way home, after she's gone – the dress was fine, needs taking in some more, I keep losing weight, I can't help it – I google Drew's name and click the news tab.

Lilly wasn't wrong. There is a mention of a dinner, some sort of finance thing back in the spring. Girls being told to wear certain clothes and expect annoying behaviour from men. And it's men only. No women.

The quotes from the girls aren't easy reading. There's a couple of pictures also, they look so young, nearer in age to Anouk, than me, babies really. And then it strikes me that I was the same age when I first met Liam.

There's a screenshot of a list of names. I click on it to open it up and browse through. There are a few names I recognise from the news, as I expect, but I keep scrolling and it's at the end of the list when I see another name I recognise, the last in the list of attendees. It shouldn't really be a surprise to see his name there but all the way home it eats at me.

I've been avoiding the past for a reason, but my mind won't let it rest. If I'm honest, I've always had questions about what happened back then. It's time now though, for answers, to get closure on this whole thing once and for all. To lay my ghosts to rest, especially Anna's.

And I know exactly who to ask.

TWENTY-ONE

Summer 2017

I'm meeting Drew for lunch. I wasn't expecting him to agree to see me without Liam, but knowing Drew, he probably thinks I'm going to proposition him. I messaged him on LinkedIn and of course, he replied immediately even though we haven't actually seen each other since Anna died, despite his friendship with Liam. I haven't avoided him exactly, more found ways to be busy when they saw each other. Besides, men like Drew are so predictable. He didn't even ask me why I wanted to meet, just said he had a standing table at the Duck & Waffle on Bishopsgate and to meet him there on Monday at midday.

I feel like I'm facing down a predator. After I saw Lilly, I figured I owed it to Anna, and to all of girls – Lilly, Noush, myself also – to get to the bottom of this. Not just for what happened in the past, but also for the future girls like us.

Lilly and Noush aren't stupid, and neither am I. There's a loose thread at the heart of all this and something in me kept tug-tug-tugging at it. It's the first time I've really acknowledged to myself the immensity of all this, accepted what I believe

Drew did to Anna, but also started to consider what he did to me. Lilly says she's proud of me, that I'm brave, doing all this, but I don't think I am, not really, not like Anna was.

It kills me that I feel a boost when Drew checks me out as I walk into the restaurant. Mostly though, I'm pleased, because it makes what I'm here to do easier, to talk to the last person to see Anna alive. I know what the official story is, a tragic accident, too many party drugs and a hot bath are a recipe for a disaster. But Anna would never have done what they say she did. And I'm determined to get the truth out of Drew, one way or another.

I'm barely at the table though, before I'm rumbled by him.

'Emily, delightful as it is to see you, what is it that you want?'

That penetrating gaze of his is exactly how I remember, as if he is firing lasers into my brain, able to see everything I'm hiding from him. Somewhere inside, that morning-after girl in the hotel room quivers, but I tamp her down, grit myself.

'How do you know I want anything at all?'

'Because you seem to have gone out of your way to avoid me since you and Liam became... *reacquainted*... and yet here we are, with you all dolled up in your finest. Clearly there's something you want.'

Somehow, over the years, he has become more refined, more well-spoken. Another silver fox. But also one that likes to play games, even though he seems direct. His bluntness makes me doubt myself for a moment. Do I really know what I'm letting myself in for? Can I handle it?

And then I think of Anna, facing off against that massive rugby player, when we were at university, how fearless she was, who was he to try to intimidate her – and me? If she can do it, I can.

'It's nothing really, just something niggling at me about

some of the stuff we used to get up to – and I didn't want to bother Liam.'

'He knows we're having lunch though, surely?'

'Of course.' He doesn't, but I'm not telling Drew that.

'Okay, well, what can I clear up for you?'

The waitress comes over before I can answer and Drew, true to form, orders for me.

Fillet steak for both of us, medium rare, pommes frites and a house salad – no dressing.

I don't stop thinking about Anna, imagining what she'd do if she were here. What she'd say. How she used to fight for what she believed in.

I took the piss out of her. But I can't stop thinking of the fervent look in her eye when she'd talk passionately about recycling or using cruelty free cosmetics, asking me if the shopping was fair-trade. When I looked in my mirror this morning, I had the same gleam in my eye. It's almost like she's here with me, part of me. Maybe she has been all along.

'I want to know more about the parties.'

'What parties?'

He dabs his napkin across his lips. I'd not noticed how fastidious he was, almost girlish in his mannerisms, the precise way he places his cutlery down on his plate when he picks up his wine glass, or selects bread to butter.

'The parties we used to go to – with your friends? And mine?'

'I went to a lot of parties, you'll have to be more specific.'

Blood leeches across our plates as we eat, mingling with the frites.

'They used to be at that members' club Liam belonged to. With the fancy ballroom.'

'Again, you'll need to be more specific. And why do you want to know anyway?'

'I... need to be sure, before Liam and I get married. About something.'

All of this is going to get straight back to Liam, but right now I don't care.

'We've all done things we're not proud of, but I'm telling you, you've got a good one with Liam. Put the past behind you, don't meddle around in things that don't concern you.'

'That's not very reassuring.'

'What is it you're worried about? Him cheating on you? That whole "marrying your mistress, leaves a vacancy"? I promise you, there's nothing to worry about. Sabine is in the past, I never thought that would last anyway. You two though, you've got something special, something different.'

His tone is placatory, as if this has been easier than he thought. It's this that makes me dig deeper, no matter how much I want to listen, to believe.

Besides, it's not going to change anything, I'm still getting married. I love our life together, the life I've created for Anouk.

'I know you're right – perhaps it's all in my head. But I can't rest until I know for sure though. Then I can leave it all in the past.'

As I speak, something in his face closes up. He clanks down his cutlery and pushes his cuffs back, checks his watch, and signals to the waitress for the bill.

'Unfortunate as it may be, there were lots of lovely young ladies and lots of parties. However, with everything going on, my legal team has advised me not to speak about it...'

He sounds like a politician, reciting lines written for him in a boardroom somewhere else, very far from him, very far from dead girls in hotel rooms.

'I take it you mean all the stuff in the papers, about that dinner you spoke at.'

His jaw clenches. I can't believe I ever found him attractive.

'I've said everything I intend to say about that, to the press. If you have any other questions, I can't answer them.'

He's spooked now – he knows something and now I need to know what it is.

'Are you sure you can't remember anything about Anna? Because I remember another, different evening that you were also at – we were both at. And I woke up in the morning with a lovely ring of bruises on my neck.'

'I don't know what you're talking about. And you should be very careful making statements like that. Liam's rich, but he's not that rich. Libel can be costly.'

His face is flushed though, and not with wine. The waitress comes over with the card machine and he taps his phone against it with a thud. In another life, he'd be putting his hand on the waitress's bum, pulling her closer, asking her if he can buy her a drink, his voice low in her ear over the braying of his peers.

He gets up from the table.

'I'd say it's been a pleasure—'

'See you at the wedding, Drew. Thanks for your time.'

He stalks out, swerving through the tables, his phone clenched to his ear. Before the door closes behind him, the strident tones of his voice carry back, berating someone.

It's not until I get the train home that I think to check my phone. Amongst the Instagram notifications and WhatsApps from wedding suppliers, I spot a LinkedIn message from Drew.

Only a few words, but it's enough for now.

> It's not me you should be asking about Anna.
>
> Try your precious fiancé.

TWENTY-TWO

Summer 2017

I don't often go in Liam's study – I have no need to. Either way, he's not protective about it. Always tells me he's got nothing to hide, and *what's mine is yours, darling, you know that*. So I don't expect to find a random phone in his desk drawer.

To be clear, I wasn't snooping, I needed a tape measure. I wanted to check something for the wedding gift list. And he keeps all sorts of crap in there. Receipts, empty painkiller boxes, a prescription for sleeping tablets he's not picked up – *I need to remind him about that*.

When I see the phone, I think for a moment he's left his usual one at home. But then I remember he was texting me this morning.

The phone comes to life in my hand though. It's got seventy-five per cent battery and it's connected to our Wi-Fi. There's no picture as a wallpaper though.

I don't remember Liam saying he had a separate work phone – or any other phone, to be honest. I suppose at this point I should assume he's using it to message other women.

I put it back in the drawer though, I know well enough not to ask questions I don't want the answer to. I keep rifling through the junk, pulling out piles of torn paper and dumping it on the desk as I search. The tape measure isn't in there, so I resign myself to having to buy a new one and start to put everything back in.

I pile back in the pens and pencils, the stapler, the old phone, but save the papers to put in the bin. God knows why he's keeping them. They're all scribbled on, so not even good as scrap paper. I never had Liam as a hoarder. When I go to grab the papers, the writing on them catches my eye. It's my writing. What the fuck? I stop where I am and spread the pieces out on the kitchen table.

He's somehow found the letters Sophie sent me. And he's torn them up, they're just scraps of paper – he's even destroyed Anna's letter to me. The one she didn't send. A blaze of heat rips through me, so strong, I'm amazed I don't combust. These letters weren't his to touch, to read. The last piece of Anna I had, and he's destroyed it. I don't know what to do. I want to believe it's a mistake, an accident, maybe he didn't realise what he had. Maybe that's why he's got them, to stop me finding out? I clutch at straws, trying to calm down. It's only mid-morning, there's hours and hours to go until Liam's home. And it might as well be aeons, the way time crawls past, sluggish and torpid, as I wait for answers. All I can do is piece Anna's letter to me back together and pace the kitchen, trying to work out what all this means.

Of course, Liam doesn't get home until late. I've bathed Anouk and put her to bed, Liam's boys are with Sabine. I sit on the sofa in the den and drink Pinot Grigio, going back and forth in my head about it all; why would he do this?

When he walks in the door though, I don't bother playing it cool. We're getting married, I don't need to coax information out of him via lace and suspenders anymore. And Liam's too smart for that anyway. Sometimes the best way to get something is to ask for it. You just need to know what and when.

I leave Anna's torn letter on the kitchen table, by the fridge, alongside a pile of my torn-apart letters to her. As soon as he comes home, he always grabs a cold drink – beer, wine, juice, whatever. I know he can't miss the pieces of papers.

'Hey! How was your day?'

He kisses me on the cheek on the way to the fridge. I can tell he's been smoking again. I keep warning him about the risks, but he likes to think he's Don Draper. I keep telling him diseased lungs aren't sexy, but he only looks at me and I remember all the times before, when we smoked in bed after. The way his face looked as he inhaled, the intensity of the pull of the nicotine and the hit to our bloodstreams. Even now, with the bubbling rage inside of me, part of me wants to take him by the hand, lead him upstairs, draw the curtains, forget the world. He has me so well trained.

'Good, thanks. Finalising some stuff for the wedding.'

'I hope that the planner we hired is helping – you're not doing too much yourself. Save some energy for me?'

And when our eyes meet, it's there again, the desire to lie back, close my eyes. Let him do to me the things we do in the dark. But I need to focus.

'What's this?' He points at the kitchen table, the letter I've reassembled.

'I don't know, you tell me. I found it in your desk drawer.'

'What were you doing in my desk?' His tone is mildly affronted, even as he uncaps a beer. He's such a politician, waiting to map out the landscape before deciding on a response.

'Looking for a tape measure. How about you tell me what my personal letters were doing in there?'

'I don't know what you're talking about.'

The never explain, never complain strategy, a play of his I

am familiar with from when we worked together. Deny all knowledge even when confronted with evidence.

'Let me explain it, then. These pieces of paper are torn up letters from me, to my friend Anna, and from Anna to me. You remember Anna, don't you?'

He has the grace to blush.

'I do remember Anna, yes – such a tragedy if I recall correctly.'

'Then what I don't understand is why you tore up the letters.'

'Darling,' he edges closer to me, the bomb disposal expert, ready with the pliers once he finds the correct wire to snip, 'I'm so sorry. I wanted to tell you, I did. I thought they were Anouk's. Just silly little letters to Beckie, her usual nonsense, and I tore them up for scrap.'

His is such a rational, logical answer. It's almost too obvious. I want to believe him, I do. I can't help but feel like I'm being managed though.

'But why did you put them in your drawer?'

'Well, I caught sight of the writing and realised my mistake – I was horrified of course, I know how close you were. I know how much you meant to each other. I didn't know how to begin to tell you and then I simply forgot. I'm so sorry.'

It's such a bare-faced lie, he tells it so well. But I'm sure he did it on purpose. It's all part of a bigger test.

He's watching me, waiting to see if I take the bait. He's got me backed up against the kitchen worktop.

'Right.'

'I said I was sorry.'

'I heard you the first time.' If I explain to him what the letters meant, I'm playing into his hands. The air is thick between us, each of us wrestling for control.

'I know I fucked up, I know I should have said something. Forgive me, please. Tell me what I can do.'

There's only one play I can make here. One way to have the upper hand. The thought of it as satisfying as the cold glass of wine I've drunk, as soothing as fresh sheets on my skin, as intense as the slap of his palm against my skin, in the dark.

'It's fine. Ignore me. I'm making a fuss about nothing. I'm being silly.'

And just like that, the tension seeps away, air from a popped balloon.

He leans forward, kisses my cheek.

'I love you.'

'Love you too.'

He steps back, drinks his beer, looks at the table, the letters.

'Want me to help you stick them back together?'

'It's fine. I'll put them in the recycling.'

In some ways, he's done me a favour. Anna's words are burned into me anyway, seared by the memories I have of her. I don't need the letter to remind me. I need to focus on my future. I know I need answers to questions though. And this only makes me realise this more.

Because if he's lying to me about the letters, what else is he lying about?

And does he realise he's not the only one lying in this relationship? Or at least, withholding the truth.

If he ever chose to look, he'd see it – living right under his roof.

TWENTY-THREE

Autumn 2017

I know it's a cliché, but your wedding day really does go past in a blur, no matter how many times you've been around the block. When I look back on the day, there's only a few snapshots left in my mind. Because there's nothing to eclipse the day you become someone's wife, like becoming their widow.

We arrived in Sorrento for what the wedding planner termed a 'week-long pre-moon', and what Liam termed, 'the calm before the storm'. The reality was somewhere in between. As a result, I took a dip in the plunge pool on the hotel's roof terrace at the end of each day. The pool is unheated, and as such, often empty. It is there for the hotel Instagram, for people to take pictures of the molten ball of the sun to drop into the bay of Naples, for people like us to arrange their bronzed, toned limbs for the camera.

I like to swim lengths, underwater, breaststrokes, holding my breath for as long as it takes for black poppies to form in my vision. For my skin to pebble over with cold and my lips, hands, and feet to become bloodless. When I emerge, minutes – or decades it seems – later, I am a nereid, a goddess, a nymph, in time to watch the world turn to gold and the endorphins to swarm my blood the way the mosquitos pester people staying on the ground floor.

Liam tells me to stop, that I'll catch a chill, offers to order champagne, a negroni, an Aperol spritz, anything to get me out of the pool. It is a rebirth of sorts, a baptism.

When I look back at our wedding day, this is what I remember: walking down the aisle of the ballroom, my silk skirts blowing in the light sea breeze. The walls of the room were buttercup yellow, with gold framed renaissance masterpieces on the walls, the wedding guests in tulle-draped Louis XV chairs. I felt like I was ascending to heaven, towards everything I'd earned waiting at the end of the aisle, Liam and Drew in their matching white suits. Anouk in her broderie anglaise tea dress, her little posy of wildflowers.

The look on Liam's face when he promised for richer or poorer, in sickness and in health. The look on his face when I promised to love, honour – and obey. The vows we were really making that day. What we were really saying. The secrets we knew about each other. The secrets we would keep about each other.

I was so stupid. It's the only thing I regret – marrying him. I wish I'd been smarter. He promised everything I thought I needed – security, love of sorts. I should have trusted my gut. I knew something was wrong, but I thought that's what I liked about him. And with weddings it's like you're on some relentless path that starts with hopes and dreams, and ends at an altar. And we all know what altars are for.

Liam only has himself to blame, the way it all turned out.

. . .

Liam doesn't say anything until we're seated at the top table for the meal. The speeches are done and everyone is in their cups, as Shakespeare might say. The amount of food at an Italian wedding feast is something to behold. Course after course of delectable dishes, each cooked to perfection. Pasta dressed with the lightest touch of oil, garlic, parmesan, shavings of truffle. Sea bass cooked with clams and mussels in white wine with tiny crisp squares of potato. Tender green beans and long stem broccoli dressed in lemon juice and butter. And then basil and lime sorbet, like fireworks in your mouth.

But now, after the lavender panna cotta, and the champagne, and the cutting of the cake, flavoured with pistachio and verbena, now we are here and heavy, replete, lounging like Roman emperors and empresses.

'I think it's really good that you went through with it all, after what he did.'

Drew is seated to my right, at the top table, as best man. My mother is on his other side, Anouk to her right, smiling as she finishes her second slice of cake before heading to the dance floor.

Drew is ruddy from the sunshine and the booze. Garlic tinges his breath and his shirt clings damply to him. He's already gotten the beautiful, young waitress with Bambi eyes and long brown curls to wait on him hand and foot, to bring him off-menu requests and drinks. He thinks she's a sure thing. She thinks he is too – but in a completely different way, more interested in the contents of his wallet and the tip he might leave her, than anything else in his trousers.

'Oh, well...'

'He's so lucky to have you. That you forgave him. It was pretty bad, even by my standards!'

And he chuckles as if everything they do is just a jolly jape, just another benefit that comes with being male, rich, white, older. Which in his – and Liam's – world, it is.

He turns so we're facing each other, puts his arm along the back of my chair. It's intimate. You'd think I'd married *him*, the chair to my left is empty, Liam is off glad-handing some acquaintance I was told we had to invite.

'Well, I love him. And you forgive the people you love.'

Liam and Drew are competitive in an odd way – I've never seen two friends who love undermining each other like they do.

'I didn't think you'd forgive him for this though, especially after the whole Instagram thing too. I know I couldn't trust someone who did that to me.'

My skin prickles at this.

'What Instagram thing?'

Drew smiles.

'I thought you knew?'

I think back to the phone on the drawer. Maybe the torn letters were only part of this?

'Drew, darling, I know you like shit-stirring, but nothing you tell me could change the fact that I'm in love with Liam.'

'Really?' He raises an eyebrow and then sips his whisky. 'So you don't care that it was him that leaked your pictures to the school?'

I still, trying to hide what I'm really feeling. 'Why are you telling me this now? You had plenty of opportunities before.'

He shakes his head.

'I thought you were smarter than this, Ems. He's not perfect, your husband. I know you idolise him.'

'But—'

'I'm just giving you a friendly warning to watch out. I know you wanted this, you did from the start – don't pretend you didn't, all those years ago. And I know about your other secret too.'

My stomach drops. *How does he know about that?*

'I see right through you, Emily, and you know I don't blame you. You've used everything in your power to get the best life for yourself and your daughter – security, wealth. I'm just saying don't relax now, not for a minute. You think you know Liam, but you don't, not really. You have no idea what he's capable of.'

He's hissing into my ear now, his breath clammy against my skin. Gone is the enigmatic tech visionary and underneath is still the skinny ginger kid who got bullied at school. Who hated Liam for his popularity and success with girls. Jealousy is a powerful emotion.

'Right. Drew, you've clearly got something to say, so say it, instead of bullshitting about how I don't know my husband. Otherwise, I'm getting up and walking away.'

Even as I speak I wonder if perhaps I've picked a scab, that maybe I don't want to hear the answer to this question. But as I used to tell clients, it's all about making informed decisions. I reach down for my bag, under the table, full of bridal necessities like breath mints and baby wipes, pull out my phone and set it to record, hiding it under my napkin.

'You asked me about Anna... well, it wasn't an overdose. He called me in a right state that night. Said something had gone wrong.'

The sounds of the crowd drop away, as I lock eyes with Liam across the room and hear what Drew is really telling me. His voice is hypnotic.

'I went to meet him and I could see her in the bed. I knew straight away it was bad, really bad.'

'So... what did you do?'

Liam is starting to walk across to us. I don't have much time but Drew carries on.

'I told him to call reception. To tell them there'd been an accident. That she'd fallen and hurt herself. And to go back to the room he had with you. I stayed there and waited for the reception staff. I told them that she'd called me, said she wasn't feeling good – but that when I got there, I found her.'

'*You* found her...?'

The papers had reported that no one was with her, that she was found in the bath, accidental drowning due to the drug overdose. Knowing that they had the presence of mind to do this – both the killing and the cover-up – is sending chills down my spine. I can't even imagine what she went through.

I need to hear him say it.

'She was dead.' He pauses for a moment, as if picturing it all. Dead bodies aren't sexy. People shit and piss themselves when they die. The indignity Anna suffered, kills me.

'The hotel manager was a friend, he didn't need the bad publicity. We agreed it was all a terrible accident – the police agreed too. Poor girl, just shouldn't have been taking drugs or drinking – well, you remember the headlines.'

I do indeed, all the victim blaming and the lies. I knew Anna hadn't overdosed; I *knew* it.

Liam is seconds away. From the set of his head, I think he has his suspicions. I rearrange my features into the smiling, seductive woman he loves. That he thinks he knows.

Meanwhile in my head, it's like all the buildings in a city are falling down, cut off at the knees, imploding. Somehow, I know Drew is telling the truth this time.

Behind it all though, is Anna's voice, whispering in my mind. *You always knew, didn't you?* Did I? I remember waking up that night in an empty bed, but then in the morning Liam was there. Surely he'd just gone to the bathroom. Hadn't he?

The idea that Liam could have done it cracks my skull open like a sledgehammer.

At the table I struggle to comprehend the enormity of what Drew is saying – implying. I know she never would have gone with him willingly. And Drew seems to be a mind reader in that respect.

'You know, he always wanted her. Even though you brought her for me. He hated her for the hold she had over you. He said he'd show her what it was like to be with a man. What she was missing out on. And you know your husband – he doesn't take no for an answer.'

'That he doesn't.'

Liam is back at the table, drawing out his chair, sitting down, allowing the waiter to replace his linen napkin on his lap, and order a drink.

'This all looks very cosy! How's my gorgeous wife?'

He pulls my hand to his mouth, kisses it, entwines his fingers with mine.

'No escape now!' Drew laughs as he says it, but his eyes shift away from mine and he pales slightly. He knows he's said too much.

I switch off my phone, tuck it away.

'Nope! Till death do us part.'

Bile burns inside me. Nails clawing at my insides. I imagine how she tried to fight him off, the way I did that rugby boy outside the pub in Oxford. How I wasn't there to defend her the way she did me.

Liam is so big, he must have snapped her like a twig, my fiery little Anna. I wonder if she decided it was safer not to fight him. To know her protests would only turn him on more. To lie there, still and silent, until it was over. The thought is killing me. And yet my face is a mask, a rictus grin as I smile and pose for photos, the blushing bride.

All the time though, I can imagine him, with his hands around her neck, smacking her head into the bedhead, pinioning her between his thighs. I can imagine it because I've been there.

Funny how something as simple as words, jumbles of sounds, can cause the tectonic plates of my life to shift and grind against each other, until it seems like the world as I know it is a completely different place, totally alien. A barren minefield, and I have no way of knowing how to cross it, without dying.

I detangle my fingers from Liam's, tell him I'm going to powder my nose, that I'll be right back.

But when I get outside the ballroom, I can't face the fancy bathrooms with their obsequious attendants and having to talk to all our guests. So I gather my wedding dress and go outside, stand on the balcony for air.

It's quiet now, past golden hour, no one spots me in the encroaching dusk, on the corner over the ocean.

What should I do, Anna? I want to ask her. *Tell me.*

Tears prick at the back of my throat. Somewhere distant, someone is playing Britpop. I can hear a song about trash, and remember Anna playing this over and over again in halls. I can smell CK One and feel the sticky roll-on glitter we'd slather ourselves in, the smudgy eyeliner Anna would tolerate, her scuffed Chucks. And how she'd sing this song to me, how she loved it, how she said it was about us.

For a brief moment in time, it's like she's there with me. I imagine what she'd say about this incredible hotel, this beach, the view, the expense.

Waste of money if you ask me, better off in the pub. Bet you don't even know half these people. Why bother?

And she'd ask me, *Are you sure? Do you love him?*

And then, I realise she'd actually say, *Is love enough?*

Right now, Anna, I want to say, *right now, it really isn't.* And I'm not sure it ever will be. But it's too late. We're married.

Liam finds me in the end, of course he does. I can't hide forever, not at my own wedding.

He corners me, a huntsman with a fox, Drew beside him, semaphoring *danger* with his eyebrows. But maybe Liam is not the only danger.

'Here you are, my lovely bride. What are you doing, hiding out here?'

He signals to a waiter and two glasses of champagne appear. It's a clever magic trick. Because isn't that what magic is, power and distraction? Drew backs away as Liam walks closer – holding out the coupe, Hades with the pomegranate.

I take the glass and drain it. Ready to hurl myself into the psychological abyss that waits.

'Look at the view, isn't it wonderful?' I say.

'Definitely worth the money,' he concurs, putting an arm around my waist, fitting me to him, the way he always has. But in place of the desire that normally fills me, no matter what, there is a different fire in my belly.

'Are you happy?' I ask him.

'Always, my love, always with you.'

'Even after all this time?'

'Of course. It's only ever been you.'

I'm sure he told Sabine the same thing.

'What were you talking to Drew about?'

'Oh nothing, reminiscing mainly about the parties and stuff.' I wave a hand.

'Oh yes?' He raises an eyebrow. 'Not remembering too much I hope.'

Immediately, I know he's talking about the night I had with Drew.

He's so confident that I don't know about him and Anna. That if I did, he'd know too.

'Of course not. Just saying that I miss Anna.'

His face doesn't change, but he stills.

'Such a tragedy when she died, terrible accident.'

He sets his glass down and cups my face in his hands, as if I am some ingenue and we are in a silent movie. 'I hate to think of you being in pain.'

It's such a pretence, I've never seen it clearly before. Any of it. The carefully orchestrated dance, the way he manipulates me, so I am exactly where he wants. I know it's always been this way. But now, when it's too late, I don't want it anymore, despite what I've done to our lives – mine, Anouk's, Pete's.

'Did you ever find out what happened to her?' I say casually. 'Her parents were devastated. Did I tell you I still speak to them?'

He blanches slightly. *Good.*

'It was an accident – she fell and hit her head.'

I have him. Drew also told me that they got the hotel to put a different story in the news, and someone – Drew didn't say who, only making a comment about friends in high places – ensured that the police didn't leak the truth to the press. It seems no one apart from Drew, Liam, the hotel, the police – and now me – know the truth. The fire inside me takes hold, crackles and ripples through me. I want to burn down the entire fucking old boys club that has led to this, all the abuse, the attacks, the cover ups, the deaths of young women, loved like Anna was loved.

'I thought the coroner said she'd died by accidental drug overdose, drowned in the bath?'

He looks at me.

'I know what you did, Liam.' I pull him close so anyone walking onto the balcony would think we were embracing, kissing, and leave us alone. I twine my arms around his neck.

'I know you killed her,' I whisper, and then I pull his head down so his lips meet mine.

Even as he kisses me, the tension in his body radiates out to meet mine. He kisses me harder, so hard I pull back and put a finger to my mouth – it comes away wet and red.

'You bit me,' I say.

'You bit me first.'

He hasn't denied it. He heard what I said.

'Who are you?'

'I could ask you the same thing,' he says, looking at me, his pupils are pinpricks. I wonder what he's taken. I wonder if he's always been taking things.

'We need to talk.'

'Sure, anytime, we have the rest of our lives to choose from.'

'You're so funny.' I take his hand and pull him back inside, swing our arms playfully. When we walk into the ballroom we're greeted with cheers and whoops. It's late, people are dancing, ties and jackets and shoes have come off. Anouk is dancing with my mum and Drew. I want to pull her away, but Liam and I join them as the music changes to a slow song.

I sway in Liam's arms and watch Anouk and Mum.

'Anouk's been great today.'

'Well, of course. And doesn't she look gorgeous?'

'She is her mother's daughter!'

I lie my head on Liam's shoulder, and then whisper, but clearly so he can hear over the music.

'She's yours, you know.'

This time he does react – pulls me away from him, tilts his head to one side.

I spin and make him pull me in close again.

'I told you we needed to talk.'

I wake early the next morning, very early, still in my wedding dress; I am alone.

Last night, we didn't make love, we made hate. Every movement, every bite and scratch and cut and kick. Afterwards, I hated myself more than him, for letting him do it again, even though I knew it was goodbye before he did. There is no way I can stay with him now.

Liam called me a parasite, crawling around under his skin, feeding off him. But the only way he could survive was to feed right back off me. But I didn't say anything, because by that stage, I knew it wasn't love anymore. Or anything other than what it was, destructive and toxic, and poisonous.

And what do you do with poison – you suck it out of yourself. There's no point in slowly waiting to die, every day for the rest of your life.

But then he told me he didn't believe me, that Anouk was his.

'You were sleeping with me, and Pete, and fuck knows who else. You were a bitch on heat back then. Is she Drew's?'

But I ignored him, because I expected this. Or at least I didn't expect any better, just showed him the paternity test I'd done, without him knowing.

'It's fake.'

'It's not.'

'You can't do these things without my consent.'

'Actually I can. She's yours.'

He laughed then. 'You think I want some bastard daughter?'

I slapped him across the face then, but he only caught me by the wrist.

'Will she be a little spitting hellcat like her mother?'

'Will she be a raping murderer like her father?'

He let go of me then.

'Keep your voice down.'

'You've not denied it.'

Behind me on the nightstand is my phone. I turn away under the pretext of taking a drink of water, but instead I again set my phone to record, my stomach churning. But he's slumped in a chair, drinking whisky.

'You'll only believe what you want. And what are you going to do with the truth anyway? Who'll believe you? Who'll even care? You're not going to drag that frigid French bitch and her cripple of a husband through some horrendous legal battle to try to get me put away, they've not got the money and he's not got the time left.'

I knew he was baiting me, mentioning Anna's family. He wanted a fight. But I wasn't going to give him that.

'I think we should stop now, Liam, before we both say something we regret.'

'Oh, it's like that is it? You want the truth but now you're all holier than thou? Fuck that. I did it, okay? I fucked your little friend and I fucking loved it. She was petrified, the stupid bitch. At first she tried to say that it was okay, she wouldn't tell anyone.

'But eventually she started screaming, and I couldn't be doing with that – someone would notice and call reception. So I got a little rough. But you know, you like that. How am I supposed to know she'd break like porcelain?'

He stops, he's panting, he wipes his brow as he looks at me.

'Tell me what you did to her, Liam.'

'You're so fucking messed up. Are you getting off on this?'

'If it helps you to believe that, then yes. But tell me, I need to know what you did to her, you animal.'

'I didn't think she was dead at first. There was very little blood. But then I shook her, and she didn't move. Her eyes were open, but she didn't blink. I never meant to kill her. But she was asking for it. She laughed at me, you know, when I was fucking her. Fucking bitch.'

I breathe in and I breathe out. Tremble inside.

I shift slightly, wary he will catch a glimpse of the light from my phone, even though I've flipped it over and put something next to it. I hope it's catching everything.

'So, there you go. Happy now? What else do you want? You're not going to divorce me. You like this life too much. You like me too much.'

Except I am. I am leaving him. I can't do this anymore.

'I'm not going to divorce you because that would be too easy. And also you'd drag all sorts of muck through the courts about me being an unfit mother. I saw you do that to Sabine, don't forget.'

'So, what are you going to do?' For a moment, I wonder if he's scared.

'Nothing. I'm going to forget you said anything. I'm going to go and wash my face and brush my teeth and then I'm going to get into bed and forget this whole conversation happened. And in the morning, everything will be like it was.'

My defence argued that it was an accident, that he was in a rage and hurrying after me, but that he tripped and fell, hitting his head on the bedside table.

I'd testified that I remembered him coming at me, reaching for me. I tried to evade him, I had my hands out in front of me to get past him – but after that, there's nothing, a blank spot in my memory.

The next morning, I woke up in the lounge of our suite. The door to the bedroom was closed and I knew I didn't want to open it. But I couldn't remember why. The psychiatrist that assessed me told me that memory problems are common after great trauma.

I called Drew, told him I had some more questions and it was fine – Liam knew and everything was okay, but as he was still asleep, could we have a quick coffee? I could come to his room?

This is all so etched in my memory, reported on in the papers, word for word from the trial. But sometimes I wonder how much my mind is filling in the blanks. How much is what I thought I did, versus what actually happened.

The media made a big deal about me calling Drew. That I was so callous as to walk out of our suite, leaving behind my new husband's corpse to have a doppio espresso with his best friend.

The media were not shocked about anything that Liam did. Because, of course, my defence team used the recording on my phone, his confession in the bedroom. But even with the protests outside the court, the press know what makes the real money. And that's stories of ageing second wives, MILFs who go crazy and kill their husbands.

In the end they got what they wanted, the media – they got a spectacle, when I was found guilty of manslaughter, despite everything. They'd been gunning for a verdict of murder, but I know there were people on the jury who believed me. Women like me. Because we're everywhere. In your offices and your shops and your schools and your hospitals. In your homes, in your families, and most importantly, in your beds. Victims and survivors.

TWENTY-FOUR

October 2023
Naomi

It's one of my last days on campus when I receive the letter from Brigham. I'm all packed up, ready to drive back down to London, without Max. It was inevitable really, our break-up. Apparently I wasn't there for him enough, too engrossed in finishing my thesis. Last thing I heard, he's dating some philosophy undergrad.

I'm moving back home so I can work on converting my thesis to a book. I signed with an agent in the summer, so now it's a case of getting my head down and cracking on. Mum wants me to come home so I can run interference between her and the girls, who are apparently *hellish teenage gobshites*. It'll be nice to see my sisters again. It's a long time since we all lived together though. In fact, we've never really lived together because I left for uni pretty soon after Pete and Mum got together.

It's an overcast, blustery autumn day, all the beauty of the leaves long gone, just dirty mush on the pavements and blocking gutters, reminding me of the first visit to Brigham in prison. When I walk into the department, the wind blows the door shut behind me, the sound echoing down the corridor. It's a quiet week – the end of October is an unofficial reading week, although I suspect it's more to enable the professors to take half term off for their kids. Or that's what it seems like in any case.

When I walk past the office, Deirdre calls me in.

'Hello there, Dr McKenzie! All set to leave us?'

I greet her with a hug and a box of chocolates. Anyone in academia knows that the office administrators and secretaries really run the show, keep the wheels on. I'll miss them, their comfort and support, mopping up tears, endless cups of coffee, their quiet chatter and gossip. Mum would be horrified; it's very anti-feminist she thinks, to have so many women supporting men in such an old school way. But I like their softness, because I know behind it is steel. After all, as anyone knows, if you want something done, you ask a woman. But she's right, they don't get anywhere near enough credit for all they do.

'I'm going to miss you so much.' To my surprise my voice cracks.

'Oh, duck, we'll miss you too. Leaving us to deal with all these bloody freshers. We're so proud of you, you know.'

Deirdre read my thesis. She was one of the interviewees. Very early on, when I was looking for volunteers to talk about their stories, their experiences, she knocked on my door. I've anonymised her in the book, but her story of groping at photocopiers, 'banter', drunken office party assaults, could be any of us. It kills me sometimes, realising how lucky I am. That the worst I've experienced is the odd catcall, the odd dick pic. And even then, I shouldn't need to count myself lucky.

'I wouldn't be here without you. Thank you so much. For everything.'

I look at her and she knows what I mean.

'You keep fighting the good fight, pet. We'll be here for you.

You let us know when that book of yours is published and we'll all buy a copy.'

Deirdre wasn't the only one in the office to share her story. There are others – men and women – who came forward. I'm not planning a #MeToo style take down of academia, but I know journalists who would be interested.

'If it's published. *If.*'

'Don't be ridiculous. I believe in you, we all do. You'll be a bestseller before you know it.' And she hugs me again. 'Before I forget, a letter came for you – it's here somewhere. I kept it for you as I didn't think you'd be back to check your pigeonhole.'

She steps over to her desk and pulls a white envelope from a pile. The stamp of the prison is visible from where I stand.

'I expect you know who it's from.'

I didn't tell many people I was interviewing Brigham. I didn't want her notoriety to colour my interactions with her, any more than they had to – dealing with Max was bad enough, and of course, our family history. I did tell Deirdre though.

When she hands the envelope over she raises her eyebrows at me. 'I thought you told her story well. Showing what she went through. Sympathetic, but holding her to account.'

'Thank you, I appreciate that.' It's true, I do, though I still worry I was too sympathetic.

'I still don't understand the relationship she had with him though. How could she go through with the wedding?' Deirdre bunches her lips.

'I know. But we have to try to be objective, just because someone isn't a nice person, doesn't mean they don't deserve justice.'

'But she took the law into her own hands. Doesn't that make her no better than him?'

It's a question I've asked myself many times over the past few months.

'I think it's about power, and privilege. And who holds the balance.'

'Is it?' And she looks at me. I wonder if I'm defending a monster. Or if sometimes monsters deserve defending. She still claims it was an accident, from what she can remember.

'That whole nature versus nurture thing. It's so fascinating. They've done studies—'

The phone rings, and I've lost her.

There's something Max said to me though, when he heard I wanted to write my book. *Who benefits here, Nay? Are you glamorising her? Isn't this why we have a justice system?*

I can't lie, I know how much the true crime industry is worth. But I need to make a living. Isn't that all any of us are trying to do, just live, just survive. Isn't that all Brigham was trying to do? Fighting for something we all want.

Freedom.

Dear Naomi,

Firstly, congratulations on finishing your thesis. I knew you'd do it. Is it weird to say that I'm proud of you? I'm sure your mother is. Sometimes it's strange to think that if things had worked out differently, you'd just be Pete's stepdaughter, Anouk's big stepsister. But now you're so much more than that.

I wanted to write to you before now, but I thought I'd give you some space. I imagine you've been busy. I miss you though. I miss our chats. The way you suspended time for me, for that one hour.

I'm sure you're surprised to hear from me though. I bet you thought we were done. After all, I gave you what you wanted, didn't I?

I hope you sell your book, I'm sure you will, I know there are many people who want to hear what I have to say. And of course, all those other women you interviewed. I know I wasn't the only one. Victim, that is, I wasn't the only victim.

You helped me see that's what I am. Victim and survivor. That my story was only ever going to end one way. Doomed from the start by society, isn't that how you phrased it?

And that's why I'm writing to you, because there's one last piece of the puzzle that I didn't tell you, but I wanted you to have it now.

Before I tell you though, I need you to do something for me. There's another letter in here – it's not for you. But if you can follow the instructions on the envelope, that would be great. Anouk might need your help too, in finding what I've left for her. Call it a gift, and what you do with it, when you find it, is up to you. You're smart girls, you'll know the right thing to do.

You know you were special to me. I saw a lot of me in you. Drive, passion, perseverance, single-mindedness; you weren't afraid of me. And that's because somewhere inside you, there's a wolf also. You hunt for answers like me, and you'll destroy anything that gets in your way.

I need you to understand that everything I did, I did for Anouk. To keep her safe. She has money now. She won't ever have to do what I did, to survive. She won't ever need to rely on a man – or a woman. She can get by, alone, on her own terms. She's safe with you and Sarah, and Pete, and Liam's money is in a trust for her when she turns eighteen. I might be in prison, but knowing this makes me so happy.

But now, the truth. If you're still reading this, that's what you're waiting for, isn't it?

You see, I've spent hours wondering how long it took Anna to die, if she begged for help. I've tortured myself with the thought of her in agony. As much as Liam said it was instant, I'm not so sure. The autopsy was false, the coroner bought off. So, I have no reason to believe any of it was the way Liam said. And also, I knew him, I knew how he revelled in power, holding the decision over life or death, balancing it all on a knife edge, would have been intoxicating for him.

It took Liam 37 minutes and 15 seconds to die. I know because I counted every single second after I shoved him. Yes, I know, we said it was an accident, that I didn't remember. And in my defence, none of it was premeditated. But once he lay there on the floor, a shadowy red pool spreading out under his head, I did nothing except watch, and think of Anna.

At first he asked for help, slurring and slow. He tried to reach out to me, to grab on to me. The look on his face moving from pleading to surprise to sorrow, to fear.

But I still didn't move. Hoping he too was thinking of Anna's last moments. After about ten minutes, he fell unconscious and after that it was only a matter of time. I didn't call for help until the following morning, after I'd seen Drew. And by then it was all too late.

I know that makes me sound heartless. I've had a lot of time to think about regret. Was it wrong? Am I remorseful? If I had my time again would I have sought help sooner? But I don't think I'd change a thing. It was the only way he'd ever face any sort of justice for what he did to Anna – and to me – and probably to countless other women. The deck was stacked against all of us. We'd never win in a court. So instead of trying to win the game, I changed the game.

I hope you'll think about that, as you get older. When you're trying to manoeuvre your way through life, like levels in a game, remember you have the choice to completely change what you're doing. And not play by anyone else's rules...

Tell Anouk I love her. Tell her I hope one day she'll visit me, please.

Maybe you could come with her?

I hope so.

All my best to you

Emily B x

TWENTY-FIVE

January 2024

It's a bitterly cold day in January when Anouk and I make the trip across London, to visit Anna's grave. It's frosty and overcast, and the sky is heavy with the promise of snow.

The envelope Brigham – she will always be Brigham to me, she never legally changed her name to Acaster after the wedding – left for Anouk, had clear instructions to find a box in her own bedroom, at the back of her wardrobe. Anouk was baffled because we've moved house since her mother went away. But Emily was clever. Inside an old shoe box, with school reports and medals from long ago school sports days, was a jiffy bag with Anouk's name on it and inside was a USB stick with a Post-it that read '*play me*'.

It's funny, being with Anouk now, having spent so much time with her mother, how similar they are in both looks and personality, despite the time apart. Under the heavy eyeliner and the nose piercing, Anouk has the same bone structure, that beautiful smile, and her mother's charisma. I'm not surprised Beckie hung off her every word even in nursery.

When we plugged in the USB stick we weren't sure what to expect. There was only a single video file. But as soon as we watched it, we knew what to do. Neither of us have a clue how Brigham smuggled this recording of Drew's confession out of Italy and into the UK – much less got it into a box in Anouk's wardrobe. All we can think of is that she paid someone to post it – the jiffy bag has Italian stamps on it, dating from her wedding. It still shows a foresight and clear thinking during a crisis that neither of us could hope to possess – but certainly shows how Brigham has been such a powerhouse at work – and in life.

As we surface at Highgate Station, our phones ping with BBC news notifications. Anouk punches the air as she reads the headline and then hugs me.

'We did it! You did it! I can't believe it.'

And then she bursts into loud sobs.

Anouk's relationship with her mother is complex. She's never visited her in prison. She doesn't want to. She has a therapist, and we go through periods of family counselling also, and she has a close support network of friends. I think maybe one day soon she will visit Brigham, especially now.

Over Anouk's heaving shoulder, as I hustle her towards a Starbucks before we head to the cemetery, I read the first line of the news story aloud.

'Drew Carson, billionaire and founder of tech mega platform BeeU, has been arrested on multiple charges of rape and assault.'

My phone bleeps with a text, telling me that none of this would be possible without Brigham's recording, which Anouk and I handed in to the police last autumn.

In the video, shot in his hotel room in Sorrento, crackly and muffled, you can just make out his face and his words as he talks about the parties Liam and his friends used to run. You'd think he'd be more discreet – and it seems like he was drunk when he said it, but apparently once Emily married Liam, he felt she deserved to know everything her husband got up to.

I wonder why Drew told her, why he was so indiscreet, openly talking about how they'd take advantage of drunk girls, plying them with drugs, evening alluding to giving them Rohypnol. He sniffs a lot during the video, rubs his nose from time to time and I wonder if the drug usage applied to him, even then.

He is guarded with names, dates, places in the video, but a few slip out towards the end and these the police dug into. Sometimes I wonder if he wanted to get caught. But it's more likely he was proud of what they did. His tone is boastful, not apologetic, even using the word untouchable. Or so he thought. Liam may have died for his sins, but Drew is finally getting his comeuppance and the satisfaction for me, even at my distance, is immense. I can only imagine what those women went through – apparently they started at university, my skin crawls at the thought.

I wonder if Brigham has seen the news too. Somehow I know she won't be celebrating. True justice for her is delivered in a very different way. But Drew's arrest is still a start. If we can bring him down, no one is safe anymore, not the men we work with, sleep with, even live with – no matter how protected they think they are. Perhaps men will learn to live with the fear women have experienced for centuries.

We're standing at Anna's grave when Anouk pulls out the letter from her mother that I gave her last autumn.

'You didn't want to read it before now?'

'She told me to save it for today – see?' She holds out the back of the envelope for me to see.

'This is weird, isn't it?'

'A bit, yeah.'

'You feeling okay?' She shivers in her padded jacket and huddles closer to me.

'Mmmmm, about as okay as I can be, standing by the grave of my incarcerated mother's dead best friend.

'Right.'

'I don't think I can do this.'

'Do you want me to read it to you?'

She shrugs, bites her already bitten nails.

'Actually yeah, would you?'

Something about her grumpy teenage girl attitude is so comforting, it's so normal, in what is such an abnormal situation. As tiny flakes of snow begin to swirl around us, I open the envelope, unfold the letter, and begin to read.

Dearest Anouk,

I've done a lot wrong in my life, but the one thing I got right was you. I've never been a maternal person, I think you know that, but I want you to know that I tried so hard for you.

Even though you weren't planned, from the second I saw those two lines on the test, I loved you. And when you were born, when they tore you from me, screaming your little lungs out, all that dark hair, I knew you were going to be my warrior queen, my little fighter. And you've never stopped fighting since, standing up for yourself and what you believe in.

Even though you don't visit, your daddy keeps me updated. I bet that's a surprise. But he does – your school reports, your achievements. But also how you are, your friendships, what you're reading and watching and listening to. The everyday stuff, the things I wish I could share with you. I wonder if you like the music I love, if you'd like Courtney Love or PJ Harvey. Women who fought in a man's world.

You probably don't realise but you're named for someone I loved once, almost as much as I love you. She was a fighter also. I think you would have liked each other. She'd be the cool aunt. And by cool, the one to help keep you straight. To remind you to study, to plan a career path, to stand up for what you believe in. She and I were very different.

Her name was Anouk too. But she preferred to be called Anna. If everything has gone to plan, you should be standing at her grave. Today would have been her 40th birthday. She died when she was 25, and it was my fault. She was my best friend.

I know you'll never understand why I did what I did. And I don't expect you to. Something I get asked a lot is if I regret what I did. It's a hard question to answer. But I've had a lot of time to reflect on it, over the years.

And my answer is, I do regret it. I am sorry. Not because I don't think he deserved it, or because he didn't have it coming, but because now I'm no better than him. I know I should have let him face the proper justice, but I would just remind you though, of the conviction rate for rapists.

I am sorry though, because even though in here I'm free in many ways that I never was before, it kills me that I haven't seen you grow up – and by the time I get out you'll be an adult.

So far you haven't wanted to see me, or speak to me. And that's entirely your right and your choice. But if you're still reading this letter, please know that with the money in trust, you have the freedom to do anything you want to do and to love anyone you want to love. To live without the unwritten rules I lived my life by. So, my darling girl, please do that. Please take my apology and my love, and be happy.

That's all I've ever wanted for you. It's not always easy to do, but just remember this – a witch is simply a woman with power. And there's nothing the world fears more than that.

I love you baby girl.

Be free.

Mum x

A LETTER FROM THE AUTHOR

Dear reader,

I can't believe you're holding my second book in your hands. This is all so unbelievably surreal still. Huge thanks for choosing to spend your precious time reading *The Second Marriage*. I hope you were hooked on Emily's journey and how she learns to take back control.

If you loved *The Second Marriage* and you want to join other readers in hearing all about my new releases and bonus content, you can sign up here:

www.stormpublishing.co/rebecca-de-winter

Also if you could spare few moments to leave a review that would be hugely appreciated. Even a short review can make all the difference in encouraging a reader to discover my books for the first time. Thank you so much!

I first had the idea for *The Second Marriage* in 2022. It came out of frustration that even in my 40s I was still having to text my friends that I'd gotten home safe, that I still get catcalled, when would it stop? And then I read an article about a woman who missed her 'pretty privilege' as she aged. And I wondered what happened to all of us who came of age in the nineties and noughties, when FHM and Page 3 and circle of shame existed, got older, became invisible to the world. And what we'd do as a result of that.

I'd also followed the trials of Harvey Weinstein, Jeffrey Epstein, Ghislaine Maxwell, the wave of #metoo stories across the world, and I reflected on the experiences I – and many of my friends – had at work, at school, everywhere really, that we would always be judged on looks first, ability second.

And I thought also about how hard it is for women to own their own sexuality, how sex workers are shamed and discriminated against, how older women and younger men are laughed at, the concept of mutton dressed as lamb.

I thought about an older woman, valued only for her looks from a young age, who used them in the only way she knew how – and what she might do when she realised how much more she could be...

Finally, thank you again so much for reading *The Second Marriage*. I'm so very grateful for all the readers that have come with me on my writing journey so far. I wouldn't be here without you.

I love hearing from you and what you're reading and what you think of my books, so please do stay in touch – you can find me on X, Facebook and Instagram – I have so many more stories and ideas to entertain you with!

Thank you again,

Rebecca de Winter

- facebook.com/rebeccadmwilliams
- x.com/stupidgirl45
- instagram.com/rebeccadwinter

ACKNOWLEDGEMENTS

And finally, the most exciting part of writing a book for me, getting to thank all the amazing people who helped this book on its way.

First up, yet again, the best co-parents a book baby could ever hope for, Alison at LBA and Kathryn at Storm. Thank you for not thinking I was totally bonkers when I said I wanted to write a book that was a modern-day cross between Madame Bovary and Belle de Jour – and then I proceeded to write a novel which was exactly not that. Thank you for helping me decide the best platforms for people to send nude pictures on, giving me a swear words allocation (how many f**ks is too many f**ks?) and particularly Kathryn, all your lovely – and funny comments as we co-edit the book! This book is definitely less violent than its older sibling, but sorrynotsorry for all the sex scenes I made you read and edit – you both make writing a book so much less lonely.

I'd also like to thank everyone behind the scenes at Storm that have helped get my book out into the world and into the hands of readers – from production to marketing to copy-editing, none of this would be possible without you all, thank you so much!

I'd also like to thank the writing community that exists mostly online, but also in person, particularly my so very lovely Debut 2023 group (our DMs give me life), and also the following people: Natali Simmonds, Gaynor Jones, Cailean

Steed, Alison Stockham, Laura Pearson, Stephie Chapman, Lia Lewis, Bella Harcourt, Chikodili Emelumadu.

I'd also like to thank the bands and artists who kept me going over the nine months it took me to get this book ready for the world, Ethel Cain, Lana Del Rey, Wolf Alice, Radiohead, The Jesus and Mary Chain, Chvrches, Portishead, Florence & the Machine, Garbage.

Thank you also to my lovely Indeedian colleagues, past and present, for supporting and championing my writing, particularly Bill, Caroline B, Dana S, Danny, Debra S, Ellie, Garreth, Jack K, Laura G, Matt, PBS, Rebecca C, and Ute.

Outside of work I'd like to thank Rowena C for the chats and inspiration, Circe and Sulis Minerva for answering some research questions, the SKMC for the climbing related distraction on Sundays and asking me how the writing is going, and also Andrea M, Genevieve, Georgia G, Trashleigh, Vitsou, Audrey, and also the Gossip crew.

Thank you also to all my local Surrey friends, in particular the Y3 + Y6 WhatsApp groups, as well as Karen C, Amy C, Rachel D, Rose, Sofia L, Aaron, Rhian, Sarah O, Helen A. I know I've forgotten people but consider yourselves thanked all the same!

Also thank you to my mum and my sister, who as I've said before and will continue to say, are the most talented writers in the family. I love you both. To my lovely Welsh family, without whom my books literally wouldn't exist – thank you for the support, love, and childcare!

Thank you to my baby dragons, Thor and Uther. I'm sorry I still haven't learned to play Fortnite, Minecraft or Roblox, but I'd like to thank the creators of such games which have enabled you to entertain yourselves whilst I write. Jokes aside, I love you both more than life itself. You make me laugh every single day. Thank you for all the snacks, memes, WhatsApps, farting, jokes, and continuing to write your own books. I love you, babies. Smooches.

Also CRW. I love you 'c'. Thanks for the climbing related distractions and putting up with living with a *tortured artiste* and generally surviving the random questions that come with having a writer as your wife. This book would be a lot worse without your help! I promise to try and set book 3 somewhere with good climbing so we can go on a research trip .

Finally thank you to all the readers who bought and championed *Best Friends*, but also to you, the reader holding this book! Thank you for choosing to spend your time with the people I've dreamed up for you.

Printed in Great Britain
by Amazon